Shakeera Frazer

7/30/10

Natalie ,

Thank you so much for your support :) Enjoy life the Fast Lane

Love always
Shakeera

1

FAST LANE

SHAKEERA FRAZER

Cover Design by Baja Ukweli
www.bajaukweli.com

*

*Thanks to everyone that supported me and my
Journey in the Fast lane*

*

Acknowledgements

First and foremost I have to thank God, without Him this wouldn't be possible. Next I have to thank my mother and best friend, Lisa Chatman for being my biggest supporter and number one fan. There was so many times I felt like I couldn't do something and she was always there telling me that I could succeed at whatever I wanted. She believed in me and then I believed in myself. Thanks Purcell for being there when my father wasn't and being supportive. Dante, I love you! Thanks India (Grandma) for being your crazy self! Grandpa I miss you so much! Wish you were here, I know you would be proud.

I'd also like to thank my friends for giving me so much inspiration and fueling my imagination to do what I love to do, Thanks! Serena, it's like we share the same brain sometimes!!! U know the real me! Always there with a funny or crazy story and being there whenever I needed you, the true definition of a friend, love you. Alicia, we completely understand each other, without words, we have been through a lot together, Love you. Anaise, I never would have thought we would be as close as we are now I can't picture you not being a part of my day, giving me my daily dose of the drama that's going on in your life! You are so crazy but I get you. Summer (Nikki) we have came a long way thanks for always listening.

Daniel (JoJo) thanks for giving me my

motivation back, you believed in me and really helped me get this project rolling. I really appreciate it. Thanks. Yadi thanks, Love you. Ru thanks for always loving me, Love you. Risa, thanks for making me laugh and playing "would you rather" LOL. Love you. Robin Ayele, thank you for believing that my book could be a success and giving me motivation. Thank you my "Mother in Law", Cheryl King- Whitehead for being so supportive, so positive, and loving me so much, I love you MIL!

Thanks to all the authors that have given me so much inspiration over the years. Thank you Omar Tyree for writing *Flyy Girl*, I read *Flyy Girl* in the sixth grade, it was the first novel I ever read and immediately I was hooked, I loved it. I think that's when my love for reading and writing started. Thank you Sheila Copeland for writing *Chocolate Star* and all the other sequels to follow, I think these were my favorite books of all time!! Thank you Mary B. Morrison for writing *Soulmates Dissipate* and the sequel, two more favorites. Thanks Lolita Files, Eric Jerome- Dickey, especially Jackie Collins, and so many others that have provided me with a world I never knew and a few hours, days or minutes to escape into the lives of one of their characters. I hope I can make an impact through my writing on people's lives the way each and every one of you has impacted mine. Anyone else if I forgot to thank you, you're not forgotten and I do apologize.

Chapter 1

Get in the closet!!!
What? Trish said groggily.
Get in the closet! Jay whispered through clenched
teeth.
Trish looked around as if she was in a daze, trying
to remember where she was. All she remembered
was meeting Jay last night at Lotus, a new club that
opened in the meatpacking district in Manhattan.
Lotus was famous for celebrity sightings and that
was exactly what Trish wanted. She needed a man
to take care of her. As far as Trish was concerned
that's all they were good for! Looking at Jay now he
wasn't that cute, but he was paid! He was a medium
brown complexion, about 5'10" and slim, but even
though he was slim he was muscular. Trish looked
at his muscles flex each time he spoke.
Trish had seen him at three other parties over the
past few months. He was always with an entourage
of people and surrounded by two or three body
guards. She could never get to him. But last night he
was alone and she was going to get him! He was at
the bar in V.I.P and when Trish spotted him she left
Nina, Paulette, and Crystal in an instant.
Trish walked over to V.I.P. and began to work her
magic. She could feel all eyes on her as she glided
across the room and she loved it. Trish was not your
typical beauty but she had a natural sex appeal that
almost everybody, guy or girl was drawn to. She
was about 5'7" with chocolate brown skin, bright

brown almond shaped eyes and a curvy shape. Trish adjusted her white BCBG strapless mini dress and glanced down at her perfectly French manicured toes peeking through her silver rhinestone encrusted Jimmy Choo stilettos. She grabbed her Louis Vuitton handbag and took out her perfect shade of MAC lip gloss, *Oh Baby*, and put on a coat as she ran her fingers through her brown long curls. Pleased with herself she strutted through the crowd and thought of what she would say to her mystery man.

When she reached V.I.P a heavily built burly dark-skinned man that resembled the late Biggie Smalls guarded the roped area.

"May I help you?" he asked in a deep voice.

"Yes you can by letting me in" Trish said as she batted her long naturally curled eyelashes. Trish usually didn't have to say anything to get her way.

"Who are you with?"

"Excuse me?" Trish asked with an attitude.

What the fuck is his problem? He must be gay.

"I said who are you here with, you don't have on a band"

"Him" Trish said as she pointed to a random man sitting on the couch in the V.I.P section.

The man took one look at Trish and smiled and nodded his head.

"Aight" The guard said as he opened the rope and let her pass.

Trish walked up the steps and looked around for her man.

She spotted him and was about to make her way over when someone tapped her shoulder and said "Where you going?" The man asked "Excuse me?" Trish turned around and asked with an attitude. Then she realized that it was the guy she pointed to on the other side of the ropes.

Trish sized him up quickly; he was okay, but definitely not her type. He was light skin, with light brown eyes, curly hair and a little on the chunky side. He was rocking tan slacks and a Bill Cosby sweater, definitely not her style, he looked broke, but what the hell, she could have a drink with him.

"Come over to my table and get yourself a drink"

He said

"Okay"

When Trish sat down there was a bottle of Rose sitting on ice, Dom Perignon at that.

Maybe he's not broke. Trish thought, because she knew that a bottle of Rose was at least $350 and at a club it was going to be double, she did her homework.

Maybe I'll give him a little of my time.

He poured Trish a glass and handed it to her.

"So what's up gorgeous? What's your name?"

"Trish"

"I'm Walter, nice to meet you"

"Nice to meet you too"

Trish really didn't give a damn about meeting him.

Just make this shit fast.

Walter began to talk about his self. His life, his job and Trish was bored to death.

10

She began to ignore him as she looked around to make sure who she really came to see didn't leave.
"Are you looking for somebody?" Walter asked annoyed.
Trish ignored him. She had completely tuned him out by this time; she didn't even know he was asking her a question.
"Hello, Trish are you looking for somebody" Walter raised his voice over the music.
"Actually I am, thanks for the drink" Trish said as she got up and walked away.
Trish walked right over to the other side of the room where she saw him. He was sitting on a couch in the corner sipping on a drink. He had on some dark True Religion jeans, black Gucci Sneakers, a black fitted T- shirt and a black blazer.
Trish walked over and stood in front of him with her legs slightly open.
"Hi I'm Trish, nice to meet you" She said confidently
"I'm Jay, have we met before?" He asked as he gently took her hand
"No, I'm sure you would have remembered me." Trish said as she licked her lips and ran her fingers through her long brown flowing curls.
"So you here by yourself beautiful?" Jay asked
Looking at him he was not typically her type but she was attracted to him anyway. He was sexy. He just had a swagger about him. He was very laid back and confident and she loved that.
"No I'm with my girls, but you looked so lonely I

decided to come keep you company"
"I'm chilling. I just got off work and wanted to stop
and get a drink before I went home." Jay said
"What kind of work do you do?" Trish asked.
"I'm a producer and I've been in the studio all
night."
"So are you going home alone?" Trish asked getting
right to the point.
"Why you want to join me?"
"I was waiting for you to ask"
Jay grinned and finished the last sip of his drink and
called the bartender over so he could close out his
tab.
"You want something before we go?" He asked
Trish
"No I'm good"
"You ready? Jay stood up and asked.
"Yeah, let me just tell my girls I'm leaving. I'll be
back in a minute"
Trish turned around and walked very slowly. She
knew Jay was staring at her ass. She walked over to
Nina, Paulette, and Crystal and she said "I'm
leaving with Jay. I'll call you guys in the morning."
Who the hell is Jay? Nina asked.
Nina and Trish met in their first year of college.
Nina was the more average looking one of the girls.
She was naturally cute, but didn't stop traffic, like
Trish or Crystal. She was brown skin with long
thick black hair that she usually wore in a pony tail.
She was about 5'8", slim with small breast and a fat
ass. Tonight she had on a white tank top, some dark

blue Joe skinny jeans, that made her butt look great and she wore some gold Prada sandals that she spent half her pay check on. Her hair was in a ponytail as usual.

"Mr. V.I.P." Trish said smiling.

"That was fast, what the hell did you say to him?" Paulette asked.

Paulette was the earthy chic one of the girls. She wore her dark brown hair in a blunt cut bob that reached her cheeks. She hardly wore any makeup except for a clear lip gloss and her body was well-toned like a track star. Tonight her calves looked excellent in her brown wedged sandals that she wore with a loose tan sun dress that stopped mid thigh. Paulette's care-free attitude always commanded attention. She just had a natural sex appeal.

"I didn't have to say anything, look at me." Trish spun around for her girls to get a full view.

"Are you sure you should be leaving with him? You don't even know him. Do you even know his last name?" Crystal asked.

Crystal was the mother of the girls. She always felt like she had to be a mother to Trish since they met in the ninth grade. Crystal was one of the few people that woke up gorgeous. She had a beautiful caramel skin tone, big light brown eyes that changed color in the sun and perfect full lips. Her mane was cinnamon brown with blond highlights that hung down to the middle of her back. Her body

13

was a well toned, well proportioned size six. Everyone always questioned her nationality. Although Crystal had the looks she wasn't as over the top and dramatic as Trish. She always dressed impeccable, but classier. Tonight she had a simple gold bronzer on her face with white Armani satin shorts that reached her mid thigh with a sleeveless silver tank top embroidered with beads around the scoop neck. She wore silver satin Manolo Blahnik pumps that matched perfectly, with her simple diamond studs and diamond tennis bracelet. Her golden tresses hung down her back in a loose ponytail.

Trish thought for a second.

"No I don't know his last name Mrs. Goodie Too Shoes and right now I don't care about his last name." Trish said.

"Okay be safe." Crystal, Paulette, and Nina said at the same time.

"Text me his license plate number when you get in the car in case you don't show up in the morning." Crystal said.

"Okay mother!" Trish joked.

Trish made her way back over to Jay and they were escorted by a bouncer out of a private exit in the back.

They quietly waited for valet to bring Jay's car around.

Trish was ecstatic when the valet hopped out of a brand new Aston Martin V-12 and handed Jay the keys. *He really is paid.* Trish thought. She knew those cars cost a quarter of a million dollars, at least.

Jay walked over and opened the passenger side door for Trish to get in and then he walked around to the driver's side. *And he has manners.* Trish thought. Trish got in the car and rolled down the window. She closed her eyes and let the wind blow through her hair.

Trish only dealt with wealthy men, lawyers, doctors, athletes, and entertainers, most of which were married, but she didn't care as long as they took care of her, which most of them did. She didn't care what she had to do to or who she had to sleep with to get want she wanted she was never going back to being broke.

Just thinking about it made Trish want to throw up. She had came such a long way from the Astoria projects in Queens.

Trish remembered her mother being too strung out on crack to feed her. She had to beg neighbors for food or dig through garbage cans because she was so hungry. There were always different men running in and out of her house. Trish was only 6 when the first man felt her up. Her mother was right there on the couch passed out. Soon it became "normal". Most of the men did it right in front of her mother. Soon she started offering Trish to them just so she could get high.

Trish could still hear her mother saying "C'mon Patty be nice for mommy"

15

Patty was short for Patricia that was what everybody called her. In the beginning Trish wanted to make her mother happy, after all she was her mother and she loved her. Trish thought eventually it would stop but it only got worse. Soon the men wanted Trish to have sex with them and they wanted her to suck their nasty dicks. Trish was sure her mother would say no to that but she didn't. All she thought about was getting high. Trish's mother would just lead Trish and the men to her bedroom in the back. Again saying
"C'mon Patty just be nice for mommy". Trish just wanted her mother to love her and she saw how happy her mother was when she got high so she did it to please her. Trish cried the entire time.
Trish's older sister Kimmy was 12 at the time. She was hardly ever home and Trish had to go through it all by herself. Kimmy was a professional booster. Anything you asked her to get she could get. That's how she made a living and stayed fly.
　　By the time Trish was 14 she couldn't take it anymore. The dirty stinking men feeling all over her and having their way with her while her mother just sat right there and did nothing. Trish was tired of fucking those men and she started fighting back and most of the time she won. Sometimes she would run around the house and most of the men got tired of chasing her and would give up. Damn! She hated her mother. Sometimes she wished she would just die. She was supposed to protect her and be there for her not be her pimp.

Soon Trish started doing her own hair and wearing Kimmy's clothes. It wasn't long before people in the hood started to notice Trish. Even though Trish had been through a lot and was hurting inside on the outside Trish had the attitude that she was the shit. So when she came around people took notice. Trish's goal was to get out the hood and never look back. She didn't care what she had to do. She would leave and forget about her mother, her sister and all the nasty ass men. *Little did she know her dream was going to become reality.*

It was a hot summer day. The first real hot day of the summer, the kind where everyone was dying to put on their new shit and look fly. Kimmy was still boosting and had got all the latest shit and Trish was in heaven because her and her sister wore the same size in shoes and clothes. Trish was a little thicker than Kimmy but the tighter the better was how Trish felt. Trish had to be careful what she took because she didn't want Kimmy to notice before she had a chance to put it back. Kimmy had so much shit that she never noticed anything missing anyway.
Trish picked out some dark blue tight Guess shorts that came right to her thigh with a matching black tank top that said guess in gold letters across the front.
She slicked her brown shoulder length hair in a ponytail with sharply cut bangs in the front, she had

just cut herself and put on a pair of Kimmy's big gold hoop earrings. She even had the newest black and gold Jordans. "Damn I look good" she said to herself.

Trish didn't have anywhere in particular to go but she wasn't staying in that hot ass apartment. She hadn't made any friends because she didn't like most girls, she didn't have time for no fake ass hood rat bitches and she didn't like getting close to people.

Trish held her breath as she ran down the pissy hallway from their apartment on the third floor. "Damn I hate this shit"

Even though she lived there all her life she couldn't get used to it. She dreamed about getting out the hood every day.

Trish walked to the store across the street with the money she had slipped out of one of the numerous men's pockets who was passed out in her living room floor.

As she was walking to the store she heard someone say "Hey pretty can I talk to you for a minute?"

Trish turned around slowly and said "Okay you got one minute"

"Damn what's the attitude about sweetheart?"

"I don't have an attitude I just don't like to waste my time. My time is valuable" Trish said with a smile.

"Here let me pay you for your time then" He said
and pulled out a $50 dollar bill.
Trish grinned and took the money" Okay talk"
"So what's your name?"
"Patt-. Trish"
"Pat- Trish?"   He said laughing
"No. Just Trish" She didn't want anyone calling her
Patty anymore. She was starting a new life she
wanted to leave all the negative shit behind her.
"Okay Trish. I'm Mike. Nice to meet you"
"Nice to meet you too"
"So can I take you out sometime?"

Trish sized him up real quick. He looked good. He
was tall about 6 feet with chocolate brown skin and
deep dimples. He wore his hair real low and he was
built. He had on some dark blue Iceberg Jeans with
a grey and blue Iceberg T- Shirt. On his feet he had
on some brand new crispy white Air Force Ones.
Trish already knew who he was. He was hustlin'
and he was getting money and that was all that
concerned Trish. He was leaning on a brand new
silver Lexus and he pulled out a wad of money
when he gave her that $50.
Trish had seen him a couple of times with her sister.
But he probably didn't even recognize her. Her and
her sister looked completely different. They had
different fathers. The only thing they had in
common were they were both tall, about 5'8". Trish
was dark skinned and shapely with brown shoulder
length hair and almond shaped brown eyes. She

19

wasn't a common beauty but she had a very exotic look. Kimmy on the other hand was a light skinned and a little slimmer than Trish. Kimmy had a slightly big pointy nose with very full lips and very dark almost black eyes. Kimmy had a very average look but she was fly so everyone knew Kimmy. She always stood out because she wore her hair in a different hairstyle almost every week. Right now she was wearing an asymmetrical bob, it was short in the back and long in the front, with red streaks.

"Yeah. Where you taking me?" Trish asked
"Wherever you want to go"
Trish was playing it off but she was nervous as hell. She had never been on a real date or ever really talked to a guy. Trish hardly ever went out in the hood and she was always by herself. She didn't really know anybody.
"Surprise me" Trish said
"Okay. Let's go right now"
"Right now?"
"Yeah"
"Okay" Trish said.

Trish was ready to go anywhere but home. Most nights she'd sit in the stairway until it got really late and she thought her mother was asleep and her "friends" were gone.
Mike walked around to the driver's side of the car and Trish got in the passenger side and let him lead the way.

"So where we going?" Trish asked
"Just relax. You like seafood?"
"Yeah" Trish said. She couldn't remember the last
time she had seafood or even a decent meal period.
"I was going to take you to City Island. Is that okay
with you?"
"Yeah" Trish said. She had never been to City
Island.
"So how come I never seen you before?" Mike
asked

"How you know you haven't seen me?"
"Because I would have remembered you"
"Well I've seen you before"
"You're a smart ass"
"I know"
"I like that"
"I know" Trish said with a sexy smile
She was relaxing more by the minute. She looked
over at him from the corner of her eye. He looked
good and he smelled good too.
"What kind of cologne is that?"
"Issey Miyaki. Why you don't like it?"
"Yeah I like it. It smells good" *Real good.* Trish
thought
"I know" Mike said and they both busted out
laughing.
Trish looked up and they were getting off the I-95 at
exit 8C, City Island.
"That was fast"
"You never been to City Island before?" Mike

asked surprised

"Yeah just not in a while" Trish lied

"So you got a man?"

"No"

"Why not? As fine as you are"

"I haven't found anyone worth my time"

Trish was surprised how everything was just flowing out of her mouth. She had butterflies in her stomach.

"Well you have now"

"I have?"

"Yes you have. You better act like you know" Mike said with a grin.

"We'll see"

"So you got a girl?"

"I did but not anymore"

"Why not?"

"Because I met you and I like what I see. I want you"

Trish smiled.

"So you leaving your girl?"

"Yeah"

"I don't believe you"

"I'm a man of my word. Trust me"

"Like I said I don't believe you. We'll see"

They pulled into a parking lot covered with gravel with a large white sign that said Valet in front. A Mexican man walked to the driver's side of the car and handed Mike a ticket.

He put the ticket in his pocket, opened the door and said

"C'mon"
Trish got out the car and looked around. It was so many people outside, young and old. They walked across the street to Sammy's Fish Box.
When they got inside Trish felt underdressed. It was very nice inside, not like anything she was used to. Huge chandeliers hung from the ceiling and there was a huge fish tank with enormous lobsters when you walk through the door. They walked over to the podium and the hostess seated them at a quiet booth in the corner.
"Enjoy your dinner" She said as she handed them both menus.
Trish looked at the menu and couldn't decide what to order everything looked so good.
She looked over at Mike and he didn't even open his menu.
"You're not eating?"
"Yeah but I know what I want. I'm a simple nigga. I just want some fried shrimp and French fries"
"You know what you want?" He asked
"Not yet I can't decide if I want the surf and turf or the lobster or the fried shrimp"
Just then the waitress came over
"Can I get you anything to drink?" she asked
"Yeah can I have a cranberry juice" Mike said
"Sure. And for you?" The waitress looked at Trish
"The same"

"Would you like to order any appetizers?"

"No. But I'm ready to order" Mike said
"Okay"
"Can I have the fried shrimp with French fries and she will have the surf and turf, lobster,   and fried shrimp"
Both Trish and the waitress looked surprised.
"I don't want all that!" Trish yelled
"Well you said you couldn't decide so get all three"
 "I'm not going to eat it all"
"Its okay. You don't have to"
"Okay"
Trish was not used to wasting any food.
"I'll get your drinks and put your orders in" The waitress said and left the table.
"You don't drink?" Trish asked
"No. I don't drink or smoke"
Trish was surprised to hear that.
"Do you?"
"No" Trish would never dare smoke anything not even a cigarette after she saw how her mother looked every day.
"How old are you?"
"How old do I look?"
"You always have to answer a question with another question"
"How old are you?" Mike asked again
"I'm 15" Trish lied
"What? With a body like that?" Mike grinned
"Yeah"

"How old are you?"

"I'm 22"

"So are you saying I'm too young?" Trish said as she blinked her eyes and gave him an innocent look.

"Usually, yeah. But you don't act 15 and you damn sure don't look 15"

"I know"

"You think you know everything"

It was turning out to be one of the best nights of Trish's life. Trish never saw so much seafood in her life. She tried to eat everything in front of her without looking too greedy, and she almost did. When she was finally done she felt like she was going to bust. After her and Mike finished eating they sat in the car for a while and just talked while they looked at the water.

"What time you gotta be home?"

"Whatever time I get there" Trish said

"Oh Word? So you make your own rules?" Mike asked with a chuckle

"Yeah, you can say that" Trish said changing the subject

The truth was nobody gave a damn what time Trish came in and nobody was going to be checking for her. As far as she was concerned she was on her own.

"What are we doing now? I really don't feel like going home" Trish asked sounding like a little kid at Disney World.

Mike didn't answer he just drove. They got on the Cross Island Expressway And in no time they were in front of the Howard Johnson. Trish smile quickly faded and she knew it was too good to be true. All men only wanted to fuck. That's all they cared about. Trish knew he had money though and if she was going to fuck him he was going to pay her. She wasn't letting him get off that easy.
"What's the matter? Why you look like that?" Mike asked.
"No reason. I'm fine" Trish lied

"Wait right here. I'll be right back" Mike said as he got out the car to go get a room.
Trish thought about what she was going to say to him when they got in the room. How she was going to go about getting her money. She was nervous. She thought about her bra and panties. She didn't have on any nice sexy ones. They didn't even match. She got more nervous.

In about 5 minutes. Mike walked back over to the car. He drove around back to look for parking and they found a space right near the back door.
"C'mon"
Trish quietly got out the car. They walked in through the back door and took the elevator to the third floor. Room 313.
When they got inside Trish was surprised at the room. It looked better than she expected. From the

outside it looked like a cruddy motel. On the inside the room was basic but comfortable. There was tan carpet, pink walls, and a queen sized bed with a paisley bed spread. There was one long dark wood dresser and a small desk in the corner. There was a 27"inch TV on top of the dresser. Although this may have been an average room to someone else, to Trish this was nice. Her mother's apartment didn't have carpet or a dresser that was in good condition and Trish didn't have a comfortable bed with fluffy pillows.

"Relax, sit down" Mike said

Trish sat on the bed quietly.

"You haven't said a word since we got here. What's wrong?" Mike asked

"Nothing"

"What's wrong?"

"I said nothing. Turn on the TV" Trish said trying to change the subject

"You said you didn't want to go home and I didn't either. It's late. Where else were we gonna go? What? You think I'm trying to fuck you?" Mike laughed

"Oh, so you're not?" Trish asked with an attitude

Mike just laughed and shook his head.

"No I'm not. I can get pussy whenever I want from whoever I want. I like you. I just wanted to chill"

Trish smiled. She liked him too.

"I mean if you want to I ain't gonna stop you" Mike laughed

"I know"

"You don't know shit!" Mike said and they both started laughing

Now Trish was turned on. Now she really wanted to fuck him just because he didn't act like he wanted it. But she also wanted to make him wait a little while. She had to get some money first. She was so confused.

Mike turned on the TV and found something for them to watch.
He settled on the Fresh Prince of Bel Air, one of Trish's favorite shows.
  Trish took of her sneakers and lay in the bed in her clothes on. Mike took of his shoes and laid behind her with his arm around her. That felt so good to Trish she couldn't remember anybody ever just holding her and not wanting to fuck her. She couldn't even remember her mother holding her. In ten minutes they were both knocked out.
The next morning when Trish woke up Mike was gone. She sat up and looked in the mirror. Her hair was a little flat from sleeping on one side. She called out
"Mike?"
She got no answer. She got up and walked in the bathroom. She pulled her pants down and squatted over the toilet and peed.
"Where the hell is he?" She thought.
"How am I going to get home? I didn't even get any money from him?"

Trish pulled her pants up and walked over to the sink and washed her hands. She cupped her hands together and filled them with cold water and rinsed her mouth out, since she didn't have toothpaste or a toothbrush.

Just then Trish heard a knock at the door.

"Who is it?"

"Who you think?"

"She looked through the peephole and smiled when she saw Mike.

She opened the door and asked "Where were you?"

"I went to get us some toothbrushes and toothpaste"

"Oh" Trish didn't expect him to say that, that was so sweet.

Mike gave her a toothbrush and toothpaste. She walked back in the bathroom and brushed her teeth. When she came out Mike walked into the bathroom.

"So what are you doing today?" She yelled into the bathroom

"I have some running around to do earlier, and hopefully I will see you later"

Trish knew what running around meant. She was so happy he said he wanted to see her later she wanted to see him too.

"What are we doing later?"

"Whatever you want"

"What should I wear?"

"I'm sure you look good in everything. Just put on something sexy"

"I don't know if I have something sexy"

Mike walked out the bathroom drying his face off

29

with a hotel wash cloth. He reached in his pocket and counted out five hundred dollars
"Here buy something sexy"
"Okay" Trish smiled and took the money.
"You want to get some breakfast before I drop you back off?"
"Yeah I'm hungry" Trish said
Mike took Trish to IHOP on Hillside Ave. When they got inside it was packed. They had to wait about fifteen minutes to be seated. Once they sat down Trish looked at the menu.
Once again Mike didn't look at the menu he just sat there.
"Oh you already know what you want again?" Trish said
"Yeah I always get the big steak omelet"
"That sounds good. I'll get that too"

During breakfast Trish laughed so hard she thought she was going to pee on herself. Mike was so silly. He always made her laugh. He was so different from what she expected. He was so cool. She thought he would be real cocky. She was wrong. When they got back in the car Mike said
"I got a few things I need to handle this morning so I'm gonna drop you off but I wanna see you later"
"Okay. What time?"
"I'm not sure yet. I'll call you. What's your cell number?" Mike asked as he took out his cell phone to put the number in.
"I don't have a cell phone" Trish answered. She was

so embarrassed.

"What?" Mike asked surprised.

"You heard me" Trish said defensively

"Well we have to get you one. I have to be able to get in touch with my girl"

"Your girl?"

"You heard me"

They both busted out laughing

"Well I have two cell phones. You can take one of mine for now"

"Are you sure?"

"Yes I'm sure. Take it"

"I'll call you twice back to back. Answer when I call you the third time"

"Okay"

Mike dropped Trish off in front of the corner store.

"I'll see you later"

"Okay. See you later"

Trish couldn't help but smile. She was happy. He looked good, smelled good, he was nice and she had five hundred dollars in her pocket. That reminded her that she had to buy something sexy.

She didn't know what she was going to buy.

She didn't have any friends to go with and Kimmy was probably out somewhere boosting, even if she wasn't, they weren't that close anyway. Besides she didn't want her all in her business and have to explain where she got the money from.

She decided to just go shopping by herself.

She walked in the corner store because she needed a little snack for her trip to the city.

"Hey Papi, let me get ten sour pours and ten fishes" Trish loved sweets. She walked down Jamaica Ave. to the train station. It was so nice outside. Trish had on the same outfit from yesterday but she didn't care because Mike was the only one that saw her. Trish hopped on the train and took it to 34th street. She decided to go the Macy's. She was sure she could find something sexy there.

Trish found the perfect outfit and she still had a hundred and forty dollars left. She bought a black leather mini skirt with a matching halter top and some strappy black sandals.

Mike was very pleased when he saw Trish that night. His face lit up as soon as she came down stairs. Trish walked to the car and spun around. "Is this sexy enough?" she asked with a sexy smile.

"Hell yeah. You look real good baby"

"Thank you" Trish was blushing.

She got in the car and put on her seat belt.

"So where are we going?"

"It's a surprise"

Trish smiled. She liked him more and more every time she was around him.

Mike took her to the View, a restaurant in Manhattan that rotates while you eat. The food wasn't that great but it was romantic and it was a nice view of the city.

Mike made Trish feel so special.

Trish couldn't believe how much Mike was turning her on. She was so attracted to him. He wasn't even doing anything in particular, she just loved his style. She wanted to fuck him bad.
As soon as Mike left the money on the table for the bill.
Trish said "I have to go the bathroom I'll be right back"
"Okay"
When Trish got out the bathroom Mike was waiting at the exit. They walked outside and waited for valet to bring the car over.
"You really look good tonight"
"I know" Trish laughed
"Oh word?" Mike said and they both started laughing.
Trish leaned over and kissed Mike. He immediately started kissing her back. They were really getting into it when they heard someone say
"Excuse me"
It was the valet attendant. They almost forgot they were outside.
Mike handed the man the money and they both got in the car.
The ride to the hotel seemed like hours to Trish. She was horny as hell.
As soon as they got in the room. They started going at it again.
Trish was all over Mike.

"Slow down baby we got all night" Mike said
Trish felt embarrassed and sat down on the bed. She
wasn't used to people taking their time.
"Don't feel bad. I want you too, but I want it to be
special, not like I'm fucking you like I would some
other chick"
Trish smiled.
Mike walked over to the bed and slowly pushed
Trish back on the bed. He started kissing her gently
on the lips and then he moved to her neck. Trish let
out small moans. It felt so good. Mike slid down
and started kissing her shoulder.
"mmm" Trish moaned
He unloosed the halter strap around Trish's neck
and pulled her shirt down to reveal her breasts.
Mike smiled.
He started licking her right nipple and then her left
and back to her right. He began sucking them and
lightly nibbling on them. Trish was going crazy.
Mike untied the back strap on Trish's halter top and
threw it on the floor. He moved down her stomach
with his tongue and kissed her along the sides of her
stomach.
Trish moaned louder.

Mike unzipped Trish's skirt and slid it down her
legs, to the floor.
He began licking and kissing her inner thigh and
then he moved back up to her stomach. He went
back down and kissed the other thigh. Trish threw
her head back and closed her eyes. She was in pure

34

ecstasy. Mike licked Trish's legs down to her
ankles. Then he came back up and went right for
her spot. First he lightly kissed her pussy. Then he
licked, in small circles.
"Oh my God!" Trish yelled out. Nobody had ever
eaten her pussy before.
He began slowly sucking on her clit. Trish grabbed
the sheets.
Mike stuck his tongue in, he moved it in and out
like he was fucking her with his tongue.
"Oh my God! Oh my God!" Trish never knew sex
could be this good and they didn't even have sex
yet.

Mike stopped for a second and Trish thought he was
done. Shit! She was. She had already came twice.
  Then Mike buried his entire face in her pussy and
started licking and sucking like he hadn't eaten in
years.
"Oh my god!" Trish yelled.
Trish was slightly moving back on the bed.
"Where are you going?" Mike asked
"It feels too good. I can't take it" Trish screamed
Mike pulled her closer to him and buried his face
again. Trish locked her knees around Mike's head.
She was coming again.
Just then Mike came up for air and opened Trish's
legs. He spread them across the bed and he laid on
top of her.
He held her thighs open while he slid inside her.
"mmm" Trish moaned.

"damn" Mike said
He started stroking her slow. In and out, in and out.
Trish's moans turned him on and he started going
faster and harder.
"Damn baby. I'm about to come" Mike said as he
looked Trish in the eyes.
"Me too"
Mike leaned over and kissed Trish. A deep
passionate kiss. And collapsed on top of her.
"Damn that was good" Mike said.
"It was. But get up I can't breathe" Trish managed
to say
They both busted out laughing.

They had sex two more times that night and it was
better each time. Trish really opened up to Mike.
She told him things that she thought she would
never tell anybody. She told him about her mother
and all the men and the things she's done. She felt
so ashamed. She thought he was going to look at
her different and think she was a nasty ho. But he
didn't he hugged her tight and just held her. Trish
cried so hard. Like a baby. Nobody ever just
listened to her without judging her. It felt so good to
get those things off her chest. She felt so close to
him. He opened up to her too and he told her things
about his past and his family. He told how he
started selling drugs at 12, mainly because of his
mother. His father was a big time drug dealer and
he went to jail when Mike was 10 and his sister was
7. Soon their money started running out. His mother

complained every day and was accustomed to a certain lifestyle. She told him that he was the man of the house now and he needed to care of her and his sister. His mother introduced him to the right people and he followed in his father's footsteps. Damn. Trish couldn't believe it. His mother was just as bad as hers. Trish thought.
The entire time he was talking Trish looked in his eyes and they were so sad. Even though he had money she could tell he wasn't happy.
"Well what did you always want to do?" Trish asked him
"Play ball"
"For real?"
"Yeah. I was real good in high school, scouts came to see me and everything" Trish could see Mike's eyes light up like a little child.
 "But then I caught a case" Mike said sadly
"Well you're still young. Don't give up so easily"
Mike changed the subject.
"So what do you want to do?" Mike asked Trish
"I'm not sure yet. I just want to get out the hood. I hate it here. I can picture my life so different. A nice place, a good job, friends"
"Me too"

They spent the rest of the night just talking. Trish felt like she knew him for years, instead of a couple of days. She knew he was special.
From then on wherever you saw Mike you saw Trish. They were always together. He kept his word

and broke up with his girlfriend the next week and made Trish his girl. He spoiled Trish and gave her anything she wanted. She had everything from Coach to Gucci and everything in between. All the girls hated her but she didn't care. She was happy. She almost had everything she wanted. But she still wanted to get out the hood. It was depressing. She hated it. Mike got them an apartment and she moved out of her mother's place. But it was only a few blocks away. Things were going good and she knew it could only get better. She loved Mike and he loved her, he was her world.

Around the same time Trish also met a new girl at school. That girl was Crystal, they had became real cool. Her and Crystal were total opposites but they instantly hit it off. Crystal had just transferred to her school and they met in math class. Trish hated math and Crystal loved it. She asked Crystal if she could cheat off her test.
Crystal gave Trish a nasty look that said "hell no bitch" and Trish gave her the same look right back. Crystal let Trish cheat off her anyway. They both got a 98% and they were tight ever since. Crystal hated the hood too she wanted to get out just as bad as Trish, they shared that common bond. Trish could immediately tell Crystal wasn't from the hood she just didn't fit in. She talked different and had a different swagger about herself.

Mike was making more and more money. Things

were going real good for him and he had a lot of money saved, he didn't want to stop hustling but he knew Trish wanted to move out of the hood. He told her to give him six months and they would move, he would do anything for Trish, she was his everything. Trish was so happy. She was beginning to look for places they should move and colleges that her and Crystal could apply to.

Then one evening on the way back from the Bel-Aire diner in Astoria Mike and Trish were driving back to their apartment. Mike made a left and then he suddenly heard police sirens behind them.
"Oh shit!" Mike said
"What?"
"They're pulling us over"
"So? You don't have anything in here right?"
"Yeah on me"
"What?" Trish screamed. Mike was usually so smart   he never had any drugs on him and as much as the police wanted to catch him, they never could. "I just came from meeting Clyde. I was gonna drop you off and go right back out"
"What are we gonna do?" Trish cried
"I don't know but I'm not going back to jail" Mike said with a scared look in his eyes. He went to jail four years ago and he was still on parole. If he got caught with anything he would have to finish his time which would be four more years.
The police sirens were getting closer and Mike

slammed on the gas. Trish could believe they were in the middle of a police chase. She was so scared. They were about to come up to a dead end and the police were getting closer. Just then Mike took the coke that he had on him out of his pockets and began swallowing the small clear plastic bags. He swallowed about 12 of them.

"What are you doing?" Trish screamed
"I'm not going back to jail"
"What are you gonna do?" Trish cried. She had never been so scared in her life. She felt like she was going to pee on herself.

Mike began slowing down and he leaned over and kissed Trish on the cheek.
"You know I love you and you are my world. I'm going to run down to Jr's if the police question you I want you to act like you don't know me and I'm crazy and this was our first date. Tell them that you don't know why I started running."
"Okay" Trish said through tears. This was all too much for her to process. She couldn't believe this shit was happening.
"I'm going to call you when I get to Jr's. I love you"
"I love you too"
Just then Mike got out the car and ran straight through the bushes and he kept running. He looked like a track star; Trish had no idea he could run that fast. The cops didn't expect it so by the time they caught on to what was happening it was too late.

Mike already had a head start.

"What's going on ma'am?" One officer asked as he walked around to the passenger side that Trish was sitting on.

"I don't know officer, we just met. We were on our first date"

"What is his name?" The officer asked

"Jason"

"Jason what? What's his last name?"

"I don't know" Trish said innocently

"You don't know?" The officer asked nastily.

"No. I told you we just met"

"Can you step out of the car?"

"Okay"

Trish stepped out of the car and let the officers search the car. They kept her there for almost an hour and once they didn't find anything they let her go and gave her a ticket for the signal light being out, that's what they were originally being stopped for.

Trish rushed home. As soon as she stepped inside the house the phone was ringing.

"Mike!" She yelled into the phone

But all she heard was sobs, like someone was crying

"Hello? Mike?" Trish asked nervously

"Nah. It's Jr. We're down at the hospital. Get down here now!"

"What? What's wrong? Is Mike okay?" Trish felt her heart drop down to her stomach.

"Just come down here now!" Jr. said. She knew

something was wrong because she could tell Jr. had
been crying
"Okay I'm on my way"
Trish hung up the phone, grabbed the keys and ran
out the front door. She couldn't imagine what was
wrong with Mike. Did he get shot?
He's in the hospital so he must be okay Trish said to
herself.
She double parked on the side of the hospital and
ran into the emergency room. When she ran inside
she saw Jr. and Clyde and they both were pacing
back and forth with red puffy eyes. Jr., Clyde and
Mike had been best friends since the fifth grade.
Trish already knew Jr. through her sister Kimmy,
Kimmy and him dated for a while. She met him
before she met Mike.
"Where is he?" Trish screamed
"Let me talk to you first" Jr. begged Trish
"No! Where is he? I want to see him"! Now!" Trish
started crying. She knew it was bad.
"I'm going to take you in the room, but I want to
talk to you first"
"What happened?"
"He told me the cops were chasing him and he left
you and he ran all the way to my house. When he
got inside he sat down and told me to pour him
some milk. I didn't know what was going on so I
just did what he asked. I poured him some milk and
he drank it and started telling me what happened.
He was about to go in the bathroom and try to shit
out the grams he swallowed when he started

choking. He started spitting the milk back up and his eyes started rolling back in his head"

"Then what?" Trish asked

"I'm sorry Trish. I tried to save him"
"What happened Jr.?" Trish screamed as she punched Jr. in the chest.
"He was shaking and choking" Jr. had to take a breath because he started crying.
Tears streamed down Trish's eyes as she listened.

"I picked him up and me and Clyde carried him to the elevator and bought him straight here. We told the doctors what happened and they started pumping his stomach but they said it was too late, he already had a heart attack. It was too much adrenaline from him running and the bags busted in his stomach, causing a heart attack. He's in the room now, but it don't look good, he doesn't look like himself. The doctors say he's in a comatose state."
"Where is he? I want to see him!"
"C'mon" Jr. said
Trish's hands were shaking as she walked to down the hall to the room. When she walked inside she couldn't believe her eyes. She fell on the floor and started sobbing. His face was swollen. His eyes were closed and he was just laying there like he was dead. This was not the same man she was with a few hours ago. This all seemed like a nightmare to

her and she wanted to just wake up.

"Why God? Why?" Trish screamed
Jr. helped her up of the floor and hugged her.
"I know Trish. I loved him too" he said
She leaned over the bed and kissed him.
"Please baby wake up. Please. I need you to wake
up baby"
He didn't move, he just laid there.
Trish stood there and sobbed for what seemed like
hours. She just wanted him to move, even open his
eyes and look at her. She needed that. She needed to
feel him next to her. She needed him to hug her and
tell her that it was going to be okay. She felt so
drained. She couldn't believe this was happening.
Then she felt a small hand tap her on the shoulder
and it was Crystal.
"Are you okay?" Crystal asked
She fell into Crystal's arms and began crying all
over again.

At 3:56am Mike was pronounced dead. The doctors
said they did all they could and it was already too
late when he got to the hospital.

Everything was a blur to Trish. This wasn't
happening.

Crystal drove Trish home but she didn't want to
stay there alone so Crystal stayed with her.

When Trish got inside the apartment she called
Mike's cell phone just to hear his voicemail.
"Leave a message" Said Mike's voice
She sobbed even more when she heard it.

"This isn't real to me Crys"
"I know. I can't believe it either"
"Why does God keep doing this to me? Why is he
punishing me?"
"He's not punishing you"
"I finally find somebody that makes me happy and
takes me away from the nightmare that I was living
and God takes him away from me. Why?"
"It may not seem like it now, Trish but you will get
through this"
"I don't think I can. He was my life. I never met
anyone that cared about me and loved me that
much"
"I know he loved you and you loved him and you
have to always remember that"
"I need him" Trish broke down and sobbed
Crystal walked over to Trish and hugged her. That
was all she could do. She didn't know the right
words to say, she couldn't imagine how she felt.

The next few days and weeks were all a blur to
Trish. Sometimes she felt like she should have died
that night too. Mike's mother and sister planned the
entire funeral she couldn't bring herself to help plan
anything. They came to Trish's and Mike's
apartment and started rummaging through his

things. She hated those bitches. They didn't even seem like they missed him, they were probably just mad that their human bank was gone. Crystal had to drag Trish out the house just to go the funeral. She slept most days and she barely ate. Crystal came over to visit her everyday but Trish just couldn't stop thinking about Mike.

Sometimes Trish still talked to Mike like he was around her. He was her best friend besides Crystal.

One day Crystal came over and said.
"Trish get up out the bed!"
"No"
"Yes!"
"Why?"
"Because you have to. You have been in bed for a month. You only left to go the funeral. When was the last time your funky ass took a shower?"
"Shut up! I don't want to do anything"
"You have to Trish. I know you loved him and I know you're hurting but you have to move on"
"Fuck you! That's easy for you to say"
"No it's not. But you didn't die that night, you're not dead, you have to get up"
"I should have died that night"
"Well you didn't and God kept you alive for a reason. Don't we always say we're gonna get out of here and go to college and never look back"

"Yeah"

"Well I have been filling out the applications for us and they should be responding soon, but you have to go to school and take your finals or else we won't be going anywhere"

"I don't have money for school, Mike was going to help me"
"I don't either, but we'll figure that out later. We have to get out of here first"
Trish knew that Crystal was right but it was so hard. She couldn't just forget about Mike and move on. Trish took a deep breath and got out the bed and walked over to her closet.
"Where are we going?"
"Somewhere. Just get dressed"
Trish picked out some jeans and a shirt and headed to the bathroom.
"I'm going to take a shower"
"It's about time"
They both busted out laughing. That was the first time Trish laughed in a while. She really loved Crystal.

The hot water felt so good to Trish. But then she thought of all the times that her and Mike took showers together and she started crying. She had to move out of this apartment soon. Her and Crystal had to find a way to pay for college and quick. Just then Trish thought about Mike's stash.
"Crystal get in here now!"
"Crystal put down the magazine she was reading

and ran in the bathroom "What happened?"
"I know where Mike's stash is"
"So you want to go get it?"
"Yeah"
"How much is it"
"I don't know but it will be enough for us to go to
college and get the fuck outta here!"
"Us? You're gonna pay for me too?"
"Of course"
"Well what the hell are we waiting for!"
….

Trish still had the keys to Mike's car. Her and
Crystal rode over to Mike's stash spot in silence.
Trish found a spot right in front of the building.
"C'mon" Trish tapped Crystal.
Crystal was in a daze.
Crystal got out the car and let Trish lead the way.
"Grab the duffel bag out of the back seat" Trish said

Trish led Crystal across the street to an abandoned
looking building. The building was boarded up and
looked like it had been in a fire. There were two
bums sleeping in blankets outside the building.
"This is it?" Crystal asked. She had a scared look on
her face. She didn't even want to go inside.
"Yeah C'mon"
"What if somebody sees us?"
"Stop being scared just c'mon"
Trish walked in the building and looked to her left
and to her right to make sure nobody was sitting in

the hallway. Crystal was right behind her, holding the back of her shirt. Crystal held her nose to try to block the strong urine smell.

"Damn it stinks in here"

"I know" Trish held her nose too. She had only been there twice with Mike.

Trish walked quietly up the two flights of steps. She stopped in front of a door that looked like it used to say 217. Trish pulled a set of keys out of her pocket. She tried both keys, they didn't work.

"Shit!" Trish said under her breath

Then she remembered that Mike told her that she had to turn the knob at the same time she turned the key. She tried again, the first key didn't work. She was beginning to get frustrated.

She put the second key in and turned the knob at the same time and the door opened.

Trish walked inside. Crystal stood in the hallway.

"C'mon"

Crystal took little baby steps inside the apartment.

"Close the door" Trish said

Crystal turned around and closed the door behind her.

It was dark inside.

"I can't see, try and find a light" Trish said

Crystal turned on the light switch by the door and that didn't work. Trish found a lamp on the floor and plugged it in. It came on.

"Okay where is it?" Crystal asked. She did not feel comfortable. She was antsy and ready to get outta there.

"I'm not exactly sure. It's under one of these floor boards near the kitchen"

Trish got down on her knees and started trying to lift up some of the boards. None of them moved.

"Bitch you better stop acting cute and help, if you want to find this money" Trish said

Crystal put the duffel bag down and got down on her knees next to Trish and started helping her.

"Trish this one is loose, pull the other side"

Trish lifted one side while Crystal lifted the other. Trish put her hand under the floor board and she should feel a paper bag.

"This is it Crystal"

They tried to move the next floor board and it wouldn't budge.

Crystal tried to break it.

"Be careful, I don't want to break it because we have to put it back"

"Help me. Try to lift the other side"

They lifted another floor board up and now they could see the large brown paper bag underneath. Trish tugged at it but it wouldn't budge.

"We have to take one more board off and then we should be able to get the bag out"

"Okay C'mon"

They both tugged at the floor board to the right. It wouldn't budge. Crystal was sweating.

Trish was out of breath.

"C'mon take a deep breath. On three. We need this

money Crys"
"I know"
"One-two- three"
It didn't budge.
"Okay let's try again" Trish said
"One- two- three"
It didn't budge
"One- two- three"
The floor board came off.
"Damn I got a splinter" Crystal said as she sucked
on her index finger.
Trish pulled the brown paper bag out. It was heavy
as hell. She opened it and looked inside. It was full
of stacks of 5's, 10's, 20's and 50's with rubber
bands tied around the stacks.
Trish smiled.
"Yeah this is it"
She handed the bag to Crystal
"Put it in the duffel bag"
Crystal took the brown paper bag and put it inside.
"There's another bag under here" Trish said
surprised.
She took out the other brown paper bag and opened
it. Trish couldn't believe her eyes. The second bag
was filled with money too.
She gave the bag to Crystal.
"Put this in the duffel bag too"
"That's more money?"
"Yeah"
"That was all Mike's money?"
"I don't know and I don't care. I know Jr. knows

about the stash too but if he finds it first, I know he's not gonna give me shit. So fuck him"
"Are you sure?" Crystal asked
"Yeah I'm sure. Stop being a punk"
"But he's going to know it's us"
"That's why we have to hurry up and get outta here. We have to go home and pack a bag and get outta town for a while.
"We have to finish our finals this week" Crystal said
"Well maybe we can take them early, we have to get out of here soon"
This was all too crazy for Crystal. But lord knows she was ready to leave. She couldn't stand being in that house with her mother and her nasty ass step father Harold.
"Okay" Crystal said
"C'mon help me put these floor boards back"
Crystal and Trish paced back and forth across the apartment. They were both so nervous.
"So how much money do you think is in there?"
"I don't know. We can count it later. It looks like enough to get us outta here though"
"I know" Crystal said as she smiled.
"C'mon lets go. I don't want anybody to see Mike's car outside."
...
"197,000 dollars" Crystal screamed
"I know!" Trish said as she jumped up and down on the bed.
"I didn't expect it to be that much!"

"C'mon let's put it back in the duffel bag and get
outta here"
"Where are we gonna go?"
"I don't know yet, but if Jr. finds out all this money
is gone. He is gonna be looking for us"
"I just have to stop by my house and grab some
things"
"Okay cool"

Chapter 2

"Hello. We're here" Jay said waving his hands in front of Trish's face to get her out of her daze.
"Sorry I zoned out for a second"
Jay pulled the car into his five-car garage and they entered the house through an inside entrance.
The house was even better inside than it was outside. Everything was immaculate. The entire house was an array of different shades of beige, browns, gold, and mahogany. It looked like something out of MTV cribs, like nobody actually occupied the space, it was just for show.
"Sit down, make yourself comfortable." Jay said
"You have a beautiful home." Trish said as she looked around and inspected everything.
"Thanks, would you like something to drink?" Jay asked.
"Sure, do you have Grand Marnier?" Trish asked.
Jay laughed
"What's so funny?"
"Most women don't drink that." Jay said
"Well I'm not most women." Trish said
"I can see that, would you like that straight?"
"No, with a little pineapple juice"
"Coming right up" Jay said as he walked over to the bar.
When Jay came back with the drinks they talked for a while.
He asked her a lot of questions about herself and she was surprised at how down to earth he was. But

54

after awhile Trish just wanted him to shut up and fuck her.

She was tipsy and horny.

Two drinks later she couldn't take it anymore. She walked over to him and kissed. First she lightly tapped kissed him and then she tongue kissed him. They started kissing wildly and Trish started moaning, she was so turned on. He moved his hands all over her body. He palmed her ass with both hands and grabbed it as he kissed her harder and pushed his tongue deeper down her throat.

Trish lifted Jay's shirt up and moved her hands under his shirt and felt his chest. She was surprised at how muscular he was. Jay pushed Trish skirt right up over her hips and grabbed her ass even harder. Trish moaned louder. She wanted him so bad. She was soaking wet. Jay moved Trish's white lace thong to the side and stuck his finger in her pussy. "Damn" He said when he realized how wet she was. That turned Jay on even more. They took a break from kissing long enough for Jay to say

"Take this off"

Trish didn't hesitate as she unzipped her dress from the back and pulled it over her head. She stepped out of her panties and threw them on the floor. She left her pumps on.   Jay smiled when he got the full view of Trish naked.

Jay unbuckled his belt and stepped out of his jeans. "Come here" Jay demanded

He pulled Trish close to him and pushed her back on the couch. He got down on his knees and buried his face in Trish's pussy. She wrapped her legs around his neck and closed her eyes. He stuck his tongue in and out of her pussy. Trish moaned. Trish's moans turned Jay on.

"You like that?" Jay asked
"Mmm Hmm"
Jay sucked on Trish's clit and she moaned even louder. She surprised herself.   Trish felt herself coming and she grabbed Jay's head and grinded her pussy on his face. She wanted some dick now!
Jay came up for air and said "Get up"
Trish couldn't get up quick enough. She was so open that if he would have told her to stand on her head she would have.
"Turn around" Jay said
Trish bent over on the couch and Jay slid his dick inside.
"Mmm" Trish and Jay moaned at the same time.
Jay's dick was long and fat, it felt so good to Trish.
"How you want it fast or slow?"
"Fast"
Jay began to pump Trish hard and fast just the way she liked it. After two minutes she felt herself coming again.
"You want me to go harder?"
"Yeah"
Jay pulled a hand full of Trish's hair and began pumping harder from the back.

"You like that?"

"Yeah"

Jay smacked Trish's ass as he pumped harder.

Damn that hurt. Trish thought but she was so turned on.

"You got some good pussy" Jay whispered

Jay smacked Trish's ass again.

"I'm coming" Jay moaned.

Jay pulled out of Trish and they both collapsed on the couch.

"Damn that was good" Trish said as she felt her hair. It was damp with sweat and all over the place.

"Yeah it was real good"

A few minutes later they drifted off to sleep right on the couch.

...

"Did you hear me? Get in the closet!" Jay said.

"What?" Trish asked as if Jay was speaking Japanese. She didn't even remember getting into the bed.

"Get in the damn closet!" Jay said as he raised his voice.

"Why?"

"Because my wife is home!" Jay said

"Your wife?" Trish asked surprised. *She really didn't care that he was married but it sounded good.*

Trish wrapped the sheet around her naked body and picked up her dress and shoes and walked in the closet.

She put on her dress and shoes. *Shit! I left my*

panties out there! Oh well!
I can't believe this shit! He should have told me his
wife was coming home and I would have left
sooner! I don't have time for this shit! I have never
been so humiliated. I don't know how long he thinks
I'm staying in here. Trish said to herself.

Just then Trish heard.
Daddy, Daddy we missed you! From what sounded
like two little girls. *He has kids too?* Trish sat down
in a corner of the closet. *This might be a while.* She
thought.
...
Brr-ring. Brr-ing.
"Hello?" Nina said.
"Hey Nina, have you spoke to Trish today?"
"Oh what's up Crys? No I haven't spoke to her
since she left last night, why?"
"I was worried about her, that's all." Crystal said.
"Will you relax, she's a big girl. She can take care
of herself" Nina said.
Crystal knew that Trish was grown, but she always
had to take care of Trish.
"I know but she scares me sometimes with all the
crazy shit she does, anyway what's up with you?"
Crystal asked.
"Oh my God! Let me tell you what happened to me
last night!" Nina screamed.
"Last night when? We were together all night."
"When I dropped you off I went home and called
Rick. I needed some dick"

"Rick, who?" Crystal asked.

"Remember the guy I met at that fashion show?"

"Oh yeah, what about him?"

"Well he came over last night and he bought me some takeout from this after hours Thai restaurant."

"And?"

"Well, we ate and then we were just lounging around listening to some music and sipping some wine"

"And?" Crystal asked.

"I asked him if I could I see his dick." Nina said.

"Why do you always ask that?" Crystal asked.

"Because I want to know what I'm getting before I even decide to waste my time. I need a certain amount of inches." Nina joked.

"Anyway, what happened?"

"He took it out and I looked at it and I felt it. Then he asked me if I could jerk him off."

"Was it big?"

"It was medium sized, not too big and not too small. I might have let him get some"

"And what happened next?" Crystal asked.

"I jerked him off and then I asked him if I could give him a massage. He said okay and he took off his clothes and laid on his stomach."

"Okay, get to the good part!" Crystal said.

"I am shut up! So I began massaging his ass and feeling around his ass" Nina said.

"What is with you and guy's asses?" Crystal asked.

Nina is always trying to play with a nigga's ass.

"You know that's my gay test. If a guy lets me put

my finger in his ass, he is gay." Nina said.

"You are really crazy."

"Anyway, I began putting my fingers near his crack and he didn't move or even seem surprised like most guys would, so I put a finger near his hole."

"Did he jump?" Crystal asked.

"No! He just laid there." Nina said.

"Okay, what else?" Crystal asked as if she was reliving it herself.

"So I put my finger in his ass" Nina said.

"You are so Nasty!" Crystal screamed.

"And he still didn't move. First I had the tip of my finger and them I put it deeper, past my knuckle." Nina shouted.

"Eewwl." Crystal said as she pictured it in her head.

"Then do you know what he said?" Nina asked.

"What?"

"You're not doing it right!" Nina screamed as she jumped out of her bed.

"You're lying!" Crystal yelled.

"No I'm not girl! He told me to put another finger in, he said didn't feel anything!"

"So what did you say?" Crystal asked.

"I put another finger in." Nina said.

"You are one nasty bitch!" Crystal screamed.

"Fuck you! I wanted to see how far he would let me go."

"Whatever, nasty ass" Crystal said.

"Then he said do it harder and I felt like I wanted to throw up, because he was so cute"

"What did you do then?" Crystal asked.

"I put another finger up there." Nina said.

"I'm hanging up. You're lying." Crystal said as she laughed so hard she felt like she was about to pee on herself.

"No I'm not, I had three fingers up his ass and it was still loose." Nina said.

"Oh that is so nasty."

"He looked like he was starting to enjoy it and then he asked me to put another finger up there!" Nina screamed.

"And you did?"

"Yeah" Nina said.

"You are disgusting, remind me to wash my hands when I come around you." Crystal joked.

"I had four fingers up his ass and it was still loose. I am so hurt."

"Why?" Crystal asked.

"Because he is gay and I thought he was so fine!"

"Yeah girl, You need to leave him alone he does sound gay" Crystal confirmed.

"Wait I didn't tell you the craziest part"

"There's more?"

"Yeah I asked him has anyone ever fucked him in the ass and he said no. He said he used to be gay but that was a long time ago" Nina screamed as she busted out laughing.

"What? How the fuck do you used to be gay?" Crystal asked. She was on the floor now because she was laughing so hard.

"Girl, I don't know. That's the same shit I said. I told him nigga you used to smoke, you used to be a

Christian, you didn't used to be gay!"
Crystal busted out laughing.
"You are crazy! What did he say?"
"Nothing, he didn't have a chance I gave him his
clothes and went to the bathroom to scrub my
hands. He was gone when I came out"
"That is crazy girl" Crystal screamed
"Hey" Keith, Crystal's boyfriend said in the
background.
"Hey" Crystal said
"Who you talking to?"
"Nina"
"Mmm. What did you cook?"
"Nothing yet. I was about to"
"When? Now?"
"I don't know how you deal with his ass. Go ahead
and call me back"
Nina said.
Nina couldn't stand Keith. He was so fucking rude
and nasty, she didn't know what Crystal saw in him.
She could do so much better.
"Stop it. I'll call you later girl"
"Okay Bye"
"Bye"
Crystal knew Nina hated Keith. All her friends
hated him, but she loved him. They didn't
understand him like she did. He did have a bad
attitude at times but she knew that deep down he
truly loved her. He just didn't always show it.
He had been through a lot in his childhood and so
had she, she felt like they shared that common

bond.

Crystal seemed to have it all from the outside. She was smart, pretty and successful. She was the youngest person at her well known entertainment law firm and she was so driven and motivated. Most people called her a workaholic.

But Crystal became a workaholic out of habit, mostly to take her mind off the other things that were happening in her life, rather than dealing with them.

Crystal grew up in an upper class part of Long Island with her mother and father. She was the only child and life was perfect. She was daddy's little girl. Crystal's parents Marie and Luke met when they were 16. They were high school sweethearts. Right after high school they went straight to college at LIU. It was never really Marie's dream to go to college but it was Luke's and she couldn't stand to be away from him. Marie got pregnant with Crystal in their second year of college.

She was so happy she stopped taking those birth control pills and she was going to be having Luke's baby. Luke wanted to finish college and was not pleased with the idea that Marie was pregnant, she was supposed to be on birth control. Luke loved Marie and decided to marry her. Marie dropped out of college to have Crystal and Luke continued he transferred to M.I.T. They lived in a small apartment in Queens when Crystal was born but

Marie didn't care because she was so in love. Shortly after Luke graduated from M.I.T. he was offered the position as a stockbroker. When Crystal was 3 years old they moved into their huge house in Long Island. The house was beautiful Marie almost passed out when they pulled into the drive way. She couldn't believe that all this was going to be hers. She had never seen anything like it.

She looked up to a beige stone house with four large pillars in front. There were four wide matching stone steps that led up to the huge glass double doors. One the second floor there were to huge bay windows that were enclosed by small balconies. It was beautiful.

Life was going great and Marie and Crystal got everything that they wanted; anything they asked for was theirs. They took family vacations two times a year to the Caribbean.   Luke's position as a stockbroker on Wall Street made it easy for them to afford the life they had. He made excellent money and his bonuses were even better. Marie was a stay at home mom and Luke never asked her to work. Crystal and Marie were his world.

Life seemed perfect until Crystal turned 12. She noticed arguing between her mother and father. Little arguments in the middle of the night once or twice a week soon turned into yelling matches that kept Crystal up almost half the night. Most nights

Crystal cried herself to sleep. She watched her
father stay at work later and later and soon she felt
like it was just her and her mother in the house all
alone. Marie was crushed. Luke was the love of her
life. She was a virgin when she met him and he was
her first and only lover. Marie took her hurt out on
Crystal daily. She instantly turned from her loving
sweet mother to an evil bitch. She made Crystal
cook dinner and do chores everyday. Crystal had to
miss her ballet and tap classes and she barely saw
her friends anymore. Slowly Crystal's mother began
drinking. She was usually a social drinker, but lately
Crystal noticed her drunk on the couch when she
came home from school.

What is happening to my life? Crystal thought.
Even though her mother was in pain Crystal still
loved her father deeply. She usually waited at the
top of the steps for her father to come home at
night. Crystal watched him come in the door, put
his briefcase down in the corner, and hang up his
long trench coat. He would walk into the living
room and shake his head and look at her mother in
disgust because she would be drunk and passed out
on the couch. Crystal would just run to her room
and cry. She remembered when they were so happy.
    She wasn't surprised when she was 13 that her
mother and father told her that they were getting a
divorce. (Her father actually told her that he was
divorcing her mother). Even though Crystal
expected it, it felt like someone had ripped her heart

out of her chest. What did this mean now? What were they going to do? Where was she going to live? Was she going with her mother or father? This was too much for Crystal to process.

Two months later, the day after Christmas Luke told Marie and Crystal at breakfast that he was moving out. He said that he paid the mortgage for the next six months and that should be enough time for Marie to get on her feet. He said that he would be moving out right after the New Year. He kissed Crystal on the forehead and excused himself from the table. Crystal sat across from her mother and saw the blank look on her face. She looked so empty like she had just seen a ghost.
Over the past few weeks Crystal was beginning to think there was hope for her mother and father's marriage. Her mother had slowed down on the drinking and she didn't hear them fight as much. *I guess they were just being civil until everything was over.* Crystal thought.

The day the movers came was the worst day of Crystal's life. She watched her drunk mother curse out every single mover and lay across the doorway to try to stop them from leaving. They all asked her to calm down while they looked at her like she was crazy and stepped over her like a pile of trash on their way out. Crystal cried and tried to help her mother off of the floor.
"Get the fuck off of me!" Marie screamed
"This is your fault!"

Those words hurt Crystal so much. How was this her fault?

She didn't want him to leave. She wished that he was taking her with him. She loved her mother but she loved her father too. He explained to Crystal that he worked long hours and it would be best if she stayed with her mother.

"She needs you to look after her" Luke told Crystal.

Crystal knew that was true but that was the scariest part. Her mother should be looking after her. She should be a mother to her, not the other way around. The next six months were a living hell. Everyday Crystal looked through the classifieds and tried to look for a job for her mother. She wanted them to be able to stay in their house. Crystal wanted to stay at her school with her friends, she wanted her life to stay the same. Crystal did not know what her mother was qualified to do. She had never had a job in her life. When Marie met Luke in high school he rescued her from her crazy family and she hadn't seen them since, Marie never worked a day in her life.

Every time Crystal showed her mother a job she came up with some excuse why she couldn't take it. Crystal would even disguise her voice as her mothers and set up interviews for her mom. She even laid her clothes out for her. She prayed while she was at school that her mother went on the interview and got the job. But when she came home her mother was usually in the same spot watching TV with a drink in her hand or sleep on the couch. She always had some excuse why she missed the interview.

Crystal was getting sick and tired of her mother and she hated her father. How could he do this to them? How could he just leave them? Didn't he love them? They needed him.

All these thoughts went through Crystal's head ten times a day. Her conversations with her father became less frequent. She went from speaking to him everyday to speaking to him once a week. Crystal was getting scared because they only had two months left before their six months were up. If they couldn't pay the mortgage where would they go?

Crystal got a job at a supermarket to try and help out. She had got a job way out in Queens near Forest Hills so that her friends wouldn't see her. She had to ride on the bus for an hour. She went to work straight after school and stayed there until midnight almost every night. She even worked the weekends. She did her homework when she got home and usually didn't go to bed until 3am. She woke up at 7 every morning. She was tired everyday but somebody had to work. Her mother damn sure wasn't. Crystal saved every pay check that she got for two months.

Their six months were finally up. Crystal dreaded

that day. Although Crystal saved every penny from every paycheck it wasn't enough. She had saved enough to pay the mortgage for one month, but that didn't include all the other bills. The gas, electric, phone bill, cable, landscaping. These bills were the same amount as the damn mortgage!
Crystal felt like all the work she was doing was useless.
Damn she hated her mother! She hated her father too! How could they both do this to her?
What are we going to do now? Crystal thought.
They didn't have any real family and they would be too embarrassed to go their "booshie" friends.

Crystal's mother was drinking more and more. She didn't want to face reality. Crystal couldn't take it anymore.
She came home from school one day and her mother was laying on the couch drunk.
She walked over to the couch and turned off the TV and took her mother's bottle of Jack Daniels and poured it down the sink.
"What the fuck are you doing?" Marie yelled
"It's only 3:15 in the fucking afternoon" Crystal yelled back
Her mother was shocked that Crystal took that tone with her.
"Excuse me. Who are you talking to like that?" Her mother slurred
"What the fuck are you doing?"
"Minding my fucking business. You're not too old

to get a beating"
"Oh please don't try to be a fucking mother now!
You haven't been one"
"I have been doing the best I can"
"No you haven't! Do you realize that any day now
we are going to be out on our fucking ass! Where
are we going to go? Mother!" Tears streamed down
Crystal face.
Although she knew it was going to happen, saying it
out loud made it reality and it scared the shit out of
her. Marie fell down to her knees and started crying.
"This is all his fault! Don't blame this on me!" She
screamed

"I know you're hurt mommy but he left us! We
have to move on"
"I don't know how" Marie cried
The truth was Crystal didn't know how either but
she had to be strong. They had to find a way
"Well you have to stop drinking the way you are"
"Don't tell me what to do!" Marie said defensively
"Where are we gonna go mom?"
"Honestly. I don't know. The only family I have is
back in the projects. Your grandma Tammy and
your aunts Keisha and Chanel"

Crystal hadn't seen her grandmother or her aunts
since she was nine years old. She couldn't
remember the last time she saw them before that.
Once Marie met Luke she moved out and didn't
look back. Marie felt bad that her mother had never

met her own grandchild so she decided to take some gifts over there one Christmas, when Crystal was nine years old. Crystal remembered it like it was yesterday. They stared her up and down and treated her like shit. They made her and her mother feel so uncomfortable. Her aunts each had three kids and they were all mean to her too. They quickly dropped off the Christmas gifts and got out of there. They never went back.

"Its nowhere else we could go?" Crystal cried
"No. I guess I better call them"
Crystal ran upstairs to her room and fell across her floral bed spread and cried.   She screamed and punched her bed.
"Why are you doing this to me God?"
After about twenty minutes she made herself get up. She walked around and looked at her room. She had a feeling that this may be one of the last times she would be seeing it like this for a while.
She looked at her light pink walls and her big bay window. Right in front of her window was a chest full of all the stuff animals that she ever owned. She looked at the trophies she had from cheerleading competitions and she looked at her pom-poms and started crying.

She walked over to her closet and looked at all her clothes. She sat down on the floor of her closet and pulled out a big hat box filled with pictures. It was pictures from their family vacations over the last few years. They all looked so happy. She looked at one of her mom and dad. It was from the Bahamas two years ago. Luke was shirtless in a pair of white swimming trunks. Her mother had on a black bikini with a big black sun hat and big black diva shades. Her father was holding her mother like he was carrying her over the threshold. Crystal cried because she remembered taking that picture. She remembered how happy they were.

What went wrong?

Crystal reminisced for a few more hours before she began packing up some of her stuff.

...

"Did you call them?" Crystal asked her mother

"Yeah"

"What did they say?"

"They said we could stay there, but it's not much room so were going to have to give them some money"

"Did you tell them that we don't have any money?"

"No"

"Well I was just thinking that we could have a yard sale" Crystal said

"What?"

"A yard sale. We should be able to get some money for our things"

Crystal's father took most of everything but they still had their bedroom sets, living room furniture, and kitchen set. He even left some art. He cleared out most of the other rooms and took most of the

things he thought was valuable. But Crystal knew
that they   wouldn't be able to take their furniture
with them, so they might as well sell it.
She could see the look of shame on her mother's
face.
"What will the neighbors think about us selling our
stuff?"
"I don't know and I don't care. We need the money.
Besides there is a big for sale sign in front of the
house anyway. Who cares what they think?"
She really couldn't believe her mother sometimes.
Their life was falling apart and she was worried
about what the neighbors would think.
"Well when are we going to have it?" Marie asked
"Tomorrow" *Must I do everything?* Crystal thought
Crystal was happy because for a moment her
mother seemed like her old self again.

...

Living in the projects was the worst experience of
Crystal's life.
Crystal never knew that your own family could treat
you so bad.
As soon as Crystal and her mother got there they all
had their hand out.
Crystal didn't know why her mother didn't tell them
that they didn't have any money.
They did get about 2,500 dollars from the yard sale.
But Crystal wanted to save that money. She didn't
plan on staying at her grandma Tammy's for too

long. It wasn't any space for Crystal or Marie. There were already six people living in a two bedroom apartment. Now it was eight. It was Grandma Tammy, her aunt Keisha and her three kids. Jay Jay, Janice, and Jake and her other aunt Chanel. All Chanel's kids stayed with their daddies. Now it was Crystal and her mom too.

Janice and Crystal were the same age and about the same size, Janice was a little thicker. Crystal was happy when she met her because she thought that they would get along and be friends. But Janice was the worst of them all. She wore all Crystal's clothes and she stretched half of them out because she was a little bigger than her. And if Crystal asked her for something back she wanted to fight. They fought almost every day because Crystal wasn't no punk. But she wasn't from the projects either and she couldn't fight like Janice.

    Janice would grab anything from anywhere in the house and hit her with it. Shoes, boots, lamps, books, nothing was off limits. Crystal's mother wasn't there most of the time, surprisingly she found a job quick. She worked for a cleaning service at night. But she still didn't seem happy. Crystal knew she missed her father. Marie acted like she was miserable most of the time. She worked from 4pm-12am. She only saw Crystal when she came home from school. It was usually for about twenty minutes and then she was out the door on her way to work. When she got home

Crystal was sleep.

Crystal was happy her mother got a job because then they could get out of there quicker, but she hated to be there with her grandma and her aunts by herself. Her mother promised her that they would only be there three months, tops. Three months didn't seem long but Crystal didn't know if she could hang. It had only been a month and she felt like she wanted to run away already.

Crystal would tell her aunts and her grandmother about Janice and about their fights and she would expect them to be on her side or at least yell at Janice but instead they would laugh and say "Shut the fuck up you high yellow bitch! You get everything you deserve"

When Marie came around they treated Crystal nice. And as soon as she left they treated her like shit. They would cook dinner and give her a smaller plate than Jay and he was only nine. Most nights she went to bed mad and hungry.

They were all so jealous of Crystal. She couldn't understand why they hated her so much. Even her grandma hated her.

Crystal knew it would be bad but she didn't think it would be this bad. She had to transfer to a new school and she hated that too. Everyone looked at her funny because she was the new girl. She didn't hang with anyone, she even ate lunch alone. A lot of the guys tried to get with her but she wasn't feeling them. She threw herself into her school work. The only person she liked at school was her math teacher Ms. Bryant. Ms. Bryant was young and black and she didn't take no shit. She was cool as long as you did your work. She really wanted her students to succeed and Crystal liked that. She wasn't used to that because at her old school, Chaminade was very prestigious and all her teachers were white and most of them were old. She couldn't relate to them.   Math was Crystal's favorite subject and now she loved it even more.

But she hated one girl that sat in the back of the room. She was so loud and she always had something smart to say. She disrupted the class almost everyday with some smart ass comment or joke. But Crystal had to admit that she was funny as hell.
On the day of their midterm Ms. Bryant said
"Trish would you please get your books and move to this seat right here in the front"
"Why?" Trish asked
"Because I said so"
The class busted out laughing.
Crystal looked at the empty seat right next to her.
Why did she have to move her ass next to me?

Trish sat down next to Crystal and nodded her head.
"Hey" Crystal said
"Everyone place your books on the floor underneath your desk. Take out your calculators and your number two pencil. If you need a pencil raise your hand"

Trish raised her hand and Crystal grinned. She had three perfectly sharpened number two pencils on her desk.
"Can I borrow a pencil?" Trish asked
Crystal handed it to her without saying anything.
"Okay everyone you have 45 minutes to complete this test. There is no talking. Keep your eyes on your own paper" Ms. Bryant said

Fifteen minutes into the test Crystal was almost finished. She checked over everything and she was sure it was right. She looked over at Trish and she was staring into space.
 Five minutes later Trish turned to Crystal and said "What's the answer to number 6?"
Crystal acted like she didn't hear her.
"What's the answer to number 6?"
Would this bitch leave me alone. She should have studied.
"57" Crystal whispered.
"Thanks"
Crystal didn't say anything. She didn't want Ms. Bryant to catch them cheating.
"What's the answer to number 8?"
"I don't know"
"Stop lying"
"17" Crystal said with an attitude.
She didn't know why she was helping her.
"What the answer to 21, 22, 23, 24, 25, 26, 27, and 28?"

Crystal busted out laughing.

Ms. Bryant looked over in their direction.

Crystal instantly started coughing to try to hide the fact that she was laughing. She knew Ms. Bryant knew she was laughing, but she didn't say anything because she was her favorite student.

Crystal slid her paper over and moved her arm and let Trish see the answers.

When the test was over Trish said

"Thanks"

"You're welcome"

"I'm not good in math. I hate this shit. Why do you like it so much?"

"I don't know I just do"

"You going to lunch now?" Trish asked

"Yeah"

"Me too"

They talked all the way to the cafeteria and during the whole lunch. Crystal hadn't laughed that much in a long time. Trish was crazy.

She didn't understand why Trish didn't hang with anyone either.

Crystal and Trish were complete opposites, but they hit it off.

Her and Trish started hanging with each other everyday after that.

...

"Where you getting dressed up to go?" Crystal asked her mother

"I have a date"
"But we were supposed to go to the movies today"
Crystal said.
She was used to her mother not being in the mood
to do anything. When she came home from work
she was so tired and she usually slept all day on the
weekends. But Crystal had planned for and her
mother to spend the day together two weeks ago.
"Oh I totally forgot. We can go another day"
"Yeah whatever" Crystal said as she walked out the
bathroom.

Crystal decided to call Trish and see what she was
up to. Trish was probably doing something with
Mike but she always invited Crystal to come with
them. Sometimes Crystal felt bad about tagging
along but she would rather do anything than be in
the house with those nasty bitches.

She snuck and dialed Trish's number.
She wasn't allowed to use the phone.
"Hey girl"
"Hey what's up?"
"Nothing, just chilling with my boo"
Crystal laughed
"Are you guys busy?"
"No"
"Okay I'm coming over"
"Alright I'll see you in a few"
"Okay later"
Crystal grabbed a bag and threw some clothes in it

quickly. She usually spent the night at Trish and Mike's place. She hated staying home. She loved them both so much. Mike was like a brother to her. Crystal grabbed her keys and walked to the bathroom to tell her mother she was leaving. Marie was on the phone.

"I'll be downstairs in one minute. I'm trying to look my best for you honey"

Who the hell is she talking to? Crystal thought

"Mom I'm-

"Okay sweetie" Marie said barely looking at her.

Sweetie?

Crystal looked at her mother grinning into the phone. She was cheesing so hard her face could have cracked.

Crystal turned around and walked out the bathroom. She opened the front door and slammed it on her way out.

Chapter 3

"Harold and I are getting married!" Marie said as she jumped up and down
"What?" Crystal asked
"He asked me to marry him today" Marie said showing off her ring.
Crystal couldn't believe it. She could count on one hand the number of times that she met Harold. But it was still something about him that she didn't like. He made her feel uncomfortable. She couldn't believe her mother was going to marry him and they had only known each other for a few months.
"And you said yes?" Crystal asked with an attitude
"Yes. I said yes" Marie said as she rolled her eyes
Crystal could tell her mother seemed upset.
"That just seems fast"
"Look I'm grown. I don't need your smart ass comments. I've been busting my ass cleaning toilets for the last few months to get us out of here. Harold is a good man. He works hard and he has a nice house. He wants us to move in with him right away.
"Finally I can quit that stupid ass job"
"I'm sorry mom. It's just that I thought we were going to move out. Just me and you"
"We were. But things change. I met Harold and I love him"
Crystal was happy that they were moving out but she didn't know how happy she was about moving in with Harold. She didn't even know him. But anything had to better than it was now.

...

Harold's house was nicer than Crystal expected. It wasn't as big as their old house but it was comfortable. There were three bedrooms and a small backyard. He seemed pretty neat for a man that lived alone. Him and his wife got divorced 4 years ago.

Crystal was happy because anything was better than Grandma Tammy's. She never wanted see those bitches again for the rest of her life.

Harold tried his best to make her feel comfortable. There was still something about him that Crystal didn't like but she couldn't put her finger on it. She decided to stop being so mean to him because her mother seemed so happy. She hadn't seen her this happy since her father.

    Marie's attitude had completely changed. Crystal felt like she turned back into her old mother. She was nice to Crystal, she took her shopping and they spent time together. Marie had more free time now. The day they moved in with Harold Marie quit her job at the cleaning service. Crystal still wasn't completely nice to Harold because he wasn't her father. She missed her father so much. She was definitely daddy's little girl and it hurt her so much that he didn't care anymore. He hardly ever called. She hadn't seen him since he came to pick up his things from the house.

How could he just forget about me? She thought

...

"Crystal get ready we're going out for dinner"
Harold called out from downstairs
Crystal was sitting on her bed reading Word Up
magazine.
She had to admit Harold was really trying. Living
with him wasn't so bad, it was actually kind of
good.
He gave her anything she asked for and most of the
time he was nicer to her than her mother.
Life still wasn't like it used to be, but it was close.
Her mother was finally happy again and they were
really becoming a family.
Crystal still missed her father, but she missed him
less and less every day.
...

"That was really good thanks Harold" Crystal said
as she headed upstairs to her room.
They had just got in from dinner. Harold took them
to a really fancy Italian restaurant Trattoria
L'Incontro.
Crystal ordered shrimp parmigiana, it was delicious.
"I'm going to the supermarket to pick up a few
things. I'll be back in a few" Marie called out.
"Okay honey" Harold said as he kissed her on the
cheek .
Crystal walked in her room and picked out some
shorts and a T-shirt out of her bottom drawer to
sleep in. She threw them on her bed and grabbed
her towel off her closet door and walked in the

bathroom. She turned on the shower and began undressing. She stepped in the shower. The hot water felt so good. She loved taking steaming hot showers. She stayed in the shower for about fifteen minutes. She stepped out of the shower and dried off. She walked in her room and she screamed when she saw Harold sitting on her bed.

"What are you doing? Why are you in here?" Crystal asked startled.

"Relax I just wanted to talk to you"

"Well you can talk to me after I get dressed"

"Don't be so mean Crystal"

"What are you doing?" Crystal hoped he wasn't trying to do what she thought he was. He was married to her mother.

He walked got off the bed and walked over to Crystal and stroked the side of her face. Crystal flinched.

"Get off me. You're married to my mother"

"You are so beautiful"

"Please get out!"

Harold leaned forward and kissed Crystal on the lips.

Crystal pushed him away.

"Stop!"

"You know you like it. Life could be really good for you Crystal"

"What is that supposed to mean?"

"It means that if you keep our little secret you can have whatever you want"

"I don't want anything, just leave me alone"

"Stop playing with me. I see how you look at me
when your mother isn't around"
"What?"
Crystal couldn't believe what he was saying. She
never looked at him like that. He was attractive for
an older guy, but she never thought about him in
that way.
Harold grabbed Crystal by the back of the head and
pulled her face close to his. He kissed her hard and
shoved his tongue down her throat.
Crystal started crying.
"Please stop. Please. My mother will be here soon"
"No she won't I asked her stop a few more places
for me on the way home"
"My mother loves you. Please stop"
Harold ignored what Crystal said and pulled the
string on her robe. He opened her robe to reveal her
naked body. He smiled when he saw her naked. She
looked better than he imagined.
Crystal closed it back and tried to run out of the
room. Harold grabbed her arm and closed the door.
He grabbed her robe and threw it on the floor.
Crystal tried to cover her naked body.
"Stop, Stop! Please!" Crystal screamed at the top of
her lungs.
Harold covered her mouth with his hand and she bit
his hand. He slapped her right across her face.
Crystal cried even harder.
He pushed her back on the bed and pinned her
down.
"Stop putting up a fight. You know you want it.

This can be our little secret"
"No! get off of me!" Crystal screamed
"Now this can go two ways. You can be a good girl
and do as I ask and we can have a lot of fun or I will
have to tell your mother that you tried to seduce me.
I will tell her that you came out the shower naked
and tried to have sex with me. Who do you think
she will believe? Me? or you?"
"You know she won't believe you; She will hate
you" Harold said with a grin on his face

Crystal cried. It was sad but she knew if Harold told
her mother that she probably wouldn't believe her,
she would believe him. She knew her mother loved
him and she didn't want to hurt her. Her mother was
finally happy again. It would crush her mother to
know that he was a pervert. *What if she left him?*
Then they would have to go back to the projects and
what if her mother started drinking again? A million
thoughts were going through Crystal's head. She
cried even more.
Harold wiped her tears.
"Stop crying. I won't hurt you"
"Please stop. I won't tell my mother anything. I
promise. Just please stop"
Harold ignored her and kissed her on the lips.
He felt all over her breasts and Crystal cried "Please
stop"
She tried to get up but she couldn't move. Harold
was too strong. Harold unbuttoned his pants. And
took his dick out of his boxers. He laid on top of

Crystal and found her spot.

He jammed it inside her. Crystal cried more and
more. She couldn't believe what was happening.
He couldn't get it in and became frustrated.
"Oww you're hurting me! Please stop!"
Crystal was a virgin, so she didn't know what to
expect, but she knew it would hurt and it was
hurting her right now.
Harold pushed even harder.
"Ahhhh!" Crystal screamed. He got it in and it was
the most excruciating pain of her life.
"Please stop, Please" Crsytal cried.
Harold ignored Crystal pleas and pumped harder.
Two minutes later he was done.
"Look how easy that was. Go clean yourself up"
Harold said pleased with himself.
Crystal just laid there in a daze. She couldn't
believe what just happened to her. In a matter of six
months her life had been turned upside down.
Why God? She asked as tears streamed down her
face.
Crystal couldn't move she just laid there on her bed.
Harold peeked back in her room and said
"Get up and go clean yourself up now. Remember
this is our secret. You wouldn't want to hurt your
mother would you?"
Crystal didn't respond.
"Would you?" Harold asked again
"No"

Crystal got up off the bed. She could hardly walk. She was in so much pain. She picked her robe up off the floor and put it on. She walked into the bathroom and turned the shower on. It was steaming hot. She stepped in the shower, under the hot water and cried. She fell on the bathroom floor and sobbed like a baby. She didn't understand what just happened to her. She wanted to tell her mother but she knew she couldn't. Her mother wasn't strong enough. She couldn't handle it. If she told her mother she would be crushed and now she quit her job they would have to move back into the projects. Crystal didn't know what was worse. Living with Harold or living at her grandma Tammy's. Just when she thought her life was getting better this had to happen.

Where are you daddy? She thought
Maybe I can move with him. She smiled for a second.

Crystal jumped when she heard a knock at the door.

"You okay honey? You've been in there for a while" Her mother called from the other side

"Yeah Mom. I'll be out in a minute"

...

"You're pregnant? Who you been fucking?" Trish asked

"You don't know him"

"What do you mean I don't know him? You tell me everything?"

"You don't know him?"

"What his name?"

"Just leave it alone Trish"

"No. I'm not going to leave it alone. You're pregnant and you won't tell me who the daddy is"

"I'm not keeping it so it doesn't matter"

"Who is it?"

Crystal busted out crying.

"I'm sorry Crys. I didn't want to make you cry. If you really don't want to tell me then fuck it"

"Its Harold"

"Harold who?"

"Harold"

"Your mother's Harold?"

"Yeah"

"Your mother's husband Harold?"

"Yes"

"You been fucking him?"

"Not exactly"

"Well how exactly did you get pregnant?" Trish asked

Crystal began to tell Trish how the whole thing started. How Harold first came in her room when she was in the shower and how now he did one to two times a week.

"How long has then been going on Trish?"

"A little over a year" Crystal said. She was so ashamed.

Crystal was 16 now.

"What? And you never told me?" Trish knew exactly how Crystal felt. Being violated was the worst feeling in the world. Those men didn't understand what they were doing to you for their two minutes of pleasure. Nobody could ever give back what they take away.

"I haven't told anybody" Crystal cried.

Trish hugged her

"Why haven't you told your mom?"

"Because I know she won't believe me. She worships the ground Harold walks on. And if she does believe me and she leaves him, we will have to go back to the projects"

"That fucking bastard! I never liked him!" Trish screamed

"I know me too. It was something I didn't like about him when I met him. But I could never put my finger on it" Crystal said

"So what are you going to do now?"

"I want to get rid of it, but I don't know where"

"I do, don't worry" Trish said

"I only have $150 dollars"

"I'll get some money from Mike. Don't worry about it"

"Thanks"

"Now what are we gonna do about Harold?" Trish asked

"What do you mean?" Crystal asked

"I mean. Mike can fuck him up or get somebody to fuck him up real bad"

"For real?" Crystal asked

"Hell yeah. I don't know how you even stay in the same house with that pervert"

Crystal thought about it for a moment and she

would love to have someone fuck Harold up. She couldn't count the number of times she prayed that he would die in his sleep or he would get robbed and killed on the way home from work. But then she thought about her mother and she would be devastated if something happened to Harold and she couldn't live with that.

"No Trish, just leave it alone"

"So you gonna keep letting him hurt you? What if you get pregnant again?"

"I can't hurt my mother Trish. Besides we are supposed to go away to college in less than a year"

"Yeah but that's still a long time to live with that bastard, you could stay with us"

"Thanks but my mother won't let me move out, you know how she feels about you Trish but I could stay with you sometimes"

Marie couldn't stand Trish, she felt like she was a bad influence for Crystal, she didn't like them hanging out. She couldn't stand how Trish came always came to the house to meet Crystal in tight revealing clothes and she couldn't understand how Trish managed to have all the latest designer clothes and she was only in high school, she knew she had to be doing something illegal and she didn't want Crystal involved in it. Marie wouldn't be surprised if Trish was a prostitute.

"Okay" Trish said

She knew how Crystal's mother felt about her, she made it very obvious every time they saw each other, but she didn't give a shit.

Chapter 4

"So, Paulette you are not due back for your next annual until June of next year" Dr. Patterson said "Okay" Paulette responded nervously.
She always hated going to the doctor's office it always made her so nervous. Before every doctor's appointment she always got down on her knees and prayed the night before. She asked God to please let her be healthy and free of any diseases and she promised she would stop her not so smart behaviors. So far she had been successful for the past 26 years, but thinking back on the past few months, she had done some dumb shit. So now she wasn't so sure.
One event in particular stood out in her mind.

It was a Friday night and Paulette had a date with Gabriel, a guy she had met the previous week on Myspace.
It started out with him asking to be added as one of her friends.
She looked at his pictures and he looked good, he was sexy as hell so she accepted. He looked like he was mixed, maybe Puerto Rican and Black with a nice tan and a banging body. He wore his hair in a low caesar hair cut. Almost all his pictures had his shirt off and his body was perfect.
    The first day she added him to her friends he left her a comment saying
"Hey sexy. You look beautiful in all your pics"

Paulette responded with a simple "Thank you. You do too"

"Your profile sounds good are you single?"

"Yeah. What about you?"

"I'm single too. I'm still looking for the right girl"

"Where do you live?"

"I live in Harlem"

"Me too"

"Can I call you?"

"Yeah" Paulette responded as she typed her phone number.

Their conversations went on for a week. Paulette was open. She was checking her Myspace page every chance she got. At work, at home, on her blackberry, everywhere. And if she wasn't on Myspace then her and Gabriel were on the phone or text messaging each other.

After about a week Gabriel texted

"I'm tired of talking online and texting let's meet in person ☐"

Finally! Paulette thought. She was a little nervous at first but she liked something about him and she liked talking to him on the phone, she wanted to meet him too. Shit! She needed a man.

"Okay when?" Paulette asked

"Tomorrow"

"Tomorrow's cool. Let's meet in Soho by my job. We can meet at this little restaurant/lounge called the Aquagrill ☐"

"I've never been there before. Text me the address"

"Okay ttyl"

"ttyl"

Paulette was so nervous about their date. She needed to relax. She couldn't get in touch with her weed man so she bought a bottle of Bacardi and a container of Orange Juice on her way home from work.

"What if he looks different in person?" Paulette asked herself as she sipped on her Bacardi and Orange Juice.

"What if he thinks I look different in person?" She asked herself as she paced back and forth in her room.

Paulette's apartment was very small and barely had any furniture. She didn't care as long as she had a bed and a T.V. She wasn't your typical "girly girl". She had more of a bachelorette pad than a grown woman's apartment. She loved abstract art so there were very eclectic pieces of art on the walls. But besides the art there was a black futon in her living room with a small 19" television on top of a coffee table that she got from a thrift store. Now her bedroom was a different story, she took pride in her bedroom. She had a Queen sized cherry wood sleigh bed with matching dressers and end tables. She had a huge picture of an African Queen above her bed.   Her bedroom set was the most expensive thing in her apartment because she loved to be in the bed. Whether she was entertaining someone or sleeping in it. Those were her two favorite things to do.

"What am I going to wear?" Paulette asked herself as she stood in front of the mirror in her tan lace bra and matching boy shorts. She had just bought the set today from Victoria Secret's. The sales woman was trying to convince her to get a thong set, but she hated wearing thongs, she felt like something was stuck up her ass all day.

She pulled out a pair of dark blue skinny Seven Jeans. They were her favorite jeans. They made her butt look perfect. She took out a low cut black tank top.
Gabriel told her he would be wearing a black shirt and she remembered what he looked like from his pictures online.
At 8:30 Paulette walked in Aquagrill wearing a tight tank top her low-rise skinny jeans and sexy Gucci stilettos she got at a sample sale, she wouldn't dare pay full price.
She looked around to see if she saw Gabriel , and she spotted him sitting at a table in the corner, but he looked like he was already with someone.
Paulette walked over and introduced herself to Gabriel and his friend.
"Hi Gabriel, It's me Paulette"
"Hey Paulette, it's good to finally see you in person" Gabriel said as he stood up and hugged her.
"This is my friend Jaime"
"Nice to meet you Jaime" Paulette said wondering why the hell she was chaperoning their date.
"Do you mind if Jaime joins us for some drinks?

She's my best friend and I thought you guys should meet" Gabriel said

"No not at all" Paulette answered lying her ass off. *Hopefully she leaves soon.*

To Paulette's surprise Jaime ended up being very nice and she spent more time talking to her than Gabriel.

Everything was going fine until Paulette saw Jaime put her hand on Gabriel's thigh. And not the friendly way you would tap someone, the affectionate way, like they were a couple. Paulette decided to brush it off, she had had three drinks and maybe it was her imagination.

Then Jaime leaned over and kissed Gabriel on the neck.

Okay this is getting a little weird. Paulette thought.

Paulette gave them a weird look as to say "What the fuck is going on?"

Then Jaime turned Gabriel's face to hers and tongue kissed him.

At that moment Paulette stood up like she was going to leave and Gabriel said "No wait, let me explain"

"What the fuck is going on?" Paulette asked confused.

"This is not my best friend, its my girlfriend"

"What?"

"Jaime is my girlfriend?"

Paulette shook her head as if she didn't understand what he just said and then she asked "So why the fuck have you been calling me and why did you ask

me to meet you here?" Paulette asked
"Because we were looking for a girlfriend"
"We?" Paulette asked
"Me and Jaime" Gabriel said
"What? This is crazy, I'm leaving" Paulette said as
she gathered her jacket and purse.
"Let us explain" Jaime interrupted
"We have an open relationship" Gabriel said
"Good for you two but I'm not into this shit!"
Paulette said
"We were looking for someone else we could have
as our partner so it could be just the three of us"
Jaime explained
"Why can't it be just the two of you?" Paulette
asked
"Because we feel that it would be more fun to have
three people, but we can't go outside of each other,
we must be faithful to one another" Jaime said
Although it sounded weird for some strange reason
it made sense to Paulette.
"I have never heard no shit like this before, this is
all very new to me" Paulette said
"We understand that" Jaime said
"That's why I wanted Jaime to meet you, so I could
make sure we all got along" Gabriel said
"Well I have to think about this and I'll call you
guys" Paulette said as she began to walk towards
the exit. *I have to get the fuck outta here.* She
thought
"Well let us at least drop you off home" Jaime said
"I'm okay I'll take the train" Paulette answered

"It's late we'll drop you off" Gabriel said
"Okay"
"Lets have one more round of drinks before we
leave" Jaime insisted
Knowing she should say no, because she was
already way past tipsy Paulette said
"okay" anyway.
On the drive home Paulette sat in the back and
Jaime sat in the front. No one said a word for a
while. Suddenly Jaime bent over and began to
unbuckle Gabriel's belt and unzip his pants. She
took out his dick and licked her lips as she looked at
Paulette in the backseat. She covered his entire dick
with her mouth and Gabriel was not small. She
began slowly going up and down, looking at
Paulette the entire time. Even though it seemed
crazy it was turning Paulette on. Jaime must have
noticed this and she began going harder and faster.
Gabriel began to moan and stepped on the gas as he
ran through red lights back to back. Paulette
watched in amazement.

He flew through all the lights on the way to the
Westside Highway.
"We're here" Gabriel mumbled through moans
When Paulette looked out the window they were in
front of a huge high rise building on 92nd street and
Broadway.
"Where are we?" Paulette asked"
"I had to stop at my apartment and get something"
Jaime said

"Come inside it will only take a minute" Gabriel
said
"One minute right?" Paulette asked
"Yes one minute, just relax" Jaime said
When they stepped out of the car Paulette's head
was spinning and she could hardly stand up. They
walked inside the building they were greeted by a
doorman as they stepped into a plush elevator and
Jaime pushed the ninth floor.
Jaime pulled out the keys and they stepped off the
elevator and walked to the first apartment on the
right. As soon as they were inside Jaime pinned
Paulette against the wall and started kissing her.
Paulette had never been with a woman before but
she didn't stop Jaime. Jaime was sexy. She was
Puerto Rican, tall and slim.. She had long curly
black hair and a long slender nose, she had an
awkward look, but a lot of sexy appeal. She
definitely looked like a model.   Gabriel just stood
there and watched.
Jaime began feeling Paulette's breasts and she lifted
up her shirt and started furiously sucking on her
nipples.
"Mmm" Paulette moaned
Gabriel interrupted and grabbed them both by the
hand and led them to the bedroom.

Jaime started right where she left off and began
taking Paulette's jeans off.
Just then Gabriel stepped in and started kissing
Paulette while Jaime rubbed her everywhere else. *It*

was all happening so fast but felt so good Paulette thought.

The last thing Paulette remembered was Gabriel sliding in her while Jaime watched. Paulette threw her head back and closed her eyes.

"Just give your chart to Mary Ann at the front desk and have a great afternoon" Dr. Patterson said as she handed Paulette her medical chart and walked out of the exam room.

"You too" Paulette said snapping out of her daze and gathering her belongings. Just then Paulette's cell phone rang.

"Hey what's up Trish?"

"Sure I'm on my way" Paulette said.

...

"Over here Paulette" Trish waved to get Paulette's attention as she walked through the door of the always crowded diner.

Trish smiled as she looked at her friend. She was so pretty and stylish in her own quirky way. Paulette wore a brown bob that complimented her caramel skin perfectly and she hardly ever wore makeup. They were such opposites but equally beautiful. Paulette loved shopping at thrift stores and always wore bright colors that Trish would never dream of wearing but Paulette always pulled them off. Trish on the other hand wouldn't dare buy anything if it wasn't designer.

"Hey girl" Paulette said as she leaned over and kissed Trish on the cheek.

"I ordered us two turkey burgers and fries" Trish said

"Great I'm starving"

"Me too"

"Why do you have on the same clothes from last night?" Paulette asked

"It's a long story girl" Trish said as she began filling her friend in on the previous night's events.

"So he was married?" Paulette asked

"Yeah, that doesn't bother me though. What bothers me is that he didn't tell me she was coming home"

"You are such a ho" Paulette said laughing

"Why because you fuck for free?" Trish asked

"Shut up!" Paulette said

"It's true, so many women have sex with men and don't expect shit from them, not even dinner! I have standards and expectations" Trish explained

"So did you get dinner last night?" Paulette joked

"Shut up bitch! Don't worry he is going to give me what I want. I will make sure of it" Trish said

"He didn't even drive you home?" Paulette asked

"No, when his wife and kids came upstairs he told them all he would take them to breakfast and they left"

"How did you get home?"

"I called a cab"

"So how are going to speak to him again, you didn't even exchange numbers?" Paulette asked?

"I'm not worried about that. I left my phone number in his underwear drawer so he has to find it the next time he gets dressed. And I called my cell phone

from his house, so I have his home number too"
Trish said
"Please say you are not going to call his house"
"I wouldn't do that but if I have to I will"
"You are really crazy"
"Trust me if he knows what's good for him he is
going to call" Trish said as she thought of all the
new things he was going to buy her.

...

"Please hold while the Nextel subscriber you are
trying to reach is located" the operator said.
It was about the fifteenth time Crystal had called
Keith tonight. She rolled over and looked at the
clock. It was 12:16am and she hadn't heard from
Keith since he left her house this morning. She
called him a few times and once she even thought
she heard him pick up and hang up as soon as he
heard her voice.

"Damn I hate him!" Crystal said as she threw her
cordless phone on the floor.
But the fact was she loved him. She knew he had
faults but she was hoping he would change because
she loved him. Whenever she tried to leave him he
cried and sobbed and told her how much he loved
her and couldn't live without her. He promised her
he would change and she wanted to believe him.
Crystal began to cry as she thought about what her
relationship had become. She never thought she
would be one of those girls that always made

excuses for her man and justified the things he did, but now she was.

In the beginning everything was great. Keith seemed so nice and sweet. He called Crystal ten times a day just to tell her he was thinking about her. He would send mushy text messages and romantic cards.

They would take long walks and talk and look at the stars. Everything was going so good that Crystal didn't find anything strange when things started moving very fast. After about two months they were saying "I love you" and after six months he began spending the night so frequently that he slowly moved in.

Crystal loved being in love and didn't mind at all the fact that they didn't go out as much and they spent almost every minute in the house. She loved to cook and she wanted to keep Keith happy.

She also didn't mind when he started borrowing money from her. She actually found it a little strange but he was her man and she loved him.

It wasn't until one day Crystal forgot her wallet when on the way to work. She turned her car around and double parked in front of her building. Keith had left a few minutes before Crystal on his way to work too. She ran up stairs and put the key in the door and found Keith sitting on the couch in his pajamas watching T.V. Crystal couldn't believe her eyes. *He just left in a suit and tie.*

"What are you doing home? She asked

"Oh I didn't feel well so I decided to call out" Keith

said

"But you looked fine when you left" crystal said.

"Well I began feeling sick on the way to work" Keith snapped

"So why aren't you laying in bed?" Crystal asked

"Because I wanted to watch a little T.V., is that a fucking crime?" Keith asked

Maybe he really is sick. Crystal thought

"I'm late for work, I hope you feel better" Crystal said as she grabbed her wallet and walked out the door. Crystal thought about what happened with Keith all day at work. Something seemed very funny about the situation.

Keith seemed very comfortable at home as if he wasn't sick at all.

The next morning as usual Keith left a few minutes before Crystal. Crystal walked out at her usual time 8:10 am but instead of walking downstairs she hid at the end of the hallway. Crystal waited for a few minutes and just as she was about to leave Keith came walking up the stairs and headed to her apartment. She waited for him to go inside because she didn't want the neighbors all up in her business. As soon as the door shut she put her key in the door and walked in to find Keith getting some juice out of the refrigerator.

"What are you doing home?" Crystal asked

"What are you doing home? Keith asked

"Don't change this around on me?"

"Um I forgot my wallet" Keith said

"Oh you did?" Crystal asked

Crystal knew he was lying.
"Yeah, you forgot yours yesterday right?" Keith
asked
"Yes but-
"And did I run in the apartment questioning you?
Keith asked
"No but-
"But nothing, I don't need this shit!" Keith said as
he slammed his glass on the counter and walked out
the door
"Keith wait, I wasn't accusing you!" Crystal yelled
behind Keith but he was already down the steps.
Crystal felt so bad for accusing Keith. He was right
it wasn't a crime to forget your wallet.
She had to make it up to him.

Chapter 5

Damn I look good! Nina said to herself as she
looked in the mirror. Nina stared at her brand new
haircut and smiled with pleasure. She got her long
black hair flat ironed straight and she cut sharp
bangs in the front. She loved it!
She spun around in her brand new turquoise
strapless BCBG dress to get a better look at herself.
It went with her strappy gold sandals perfectly.
Nina was so excited about the date she had tonight.
She had been on so many dates in the past few
months looking for Mr. Right and she always found
Mr. Wrong; she was beginning to give up on dating.
The only reason she was so excited was because
Trish made him sound like such a catch.
"I found someone that will be perfect for you girl"
Trish said
"What does he look like?"
"He's nice, and he's kind of cute"
"You said nice first, then he must be ugly"
"No he's not ugly at all, I've never actually met him
though"
"So why is he perfect for me?"
"Because he is single and a millionaire?"
"A millionaire?"
"Yes a millionaire, I dated his twin brother Dave a
few times. Dave's twin brother Darius got into an
accident a few years ago, he sued the hospital and
got a hefty settlement, a couple million. He helped
his brother out and since then they have invested

their money and they are doing very well."
"So why is he single?"
"I don't know I guess he hasn't found the right lady yet"
"Mmm. Hmm" Nina wasn't sure if she believed that but she needed a man.
"Anyway, Dave called me last night and asked me to go with him to a dinner party on Friday. He also asked if I knew anyone that could go with his brother Darius because he didn't have a date".
"You know I do not do blind dates"
"Trust me. You will have a nice time".
"Ok. I better"
...

Br-Br-ing Br-ing
"Hello?"
"Hey Nina, you can come outside we're on our way."
When Nina got outside she looked around to see if she saw them. She waited a few minutes and then she heard loud music blaring down the block. Just then a black escalade with huge rims pulled up in front of Nina's building. She stood there for a few seconds praying that this was not them in this ghetto-fied ride. Then the passenger window rolled down and Trish said hey girl, get in. *I'm going to kill Trish.*
"Hello" Nina said to everyone once she got in the backseat. *He didn't even get out and open the door. This is going bad already.*

"Hey Nina, I'm Darius" Darius said with a head nod.

"Hi, nice to meet you" Nina said. She was not pleased at all. First off he looked a little like a rat and he looked about 20 years older than her. Then to make it worse he had on a royal blue suit. Nina looked down at her dress and then at his suit, they looked horrible together. *I'm going to kill Trish.* Nina decided to make the best of the situation since they did have to spend the rest of the night together.

"So what do you do?" Nina asked

"I mainly invest, a little here, a little there" Darius said

Nina expected him to elaborate or ask her some questions but he didn't. She asked a few more questions and they rode in silence the rest of the way. They reached their destination in about 10 minutes. *Thank God we're here.*

They searched for a parking space for about 30minutes. Nina was getting so restless and frustrated.

"Why don't we valet" Nina said

"Yeah" Trish agreed

"That's a waste of money" Darius said.

And their millionaires, please! Nina thought.

They finally found a space about 7 blocks away. Nina was pissed.

"These shoes are not made for walking" Nina whispered to Trish as they got out the car.

Just then Nina looked over at Dave and he had on the same suit! The same ugly ass royal blue suit! *I can't believe this shit!*

Nina noticed that everyone got out the car except for Darius. Trish and Dave started walking so Nina walked around to Darius side of the car and said "Are you coming?"

"Yeah, can you help me out the car?"

"Help you?" Nina asked surprised

"Yes" Darius said as he put his left hand on her shoulder and used her as a crutch to get out of the car. *What the hell is going on?*

"Did your leg fall asleep?" Nina asked

"No!" Darius snapped

"Well, excuse me" Nina snapped back

Once Darius got of the car and was standing up Nina began to walk towards the restaurant but Darius looked like he was going to lose his balance. *Oh my god! He is crippled!*

Nina walked over and reached out her hand to help Darius and he waved it away. He began walking with a slight limp and dragging his right foot. Every couple of steps he had a nervous twitch. *I can't believe this shit. I'm going to kill Trish!*

They finally made it the restaurant about 20 minutes later. *I can't wait to see Trish. I'm going to smack the shit out of her.*

...

"Where have you been?" Crystal asked Keith as she saw him creeping in the bed next to her.

"I was out with Deonte"

"It's 2 o'clock in the morning Keith"

"I didn't mean to stay out that late"

"Where did you go?"

"You know he promotes parties as a second job so he asked me to come with him to an album release party he was promoting"

"Why didn't you ask me to go?"

"It was last minute, sorry"

"Whatever! It's always last minute!"

"Don't be mad at me baby. I promise next time I will invite you."

"It's not even about that! You take my car and come in late every night and then you are too tired to look for a job in the morning. I'm really getting tired of this shit! It's been 3 months already!"

"I've been looking for a job baby, you know it's hard" Keith said as he kissed Crystal's neck and started playing in her hair.

"I know it's hard, but you could try a little harder"

"I will try harder, I promise baby" Keith said as he turned Crystal face towards his and kissed her.

"Okay baby" Keith said

"Okay baby" Crystal said as she kissed him back. She let Keith undress her and make love to her. She gave in again.

...

Excuse me! Paulette said as she pushed through the crowd in lower Manhattan. She was on her way to meet Trish and Crystal at a warehouse on 24th street for a major sample sale. She loved Manhattan and all the people but not when she was in a rush. The

sale started an hour ago and Trish said it was
packed; Paulette didn't want all the good stuff to be
gone. She loved a sale. She wouldn't dare buy
things full price.

It had been a few days since Paulette's visit at
the gynecologist's office. They still hadn't
contacted her about the results of any of her tests.
She took it as a good sign because if anything was
wrong she would have probably heard from them
already. *I guessed my prayers worked. Thank you
God.*

"Hey ladies" Paulette said when she finally got to
the warehouse

"Hey suga lumps" Trish said. Trish had been calling
her that since they were about 18, when they met in
college.

"Hey" Crystal said

"Where's Nina?" Paulette asked

"She's still not talking to me since I set her up on
that blind date" Trish said

"I wouldn't talk to you either. He was crippled
Trish!" Crystal joked

"I didn't know. I told Nina I never met him" Trish
said as she cracked up laughing.

"Nina said they were tacky, old and cheap!"
Paulette said

"They were not that old, but they were kind of tacky
and cheap!" Trish said as she laughed harder.

"Here Paulette I picked up some jeans in your size I
thought you might like" Crystal said

"Thank you darling" Paulette joked

"Trish, girl don't act like you don't see me" said a loud voice in the crowd

All three girls looked around to see where it was coming from. Then they saw a handsome brown skinned man with hazel eyes, and a Mohawk walking their way. He had on fitted blue jeans and a snug black tee.

"Hey miss Trish" He said

"Hey Deonte how are you" Trish said as they gave each other two air kisses on the cheeks.

"I'm good. You know I couldn't miss a sale girl, I love to shop" Deonte said

"I know that, you are always dressed to impress. Let me introduce you to my friends, this is Paulette and Cry-" Trish said

"Crystal" Deonte finished

"You know each other?" Trish asked

"We've met" Deonte said as he looked at her and rolled his eyes

"I'm going to get back to shopping. I'll keep in touch" Trish said

"Make sure you do" Deonte joked

"It was nice meeting you Paulette" Denote said as he turned around and walked away.

"Ooh what did you do to him Crystal?" Paulette joked

"Nothing, why do you say that? Crystal asked as if she didn't notice anything.

"How do you to know each other?" Trish butted in

"Him and Keith are best friends?"

"Deonte and Keith are best friends?" Paulette asked

surprised

"Yes" Crystal said

"And you don't find anything strange?" Trish asked

"No why?" Crystal asked

"Did you see Deonte?"

"Yes and?" Crystal asked

"He is straight up gay; I mean flaming gay" Trish said

"I have to agree" Paulette said

"So now a straight person can't be friends with someone gay?"

"I have nothing against gay people, Deonte is my friend. I just don't know if I would trust him around my man" Trish busted out laughing

"And Deonte is fine!" Paulette added

"Well Keith said they grew up together and they have been friends for years. I can't choose his friends for him" Crystal said

Crystal tried not to let it get to her, but the truth was it did. She didn't need her friends to point it out to her, she thought about it a lot.

...

"Br-Brrng Brrng"

"Hello?"

"Hi, may I speak to Trish?"

"Speaking, who is this?"

"It's Jay"

"Hello, Jay. I thought you forgot about me" Trish joked

"I could never forget someone like you. I've just

been real busy with work"

"Understandable. So what made you call me tonight?"

"I felt bad about what happened, you know leaving you in the closet and I wanted to make it up to you tomorrow night, is that alright with you?"

"You could have told me you were married" Trish said pretending she was upset

"You're right I'm sorry. But things went so fast and you didn't ask"

"Well you could have at least told me she was coming home"

"I didn't know she was coming home. They were not supposed to be home until the afternoon but they took an earlier flight"

"So how did you plan on making it up to me? What do you have in mind?"

"First you have to say yes" Jay said

"Yes to what?"

"Yes that you will go out with me tomorrow night"

"What makes you think I want to date a married man?" Trish asked knowing she didn't give a damn.

"Yes or No?" Jay asked

"Yes, only because I love surprises. So it better be damn good"

"Trust me it will be worth your while. Be ready tomorrow at 7pm"

"Okay"

"Have a good night"

"You too"

Trish hung up the phone and smiled. She knew he would call sooner or later. They always did. Trish stared at herself in the mirror wondering what came over her. She never let a man have so much control so soon. She was trying to play hard to get with Jay but that was not working. It was something about him that was just so damn sexy. She didn't care if he was married.

Trish looked at the clock it was 7:28pm. *I still have some time to catch Bloomingdales.* Trish said as she grabbed her purse and ran out the door.

...

Chapter 6

"Shit!" Paulette screamed as she spilled coffee all over her white shirt. *I think I have another shirt at work.* Paulette thought.

She worked as a receptionist at a small law firm on Bleecker Street and she was supposed to be there to open the office 25 minutes ago.

Just then as if someone was playing a joke on her it started pouring raining. *Is this a joke?* Paulette looked up to the sky and asked.
She was soaking wet from her hair to her feet. Her toes were slipping and sliding out of her wedge sandals.
She stopped in a small store on the corner to get an umbrella. Either everyone had the same idea or the store was having a super sale because the line almost reached the back of the store. Paulette was already late and she didn't want to walk the next 5 blocks in the rain so she stood on line to buy the umbrella.
I'm already late. What will ten more minutes hurt?
"That will be $9.54" The cashier said

"Here" Paulette said as she handed over her only soaking wet $10 dollar bill. *I guess I won't be eating lunch today. Thank God I'm getting paid today.* She thought

Paulette looked down at her cell phone 9:47am *By the time I get there I will be an hour late* Paulette thought. She rushed out of the store opening her umbrella. When she got outside the sun was shining. She noticed people were staring at her wondering why the fuck she was soaking wet on such a beautiful day.

She looked down at her stained shirt, and her wet feet and wondered why she was having such a bad day.

As if it couldn't get any worse the phone rang.

Who the hell is this? I'm not in the mood to talk to anybody. Paulette thought.

She looked down at her cell phone and it was a blocked number. She usually didn't answer blocked numbers but she did today

"Hello?"

"Hello, may I speak to Ms. Jackson?"

"Speaking" Paulette said wondering who the hell it was.

"Hi this is Tara from the Women's Health Center, I wanted to know if you could come in so we could talk about your results"

"Is everything okay?" Paulette asked barely breathing

"I'd rather not discuss anything on the phone. Can you come in so we can talk in person?"

"Is everything okay? " Paulette screamed

"Please calm down Ms. Jackson, I cannot discuss anything on the phone, so can we please set up an appointment for you to come into the office"

"I can come this afternoon" Paulette said through tears

"Please don't cry Ms. Jackson, what time would you like to come in?"

"Four is good" Paulette said
"Okay see you then"
"Bye" Paulette said as she hung up the phone.

Paulette reached her job and turned on the lights.
Great nobody's here yet.
The lawyers usually came in at 10am.
She put her bag and keys down and went straight
into the bathroom.
She sat down on the bathroom floor and cried.
*Please God don't let me have H.I.V, please let me
be healthy, maybe it's just a misunderstanding.*
...

Crystal walked in the kitchen to grab a bite to eat
before she went to work and just the smell of food
made her want to throw up. She ran to the bathroom
and kneeled over the toilet bowl and let out all of
last night's chicken pasta. This had been happening
for a couple of days now.
Her period was about 5 days late but she still prayed
that she was just stressed and it would come at any
minute. Even though she didn't want to, she was
going to buy a pregnancy test on her way to work
just to make sure.
    Crystal hadn't mentioned anything to Keith, not
even that she might be pregnant because she didn't
want to be pressured into anything. She had just got
out of law school and she had only been at the firm
for 6 months. Now was not the time to have a baby.
Crystal drank a glass of orange juice because she

couldn't manage to keep anything else down and she showered and got dressed. Crystal was definitely a natural beauty. She almost always wore her hair in a bun because she thought it made her look more conservative and she wanted the men at her job to take her seriously. Almost every guy she met tried to sleep with her.

Crystal walked down to the parking garage and got inside her car. Just the smell of the air freshener made her gag. *This is fucking ridiculous.* Crystal thought. She drove straight to Duane Reade and bought an e.p.t. test.
"Good Morning Greg" Crystal said as she walked in the building
"Good morning beautiful" Greg said
"Crystal" She corrected.
"I'm just speaking the truth, sorry Crystal" Greg said.

Greg was one of the only black men at the firm and he was trying to be partner. He had been flirting with Crystal since her first day. She made it clear she was not interested and he still flirted shamelessly every day. *He's such a dick.* Crystal thought.
"Good Morning Alice" Crystal said she walked past her secretary into her office
"Good Morning Ms. Dawson, I placed some files on your desk for you to review and Mr. Nelson called twice this morning" Alice said

"Thanks" Crystal replied as she walked into her office

She closed the door and picked up the phone and dialed

"Hello?" A male voice said

"What do you want? And why are you calling my job?"

"Is that any way to talk to your stepfather?"

"What do you want?"

"I've been calling you and you haven't returned any of my calls"

"I've been busy"

"Well I haven't seen you in a while and I missed you"

Crystal knew what that meant and she was disgusted. She was so tired of this shit. She thought she had escaped for a while when her and Trish went away to college but whenever she came home to see her mom for the holidays Harold made sure they always had their time alone. She couldn't understand how Harold could do this to her, he had a daughter of his own that was only two years older than her.

"I'm busy Harold. I'll get back to you"

"Well it better be soon, you know your mother is getting on my last nerve. I would hate to leave her after all these years. Where would she go?"

He is such a bastard!

Her mother and Harold had been together for 11 years now. Marie's world revolved around Harold. If he left her now she didn't know what

Marie would do.

Crystal knew that she was stable enough to help her
mother financially but if Harold left her, her mother
wouldn't want help from her. This needed to stop
but Crystal didn't know what to do.

"I'll call you back"

"If you don't I'll call you and next time I won't be
so nice"

"Good Bye"

"Bye"

Crystal slammed the phone down and sat at her
desk. She put her head down and began to cry.
She didn't know how she let it go on for this long.
She wished she would have took Trish up on that
offer when they were younger. He would be dead
and out of her life now. She couldn't take it
anymore. She wiped her eyes and reached in her
purse and took the e.p.t. test out. If she was
pregnant she couldn't keep it because she didn't
know whose baby it was. She was only with Harold
once in the last two months.

She grabbed the e.p.t. test and walked over to the
bathroom. She loved having a bathroom in her
office. She read the instructions before taking
anything out of the box. It seemed easy enough.

Remove the e.p.t stick from the foil wrapper. *Done.*
Place in Urine stream for 5 seconds. *1-2-3-4-5*
Done.
Place on flat surface and wait two minutes.
A Plus sign in the round window indicates a

pregnant result. A minus sign in the round window
indicates a not pregnant result.
Crystal paced back and forth this was the longest
two minutes of her life. She walked back into the
bathroom afraid to look at the test. She picked up
the stick and it was a plus sign in the round window.
It was very light so she thought maybe she was not
pregnant and she picked up the instructions again. It
was like the paper was talking to her because right
under the picture it said:

The lines that make up the sign can be different
shades of blue and need not match the color of the
illustrations. Please see your doctor to discuss.
Just then Crystal got on the phone with the
Women's Health Center and made an appointment
for that afternoon. She wanted to make sure. She
hoped the test was a mistake.

...

"Hello ladies what would you like today" Sue asked
Nina and Trish
"Manicures and Pedicures" Trish answered
"I'm so surprised you decided to come with me"
Trish joked
"You're treating right?" Nina asked
"Well I owe you from the other night"
"You damn sure do, I will never let you set me up
on a blind date again"
I bet she thought it was real funny setting me up

with that crippled motherfucker! She's such a Bitch!
"I'm sorry but it wasn't my fault"
"Well I see you got the brother that was not
crippled" Nina joked
"Shut up!"
"Yeah, you can't say nothing about that? Can you?"
"Anyway, I'm so excited about my date tonight"
Trish beamed.
"With who? The married man?" Nina said trying to
rub it in.
"You mean Jay? Yes"
"Don't you feel bad going out with a man that is
married with kids?"
"No I don't, I'm not dating his wife or his kids and I
would rather not think about them. Plus I never fall
in love with them or get attached, they can go back
to their wives and kids at any time"
"You are really crazy, one day that shit is going to
bite you right in the ass. You are going to fall in
love with a man and he is not going to leave his
wife"
"Yeah right. Don't spoil my mood, you're always
trying to preach to someone like you're perfect"
"I don't think I'm perfect it's just that I would like
to get married and have kids one day   and it pisses
me off to know that there are bitches like you that
would be out there fucking my husband"
"Well I don't go out looking for married men"
"But most of the men you date are married and you
don't care" Nina said angrily.
Trish looked shocked. *You would think I was dating*

her husband. What the fuck is her problem?
"Most of the men I date are established and live a certain lifestyle and someone has snatched them up already so it's not my fault"
"Well why don't you find men that aren't already snatched up?"
"Because I am accustomed to a certain lifestyle, I need the finer things in life and I have no time to be dealing with no broke ass niggas that I have to help reach a certain status" Trish said
"Well excuse me because some of us have to work and pay bills, we can't all shop whenever we want and depend on men to take care of us, did you ever think of getting a job? "
"Yeah I thought about it, but it's not for me. You don't know what you are missing girl! You are a beautiful girl, you could be living the good life instead of dealing with those annoying as kids all day, getting a teacher's salary"
"Shut up, I love my job and my annoying ass kids" Nina rolled her eyes.

The truth was Nina did love the kids, but sometimes she hated her job, it was stressful, and she didn't get paid enough as a third grade teacher. She was always grading papers during her free time, including the weekends. If she wasn't grading papers she was planning a lesson for the next day or the next week and she spent so much of her own money getting supplies for her class. But at the end of the day all of her students loved her it put a smile on her face whenever she heard them say "Ms. Franklin".

What really pissed her off even more was Trish. Nina loved Trish to death they had been friends for the past 7 years, since their first year in college but she got on her last nerve sometimes.

Although Nina would never admit it deep down she was a little jealous of Trish because she worked so damn hard and hardly had anything to show for it and Trish didn't work at all and always had money, a new car, and designer clothes. It just wasn't fair!

...

Paulette looked at the clock. It was finally 3:20. The time seemed to be dragging all day. She was in a daze most of the day.

She got up from her desk and walked to the bathroom. She couldn't concentrate all day. She threw some water on her face and said

"Everything is going to be fine Paulette, calm down"

She walked out of the bathroom and back to her desk.

"Are you okay?" Mr. Morton, her boss asked

"I'm fine, I just have terrible allergies" Paulette lied.

Mr. Morton stood there and talked to her for about 15 minutes about absolutely nothing, like he didn't hear her say, she had bad allergies and she didn't feel well. *Damn I hate this job sometimes.* Paulette thought.

Paulette thought about the phone call she received all day. She thought of all of the terrible possibilities. She thought about H.I.V. and A.I.D.S, she thought about Herpes, Chlamydia, and Gonorrhea and she ran to the bathroom again. This time she threw up.

"Paulette?" She heard a voice call out.

Paulette rinsed her mouth out with some water, threw some water on her face and walked out of the bathroom.

"Hi Lilianna" Paulette said to the girl that was covering for her so she could go to the doctor.

"Hey Paulette, are you okay?"

"I'm okay, but I have an appointment at four so I have to go, see you tomorrow"

"Okay bye" Lilianna said

Paulette rushed out of the door and flagged down a cab.

"Where to?" The cab driver asked

"The corner of 57th and 3rd"

Paulette felt herself getting nauseous from the way the cab driver bobbed and weaved in and out of traffic. *There is nothing like a New York City Cab.* Paulette thought.

Paulette reached her destination in 8 minutes.

"7.50" The cab driver said

Shit I completely forgot to cash my check. I don't have any cash on me.

"I'm so sorry sir, I forgot I don't have any cash on me, if you want to pick me back up here I can pay you then"

"You don't have $8 dollars?"

"No I don't"

"Well I can't meet you back here just get fuck out!"

"Fine. Fuck you too" Paulette said as she slammed the door. *New York City Cab Drivers are so fucking nasty.*

Paulette was barely out of the cab before the cab's wheels screeched as he turned the corner.

Just as she was walking in she saw Crystal walking from her car and crossing the street. She tried to put her head down quick and look at the ground because she really didn't want to have to explain why she was here.

"Paulette?"

Shit! "Hey Crystal" Paulette said as she walked up to her and hugged and they kissed on the cheek.

"What are you doing here?" Crystal asked

"Just getting a checkup, what about you?" Paulette lied

"Me too" Crystal lied

They walked inside, signed in and sat down. As soon as they sat down the receptionist said "Paulette you can come on back" Paulette stood up nervously and began walking towards the back

"Call me later" Crystal said

"Okay"

"Hello Ms. Jackson, I'm Tara just have a seat and make yourself comfortable and Dr. Patterson will be in, in a few minutes to talk to you"

"Okay" Paulette said, she was so nervous, her leg

127

couldn't stop shaking. *Why are they torturing me, just tell me what the hell is going on.*
"Hello Paulette, it's good to see you again"
"You too' Paulette lied knowing damn well she would be happy if she never had to see Dr. Patterson again.
"Well we called you in today because your Pap Test came back abnormal and-"
"What does that mean?"
"Well based on your abnormal Pap Test you have been diagnosed with the Human Papilloma Virus, better known as HPV"
"What the hell is that?" Paulette asked as tears instantly streamed down her face
"It's a sexually transmitted disease. The HPV genital infection is one of the most common sexually transmitted diseases, it's a form of genital warts"
"Warts?"
"What exactly is it?" Paulette asked
"HPV is a virus that is the cause of common warts of the hands and feet, as well as of lesions of the mucous membranes of the oral, anal, and genital cavities" Dr. Patterson explained
"So I'm going to have warts? Paulette cried
"You may, in women, the warts occur on the lips of the vagina, inside the vagina, or around the anus. Anogenital warts may be itchy"
"What is anogenital?" Paulette asked. *I can't take this. This is all too much for me.* She felt as if she was going to pass out right there on the floor.

"All that means is the area relating to the anus and the genitals"
Is this a common disease, because I've never heard of it?"
"Approximately 20 million people are currently infected with HPV. At least 50 percent of sexually active men and women acquire genital HPV infection at some point in their lives."
"So what do I have to take for it to go away?"
"I'm sorry Paulette but there is no cure for HPV"
"What? So I have to have this for the rest of my life? I'm only 26 years old" Paulette asked she cried harder
"There is medication to suppress the symptoms, but there is no cure to make it go away, I'm sorry Paulette" Dr. Patterson said
Paulette just cried.
"Well Paulette it could have been something much worse. There is also something else I would like to address with you today"
"There's more?"
"Well based on the abnormality of the test the viruses may be "high-risk" and may also lead to cancer of the cervix, vulva, vagina, anus"
"Cancer? Oh my God!" Paulette screamed
"Paulette I know you are upset, but please try to calm down, so we can talk about everything. I want you to take another test and then if you develop some type of cervical infection you may require a colposcopy"
"What the hell is a colposcopy?" Paulette asked

"It's a painless examination to view the internal reproductive organs in women"

"Reproductive organs? So I may not be able to have children?"

"The presence of HPV by itself should not affect your ability to get pregnant. But in some cases, having HPV can increase your risk of developing precancerous or cancerous cells in your cervix, which could affect both your fertility and your ability to carry a baby to term"

"So I may not be able to have a baby?"

"It's a possibility" Dr. Patterson said

Paulette just cried.

"Everything will be okay Paulette, just make sure you inform all your sexual partners so they can be tested and treated and make sure you are always having safe sex, and try not to have sex with multiple partners"

"Okay" Paulette managed to say through sobs.

"Here is you prescription and I want you to go in the front and schedule an appointment for the other test I would like you to take. The sooner the better"

"Okay" Paulette said

"Have a good day, see you soon"

Have a good day. Fuck you! Paulette thought

"Okay" was all she could manage to say.

Paulette stood at the front desk in a daze. She hoped that in any minute she would wake up from this nightmare? HPV? Inform all my sexual partners? She didn't even know here to begin.

...

Trish paced back and forth. She couldn't decide if
she wanted to wear a white, short, skimpy Donna
Karan Dress or her black Paige Denim skinny jeans
and a blousy shirt. She loved how she looked in
both outfits but she didn't want to be overdressed or
underdressed since Jay didn't say where he was
taking her.
She finally decided on the white dress. It was short,
sexy, and fun. She put on some silver Prada sandals,
with a stacked heel that looked perfect.   She didn't
care if she was overdressed, at least all eyes would
be on her. Exactly how she liked it!
At exactly 7:00pm Trish was putting the finishing
touches on her makeup when the phone rang.
"Hello?"
"Hello, may I speak with Ms. Patricia Grand?"
*Who the hell is this? Only my mother knows   my
full name. And it better not be that bitch.*
"This is her, whose calling?"
"Hello Ms. Grand your car is downstairs" The
gentleman said and hung up the phone.
Trish just smiled.
She grabbed her Gucci clutch and walked out the
door.
When she got downstairs a black Mercedes stretch
limo sat in front of her building. The driver stood at
the door and bowed as he said "Good Evening Ms.
Grand, you look lovely"
"Thank you"
He opened the limo door and Jay stepped out

holding a bouquet of white long stemmed roses.

"Hello, Trish. You look beautiful and these are for you"

Wow. Trish thought. But she held her composure.

"Thank you, you look handsome too"

"Ladies first" Jay said as he let Trish get inside the limo.

"So where are you taking me?" Trish asked

"Shhh, it's a surprise, just relax"

"Okay"

"Would you like some Champagne?"

"Sure"

"Let's toast"

"To what?" Trish asked

"To new beginnings"

"I like that, To new beginnings" Trish said

"To new beginnings" They said as they tapped their glasses and sipped champagne.

Trish sipped champagne and admired the scenery. They talked and laughed and joked and everything was going so well.

"This is our stop" Jay said

"Where are we?" Trish asked hoping she could get a clue as to where he was taking her.

"Close your eyes" Jay said

"Are you serious?" Trish giggled

"Close your eyes please Ms. Grand"

"Okay" Trish said as she closed her eyes.

She felt something touch her face and go over her eyes and she got nervous.

"What are you doing?"

"Relax, I'm just putting a blindfold over your eyes
because I think you will peek"
"I won't peek I promise"
"I know you won't because you will be
blindfolded"
"Okay fine"
"Give me your hand please" Jay said as he took
Trish's hand and led her out of the limo.
"Watch your step we are about to walk up some
steps"
"Steps?" Trish asked trying to figure out where they
were going.
"Hold on" Jay said as he placed Trish's hand on the
rails of the steps.
"Where are we?"
"You will see soon Ms. Grand" Jay joked.
Just then Trish felt a plush carpet underneath her
feet. *Are we at a restaurant?* No, because I don't
hear any people around. *We better not be at a hotel
room.*
"Are you ready for me to take off the blindfold Ms.
Grand?"
"Yes I am"
Trish was excited like a little kid on Christmas.
Jay gently untied the blindfold and when Trish
opened her eyes she couldn't believe it. She looked
around and they were standing on an immaculate
yacht. There was burgundy plush carpet and marble
floors everywhere else. They were outside on the
deck and the view of New York City was
marvelous.

"This is beautiful" Trish said
"Was it worth the wait?"
"Yes it was" Trish said as she smiled. She tried to
keep cool. After all she was used to men going all
out for her, but this was really romantic, especially
for a first date. He was a real gentleman.
"I am glad you like it" Jay said.
Just then Jay led Trish over to a small table for two
and pulled out her chair.
"Have a seat please"
"Thank you"
There was a bottle of champagne chilling on the
table and two champagne glasses.
He poured Trish a glass of champagne and then
himself and they sipped and looked out at the water.
They sat in silence for a few minutes just taking it
all in, it was so peaceful. Trish had lived in New
York all her life and she never saw a view like this
one.
"So tell me about yourself" Jay said
Trish hated that question because it immediately
made her think of her past.
But she had completely reinvented herself a long
time ago.
"I thought you already knew everything about me,
since you already knew my full name. How did you
find that out anyway?"
"I have my sources" Jay smiled
"Well my parents died in a car accident when I was
sixteen years old. My grandparents immediately
took over. Even though I missed my mother and

father, they were wonderful, they gave me
everything I wanted. My parent's life insurance
policy and money they had saved for me took care
of most of my expenses. They sent me on trips and
vacations and to the greatest schools. I was so
devastated when both of my grandparents passed
away three years ago. "
Trish told the story perfectly with tears forming in
her eyes. She had told the lie so many times before.
"Wow. I'm sorry to hear that" Jay said genuinely
"Thank you, but I'm moving on just taking it one
day at a time" Trish said dapping her eyes with a
napkin.
"So you don't have any family here?"
"No just a few friends"
"So what do you do?" Jay followed up with another
question

Trish hated that question too. Trish had invested
wisely since Mike's death, thanks to Crystal. But in
all actuality she didn't have a "job". She didn't want
to say she lived off men or that she was
unemployed. She always felt like she had to defend
herself. She had a college degree. She wasn't broke.
So why the hell did people care what the fuck she
does?
"I'm into real estate, I invest" Trish said. Again she
bent the truth a little but that was what everyone
said when they didn't have a career or a steady job
or when they dibbled and dabbled into a few things.
It sounded good. She wasn't completely lying she

did own her condo.

"What about you?" Trish asked

"I'm a producer"

I wonder if he is a real producer. Trish learned a long time ago that "producer" is code for bullshitter or drug dealer. Everybody has a friend, cousin, uncle, brother, even father that wanted to be a rapper, and they all need a producer. Most "producers" spend all day in the studio and they never produce shit.

"Interesting, is it a fun job?" Trish asked

"It is sometimes, but it is a lot of work, and long hours"

"Are you hungry?" Jay asked

"A little" Trish lied, she was starving.

"Follow me" Jay said as he grabbed her hand and led her into a gorgeous dining room. There was a long buffet table with everything you could imagine. There were salads, shrimp, lobster, steak, caviar, varieties of chicken and much more.

"Are other people joining us?" Trish asked as she looked at the enormous spread of food that was in front of them.

"No. It's just me and you. I wasn't sure what you liked, so I got a little bit of everything"

"How sweet of you"

"Let me go get our plates"

 Jay grabbed their plates off the table and handed one to Trish. She didn't know where to begin. *I don't want to look too greedy.* She thought.

She took a little piece of steak, a small piece of

chicken, and a few shrimps.
"Is that all you are going to eat?"
"Yes, this is enough"
Trish knew she was still going to be hungry, but she
was not going to look greedy.
"The food is delicious" Trish said
They drank some more champagne and talked for
what seemed like hours. The date was perfect.
Trish hadn't felt that way in a really long time.

...

Chapter 7

"What do you mean you have 30 students, so my child doesn't matter?" Ms. Jones said with an attitude

"Of course your child matters Ms. Jones that is not what I meant" Nina explained.

I don't need this shit today. It has been such a long day. Nina was having a bad morning and her students can sense when she's not in a good mood so the day went pretty shitty. She tried to teach division and fractions and the little bastards weren't getting it and to top it off Daylan, her student with the parent from hell cut a chunk of his hair off and Nina had to explain it to his mother.

"So where were you when he cut his hair?"

"I was teaching Ms. Jones" Nina said trying to remain calm.

"So you weren't paying any attention to Daylan?"

"As I said before Ms. Jones I let Daylan go to the bathroom and when he came back he had a bald spot"

"So he cut his hair in the bathroom?"

"Yes"

"Why did you let him have scissors? Its your fault!"

"I'm sorry you feel as though I am at fault Ms. Jones but all my students are allowed to have scissors in their desk for when we need to use them"

"So you didn't see him walk out of the class with scissors?"

"No I did not. They must have been in his pocket"

"You don't check their pockets before they leave
the classroom?"
*She can't be fucking serious. Does she think I am
going to check 30 kid's pockets before they go to the
bathroom each time? They use the bathroom at
least 3 times a day. I don't know what parents
expect from me. I am a damn good teacher but they
expect me to be the parent too.*

"No I don't check their pockets Ms. Jones. As I
explained before there are 30 students in my class
and I have to see that I am paying equal attention to
all my students at all times"
"Well you obviously weren't paying equal attention
to mine" Ms. Jones said as she sucked her teeth
*I feel like picking up one of these desks and
knocking her fucking teeth out.*
*She wants to come to school and raise hell for an
issue like this but fuck when Daylan was struggling
in math, when he could barely read, when he was
fighting and getting suspended every week, when he
was constantly talking back, that wasn't important
enough, but this is. Please!*
"I'm sorry you feel that way Ms. Jones. Is there
anything else you would like to discuss or are we
done?" Nina asked politely
"Yeah we are done for now, but I suggest you keep
an eye on my child at all time 'cause if something
like this happens again I will bus-
"Have a good day Ms. Jones" Nina said and walked
out of the room. *I better not ever run into her on the*

street. I need a drink. I really don't get paid enough for this shit. Nina hated Trish at times like this. She felt like parents need to understand that teachers see their children more than they do and they need to give teachers more credit. Teachers spend eight hours a day with their child. By the time they come home from work they feed their child and put them to bed.

I am the one that has to deal with the attitudes, the crying, the screaming, the tattle-tailing and I never even get a thank you. Fuck you! Ms. Jones. And Fuck you Trish!

...

"Pregnant? Are you sure?" Crystal asked the doctor
"I think I'm sure Ms. Dawson" Dr. Richards joked
"My period is only a few days late, is the test completely accurate?"
"Yes. Our test can detect after 1 late day. Since we are not that busy today I would like you to have a sonogram and we can determine exactly how far along you are"
A sonogram? Crystal did not want to have anything to do with a baby. Now was just not the right time.
"I have to get back to work Dr. Richards. I can reschedule for another time"
"It will only take a few minutes. I can give you a gown and you can go right into the next room"
"Okay" Crystal gave in.
Dr. Richards walked Crystal down the hall. "Take everything off. Leave the opening to the back and I

will be back in, in a few minutes"
Crystal usually wouldn't like a male gynecologist
but she liked Dr. Richards, he was so friendly.
"Okay" Crystal said
As crystal waited she felt so nervous. There were
butterflies in her stomach. Crystal was pregnant
once before when she was sixteen. She was
petrified; she was so scared to tell her mother, she
knew she couldn't have it. She didn't know what to
do but of course Trish did. Trish knew where she
could get it done quick, and cheap, and where
nobody would know. Crystal remembered it like it
was yesterday. It was the worst experience of her
life. Trish went with her, Mike Trish's boyfriend at
the time drove them.

Crystal was too embarrassed to tell Harold she was
pregnant and she couldn't tell her mother. But she
managed to get $150 from her mother and Harold
over a two week period and Trish helped her with
the rest. It cost $350 dollars. When they stepped out
of the car at 7:30am on a Saturday morning there
were protesters with pictures of deformed babies
and limbs of babies cut up and thrown into
dumpsters.
They were yelling" Don't go inside", "It's not too
late", "Don't be a murderer"
One woman pulled Crystal aside said "There are
agencies that can help you, don't do this" as she
handed her a pamphlet with graphic pictures of
babies and a set of plastic rosary beads. Crystal

wondered what she was getting into. She was so scared.

The pictures were so explicit that she couldn't get them out of her head. She wondered if she was making a mistake. She felt terrible. But she knew she was too young to have a baby, especially by her stepfather. Plus Trish had already had three abortions and she was fine.

When Crystal went inside there were about 15 girls in the waiting room that all had the same look on their faces. They all had to pass the same protesters and they were probably thinking the same thing she was. Nobody inside looked over 18 years old. Some were accompanied by men, but most were with women, probably a sister or a friend.

Crystal walked up to the front desk and was asked to fill out a stack of papers about her medical history. She had to sign waivers about the anesthesia and about the procedure and that made her even more nervous. She just wanted to hurry up and get it over with.

After about an hour she was called to the back. A tall, scary, Grace Jones looking nurse gave her a plastic cup with her name labeled on it.

"Urinate in this cup and then place it in the window on the counter"

"Okay"

I hate peeing in these cups. It always looks too yellow and then I get embarrassed.

"When you are done go back out to the waiting room"

"Okay"

Crystal walked back out to Trish and sat down.

"What happened back there?"

"Nothing I had to pee in a cup"

"Why did they make you do that?" Trish asked

"I guess to make sure I'm still pregnant"

"Oh yeah"

Sometimes I think Trish is only a pretty face. Crystal thought.

"Yolanda Payton" The receptionist called

"Yolanda Payton"

"That's you" Trish said as she nudged Crystal in the arm.

"Oh yeah, I almost forgot" Crystal whispered

Crystal always liked that name as a child.   So that's what she put on all her papers. She wasn't going to put her real name. She wanted to act like it never happened.

"Coming" Crystal said

"I'm going to buzz the door and I want you to walk straight back to room 12" The receptionist said

"Okay"

When Crystal reached room 12 there was a pretty black woman sitting behind the desk. She looked a little like Halle Berry.

She stood up and said "Hello Yolanda, I'm Dr. Rodriguez"

"Hi Dr. Rodriguez"

"I'm a counselor and I am going to talk to you and just make sure you are aware of the decision you are making today"

"Okay"

"So you have decided to have a termination today, correct?"

Damn. Termination. It sounds so bad.

"Ye-e-s" Crystal stuttered.

"Are you in a relationship?"

"No"

"Have you made the father aware of this decision?"

"Yes" Crystal lied

"Is he here with you today?"

"No" Crystal said and put and her head down.

"Did anyone force you to make this decision?"

"No"

"I looked through your chart and I see that you are 10 weeks pregnant are you sure about your decision today?"

Why is she doing this to me?

"Yes" Crystal said as tears streamed down her face. *This is so hard for me. I just want to get this over with.* Crystal thought.

"There are agencies out there that can help you if you decide to go through full term with this pregnancy" Dr. Rodriguez said as if Crystal's tears did not phase her.

"Thank you, but I'm sure about my decision" Crystal managed to say through tears.

"Okay" Dr. Rodriguez said very shortly as if she was not pleased with Crystal's' response.

She has the wrong job. She should be outside with the damn protesters! Crystal thought.

"What are you going to do about birth control after

this procedure Yolanda?"
"I'm not sure, I wanted to get on birth control pills"
"Well you need to decide quickly because abortions
are not a form of birth control Yolanda"
She is such a bitch!
"I guess I'm going to take birth control pills"
"Do you have health insurance or did you pay cash
today?"
"I paid cash"
"Well we can give you some free packs today but
then you would have to get a prescription and it
would be better if you had insurance because they
are quite expensive if you have to pay for them
yourself"
"Thank you"
"Well we are done today, you can go back out to the
waiting room and you will be called shortly"
"Okay" Crystal said as she stood up and began to
walk back out to the waiting room.
"By the way, how old are you Yolanda?"
"I'm fifteen"
"mm, mm, mm" Dr. Rodriguez said as she shook
her head in disgust and walked out of the room.
Crystal ran straight to the bathroom, closed the door
and cried.
"What took you so long?" Trish said as soon as
Crystal walked back out the waiting room.
"Nothing, why?"
"They just called your name, it's your turn"
"They did?" Crystal asked like she had just seen a
ghost. She knew she had to get it done but she still

wished she was dreaming and that at any minute she would wake up.

"Yeah, don't be scared" Trish said

"Okay. Thanks" Crystal said as the tears began to stream down her face again.

Crystal flinched as she remembered laying on the cold table with her feet propped up in stirrups.

"This is Dr. Catelman" The nurse said

"Is it going to hurt?" Crystal asked like a 3 year old.

"You will feel a little pain through the procedure. It is very quick, a few minutes. We are going to give you the anesthesia now, you will feel a little pinch and in a few seconds you will be fine" Dr. Catelman said

"Okay" Crystal said even though she wanted to jump off the table and run all the way home but she knew what had to be done. She couldn't stop her knees from shaking.

The nurse came over to her right side and held her right arm. Crystal felt a small pinch and then both the nurse and Dr. Catelman began counting backwards.

"Count with us" they said

"10-9-8-7"

By the time they got to 7 Crystal looked around and everything was blurry. She felt like she was floating.

"Scoot down closer to the edge Yolanda" Dr. Catelman said

Then Crystal heard what sounded like a vacuum and her knees began to shake again.

"I'm going to begin Yolanda, you may feel a little pressure. Please don't move. It will be over quickly"

"Okay"

"Squeeze my hand if you feel any pain" The nurse said

"Ouch" Crystal cried. She felt the like someone took a little vacuum and were sucking her insides out.

"Squeeze my hand Yolanda, it's almost over"

"Ouch" Crystal cried as she squeezed the nurse's hand.

•••

Knock! Knock! "Are you changed?" Dr. Richards called from the other sided of the door.

"Yes, you can come in" Crystal said as she snapped out of her daze.

"Now let's look at that sonogram!" Dr. Richards said as if it was the happiest day of his life

"Yeah whatever" Crystal muttered under her breath.

•••

"Excuse me can I get another shot?" Paulette yelled over the music to the bartender

"Are you sure? You already had seven?"

"Matter-of- fact make that two!" Paulette yelled. After Paulette got her results from the doctor's office she walked straight to the nearest bar, club, or lounge she could find that was serving some alcohol. She needed to forget about what the doctor had just told her. *HPV?* It was just too much for

Paulette to deal with right now.
Paulette began to think about her life and started
crying. She began to cry so hard she began laughing
hysterically. A few heads turned to look at her but
she didn't care. *I have a bullshit job, I have no man,
no car, and no money.*
But honestly Paulette was okay with her life. She
wasn't and over achiever. She was okay being
average and mediocre. It wasn't until she got
around her friends or her mother most of all that
made her second guess herself and feel like shit!
"Why can't you be more like Nina?" Her mother
would say.
"She is only 25 and she already has her Master's
Degree"
Paulette hated her mother sometimes.
"And how is that sweet Crystal? She is 26 and
already a lawyer"
Even Trish managed to make Paulette's mother
think more of her than she did Paulette, her own
daughter. Every time Paulette's mother saw Trish
she looked flawless in the newest designer shoes,
clothes, and bags. She always claimed to live off
her investments and she always treated everyone to
breakfast, lunch, or dinner whatever they were
having at the time.
That alone was enough to impress Paulette's
mother, Michelle Monroe who at 51 years old still
looked 35. People always thought Paulette and her
mom were sisters. Paulette's mom was gorgeous.

Paulette often felt insecure around her mother who was so perfect. She had perfect hair, perfect skin, and perfect teeth, she even had the perfect name! Michelle always wore designer everything and she was so concerned about what everyone thought. Sometimes Paulette swore her and Trish were switched at birth, being born only one day apart. Trish seemed more like her mother's daughter on any day.

Paulette's mother was already on her third husband and each one was wealthier than the last. Her newest husband Phillip was such a pushover. He was a real estate developer that was filthy rich. He developed strip malls all over the United States. He was beginning to expand his business internationally so he was always out of town. He adored Michelle. He let her do whatever she wanted. All that Michelle asked was that Phillip leave her at least three credit cards whenever he left on business. He always did that without a problem and Michelle was fine.

Since Phillip was always gone. Michelle had all the free time in the world and she used all of it　to fuck with Paulette every chance she got. She constantly made pop-up visits at her apartment or job. Paulette knew her mother meant well but her and Paulette had nothing in common. So Paulette ducked her every chance she got. Paulette loved her mother, but she damn sure didn't like her.

"Are you ready to close out your tab?" The nosy bartender asked Paulette

"Not yet, I will let you know!" Paulette snapped
"Are you sure you are going to be able to drive
home?" A deep voice whispered over Paulette's
shoulder.
"Why do you care?" Paulette snapped back before
she turned around to look at the gorgeous man
behind her. He was so fine she almost though she
was dreaming. He looked like a brown skinned
Boris Kodjoe. He had perfect teeth and everything.
"I just wouldn't want anything to happen to you and
then I wouldn't get a chance to know you?"
"Well are you asking to take me home?"
"Are you accepting my offer?"
"First you have to tell me your name" Paulette said
"My friends call me Chris"
"So what is your real name?"
"Maybe I'll tell you one day, but for now I consider
you a friend"
"Okay, Chris"
"What's your name?"
"Paula, I mean Paulette" *Wow how many drinks did
I have?*
"Okay Paula, Paulette" Chris joked
"It's Paulette"
"Let's get out of here"
"Okay let me close out my tab"
"$146.00" The bartender said with a huge smile
What the fuck was I drinking?
Paulette left $160 on the bar, grabbed her purse and
stumbled off the stool.
"Let me help you" Chris said

"No I'm okay I need to use the bathroom"
"Okay its right in the back to the left. I'll be waiting
for you right here"
"When Paulette reached the bathroom there were
already three women standing in line.
"I gotta go" Paulette said out loud as she bounced
up and down like a two year old.
"So do I" an older white woman said shortly as she
rolled her eyes at her.
"Fuck this shit I'm going to the men's bathroom"
Paulette walked out of the women's bathroom and
right into the men's bathroom. There was one man
peeing at the urinal and another man inside a stall
with the door closed.
There was a male bathroom attendant sitting on a
stool and he said "Excuse me miss this is the men's
bathroom"
Paulette ignored him and went in the stall anyway
"Excuse me miss I said this is the men's bathroom,
and I know you heard me"
If he didn't seem so gay Paulette would have
walked over and flashed or kissed him or did
something to make him change his mind but she
knew that wouldn't have done anything for him
except maybe make him throw up.
"I'll be out in a minute, relax" Paulette said
"I don't need to relax, you should be in the
women's bathroom!" he yelled
"Oh my god this feels so good!" Paulette yelled like
she was having an orgasm
She felt so much better. When she walked out the

stall "Mr. Bathroom Attendant From Hell" was
staring at her. If looks could kill she would have
been dead right there on the bathroom floor.
Paulette looked at herself in the mirror. She put on
some clear lip gloss and turned on the water to wash
her hands. She looked for the soap and she didn't
see any soap anywhere. Then she looked over at
"Mr. Bathroom Attendant From Hell" and he was
holding the soap bottle and the paper towels.
Paulette wouldn't give him the satisfaction of
asking him for a squirt. So she rinsed her hands and
turned off the water. Then she took a hand full of
peppermints and ran out of the bathroom like a little
school girl.
"What's so funny?" Chris said
"Nothing, I'm ready"
"Okay I parked right across the street"
Paulette and Chris made their way across the street
to a black spotless Mercedes. *My mother would love
him.* She thought.
Once they were inside the car Chris said "So where
do you live?"
"I don't really feel like going home yet" Paulette
said
"You sure?" Chris asked with a smile
"I'm sure"
Chris smiled like that was exactly what he wanted
to hear.
"Well then we can go to my place"
"Okay" Paulette sat back and smiled.
...

Knock! Knock!

"Who is it?" Trish called as she slipped on her favorite silk robe with slippers to match.

"A special delivery for Ms. Grand"

Trish looked through the peep hole and saw a gentlemen holding two dozen yellow long stemmed roses with a note attached. Trish smiled from ear to ear as she opened the door.

"Good Morning" Trish said

"Good morning Ms. Grand. I have a special delivery for you from Mr. Hollis"

"Thank you"

"No thank you. Have a wonderful day"

"You too"

Trish closed the door and inhaled the roses. They were beautiful. She went over to her China Cabinet and looked for the perfect vase for her roses. She filled the vase half way with warm water and put the roses in the center of her dining room table.

She looked around her living room and there were roses everywhere. This was the third delivery in three days.

Jay had been sending her different color roses every day since their date. He was so sweet. Trish thought about him and smiled.

It scared her because she hadn't felt this way since Mike.

She couldn't believe how much she liked him already. They had such a good time on their date it seemed like a fairytale. She opened the note

attached to the flowers and it said:
Be ready at 7pm. You won't be disappointed- Jay
Trish ran to her room to look for something to wear.
...

Crystal sat at her desk and put her head down. She
couldn't stop thinking about the baby growing
inside of her. Ever since she left the doctor she felt
completely different. She went into Dr. Richard's
office thinking *I don't care what he says I don't
want any kids* and now she felt so confused. Part of
her was very involved in her career and wanted to
go as far as she could. She knew having a baby right
now would only hold her back. Another part of her
couldn't fathom having another abortion and she
did not want to relive that again. Then another part
of her knew that she was capable of being a good
mother and she wanted to have the baby. Then she
thought about Keith and she definitely didn't know
if she wanted to be with him for the rest of her life,
even though it sounded cliché Crystal had always
pictured herself married with kids and Keith had not
proposed yet.
 	She almost threw up when she thought about
Harold. What if this was his baby? Dr. Richards
told her she was 9 weeks pregnant, so there was a
possibility.
Why now lord?
Crystal needed to talk to somebody about this.
Holding it inside was killing her. She didn't want to
talk to Keith about it yet so she decided to call

Trish. Trish was the only person she could talk
about this situation with.
She dialed Trish's number and it went straight to
voicemail. *Where are you Trish?*
When Trish didn't answer she decided to call Nina.
But she couldn't tell Nina the whole truth about the
situation.
"Hey Nina can you meet me at Loft around seven, I
need to talk"
"Sure Crys. Is everything okay?"
"Yeah"
"You sure?" Nina asked
"Yeah, I'll see you at seven"
"Okay, see you then"
Crystal hung up the phone and grabbed her purse.
"Alice I'm going to run an errand I'll be right back"
Crystal said
"Okay" Alice responded cheerfully.
She is always so damn perky!
      Crystal just needed to clear her head so she
decided to take a walk. Crystal walked like she was
the only person on the sidewalk. She did a lot of
thinking but she still couldn't come to a decision,
that's why she needed to talk to somebody else. She
walked for about an hour.
Then she looked down at her cell phone. *I have to
get back to the office* She thought. It was going to
take at least 20 minutes to walk back. Just as she
was crossing the street she saw a man and woman
holding hands across the street and they looked so
happy. She wished that she and Keith could be like

that happy sometimes.

Crystal rubbed her eyes and said *Wait a minute, that looks like Keith!*

"Keith!" She yelled

"Keith!"

"Keith!"

Crystal yelled across the street and neither one of them even looked in her direction.

I must be hallucinating, but he did look a lot like Keith.

...

"I'm a put you to bed, bed, bed, I'm a rock your body" Nina crooned along with the radio.

I love that J. Holiday song! It never gets old!

Nina was leaving work on her way to meet Crystal at Loft.

Loft was a new trendy restaurant that opened downtown.

She really needed a drink after that meeting earlier with Ms. Jones and she was curious to know what Crystal wanted to talk about so badly. Nina looked through her rear view mirror at the police car behind her.

"Shit! Why are they pulling me over?" Nina said to herself

Nina pulled her car to the right side of the road and rolled down her driver's side window.

"License and registration" The officer said nastily.

"Excuse me officer but why I am I being pulled over?"

"License and registration"

"I just wanted to know why I am being pulled over" Nina said as she handed the officer her license and registration.

"You have a tail light out"

"I really didn't know that. Could I just have a warning and I will get it fixed today" Nina said in her sweetest voice. She really wasn't in the mood for this shit. She still had to meet Crystal, grade papers, and make dinner. She wasn't buying anything to eat from Loft. They were too damn expensive.

"I'm going to go check out your license and registration, if everything is okay I will give you a ticket, if you get the light fixed in a week, mail the receipt with the ticket and it will be dropped"

"Okay"

Nina looked at the clock on her dash board. *What is taking him so long?*

Everything should be fine I just bought the car 2 months ago from a woman at my church. Nina drove a 2000 Volkswagen Jetta. She wished she could have bought something newer but it was in good condition, and the mileage was good. She got mad just thinking about what Trish said when she saw her car for the first time.

"Well it looks good, for a 2000, if that's what you like"

Fuck Trish!

"Please step out of the vehicle ma'am" The officer said to Nina

"Excuse me?"

"Please step out of the vehicle"

"Why?"

"Please step out of the vehicle!" Another officer yelled on the passenger side.

"Okay"

"Keep your hands up" They both said

"What is going on?" Nina asked

"I ran your license and registration, and then I ran your plate and this vehicle is stolen"

"What?"

"Don't play dumb with me! This vehicle is stolen"

"I just bought this car 2 months ago from a woman at my church"

"I don't know what you did but this car is stolen!" The second officer yelled

"Get on the ground" The first officer yelled

"Excuse me?"

"Get on the ground!"

Nina looked down at her cardigan, knee length skirt, and shoes.

I can't believe he wants me to get on the ground.

"Get on the ground!"

"I'm a teacher, I'm a good person, why are you doing this to me?" Nina cried

"We're not doing anything ma'am, it's all part of procedure. You need to just be quiet and cooperate"

I know they wouldn't do this if I was white! Nina thought

She began to cry, her tears did not soften the officers one bit. She got down on her knees. She

cried even harder when she saw cars slowing down
as they passed by to see what was going on. She put
her head down. She hoped that none of her student's
parents saw her. She was so embarrassed.
"What is going to happen now?" Nina asked
through tears
"We have to impound the car and take you in"
"Take me in?" Nina cried.
Then to make matters worse the officer pulled out a
pair of hand cuffs.
"You are going to hand cuff me?"
"Its all part of procedure ma'am, please cooperate"
The officer walked up behind Nina and told her to
stand up.
"Place your hands behind you"
Nina did what the officer asked and just cried.
The officers walked Nina to the police car and
opened the back door for her to get in. She had
never felt so humiliated in her entire life.
"Sit tight, we are calling a tow truck"
Nina just cried.
...

Chapter 8

Paulette wiped the crust out of her eyes and rolled over to look at the clock, except it wasn't a clock there.

Where the hell is my clock?

Paulette rubbed her eyes again and sat up straight on the bed. There wasn't a clock there because this wasn't her apartment.

Where the hell am I? She thought.

Then she thought about Chris and smiled. They had fun. Then right where the clock should have been there was a note that said:

I had to run. You looked so peaceful I didn't want to wake you. There are towels and washcloths in the bathroom. The door slam locks. Thanks for the good time. Have a good day. – Chris.

Paulette smiled again and then that smile instantly turned into a frown when she thought about her results from the doctor's office yesterday. *HPV.*

Did we even use a condom? I was so drunk I don't remember.

Just then Paulette hopped out the bed her head was spinning. She ran around the house like a mad woman. She began checking all the garbage cans. She checked in the bedroom, the bathroom and then in the kitchen. She didn't see any used condoms or condom wrappers anywhere. *Maybe he threw them out.* She thought. Paulette walked into the bathroom. She found a clean washcloth and towel and turned on the shower. She barely used any cold

water, the shower was scolding hot. She needed a hot shower she felt so dirty. She jumped in and began to scrub herself everywhere. She scrubbed as if she was trying to take her skin off.
Why did this have to happen to me?
She thought about Chris while she was in the shower. He was nice and handsome and by looking at his place he probably had a good job, but she could never speak to him again. Paulette couldn't even remember if they had used a condom. She couldn't bring herself to tell him.
By the way I have HPV and now you may be infected. Please go get tested.
  Even though she knew it was the right thing to do. She just couldn't do it.
How will he look at me?
He will think I'm a slut She thought. It was better if she just forgot about him and he forgot about her. She could erase it from her mind and act like it never happened. *It was just a silly one-night stand.*
After about 20 minutes Paulette got out of the shower and dried off. She heard her phone ringing. It was alerting her that she had a new voicemail. She went over to her purse and grabbed her phone. She had 12 missed calls.
Who the hell called me 12 times from last night?
She had one call from Nina, 6 from Crystal, and 5 from Trish.
Oh my God I hope everything is okay.
She dialed Crystal's number right away.

"What? She's in jail?" Paulette screamed
"I'm on my way" Paulette said as she hung up the
phone and looked for her clothes that were sprawled
across the floor.

...

"Thank you again" Nina said
"Its fine" Trish replied
"I will pay you back as soon as I can"
"Now tell me again what happened?" Paulette said.
She still couldn't believe Nina, the school teacher
was arrested and had to post bail.
"The car she brought from the church was stolen"
Crystal answered
"Then I had two unpaid parking tickets that totaled
$620.00, with fines. My bail was $500 so the total
was $1,120.00" Nina said
"Wow, that's crazy" Paulette answered amazed
"Can you guys walk a little faster I'm double
parked" Crystal said.
"Let's go get breakfast, I'm starving" Paulette said
"Okay" Everyone replied
"You know that money came out of my party fund"
Trish replied
"I told you I will pay you back! Thank God it only
came out of your party fund, don't we all wish we
had one of those?" Nina said sarcastically.
*Trish is such a bitch! I just spent a night in jail and
all she can think about is her goddamn party fund! I
can't stand that bitch!*　Nina thought
"You're annual party is next weekend, right?"

Paulette asked

"Yes it is and please dress to impress, it will be a lot of eligible bachelors there"

"You're not worried about any eligible bachelors since you met Mr. Jay?" Crystal joked

"Shut up!" Trish yelled

"You're blushing, look at you!" Paulette said

"Well if I must say so, I really do like him a lot!"

"Will he be at the party?" Crystal asked

"Yes he will, then you all can meet him!" Trish screamed like a high school girl talking about her first crush.

"What about his wife? Is she coming?" Nina asked nastily

"What do you think?" Trish snapped back

What the fuck is wrong with her?

Crystal and Paulette sat quietly. They could feel the tension.

"We're here, everybody out" Crystal said as they pulled up in front of IHOP.

"Nina I talked to my mom on the way over and she said that Phillip can get you an excellent attorney. Then you can sue those damn people you bought that car from" Paulette said

"Thanks" Nina replied

"So what did you have to talk about?" Nina asked Crystal

Damn why did she have to put me on the spot like that? Crystal thought

"Nothing" Crystal said

Once they were seated. Crystal blurted out "I'm

pregnant"

"What?" They all said

"I'm pregnant"

"By Keith?" Nina asked

"Yes, by Keith" Crystal said nervously.

"What are you going to do?" Trish asked.

Trish knew there was a possibility that it may not be Keith's.

"I'm not sure that's why I wanted to talk about it"

"Did you tell Keith yet?" Paulette asked

"No. I'm just so confused. I want to move up at the firm and now just isn't the right time for a baby"

"Well you know I'm pro- choice. I'll support you in whatever you decide" Trish reassured her

"Thanks"

"Me too" Paulette said

"Well you know how I feel about abortions. I hate them! You have a good job. Why not have it?" Nina said

"For one I'm not married" Crystal replied

"You want to marry Keith?" Trish asked shocked

"I don't know" Crystal said

"Well you know I can't stand him!" Trish said

"Me either" Paulette said

"Me either" Nina said

"Thanks a lot! Just forget it. Can we order? " Crystal said with an attitude.

Crystal's biggest mistake was telling her friends all her damn business. Every time Keith would get on her nerves or he stayed out too late she was running to tell Trish, Nina, or Paulette. Every time they got into a fight she cried to Trish, Nina, or Paulette. So she couldn't blame anybody but herself if they hated him.

"Speaking of Keith I saw him yesterday. He was walking with this girl" Trish said

"Are you sure?" Crystal asked

"Yes and I said hi Keith and he just kept walking"

"Where?"

"Around 43rd street" Trish said matter-of-factly

That's the same place I thought I saw him. She must have been mistaken Crystal thought.

"Hi I'm Mary are you ladies ready to order?" The waitress said.

...

Crystal walked up the steps to her apartment. She was still confused about her pregnancy. She still wasn't ready to tell Keith. She had to do some more thinking.

She walked inside and saw Keith and Deonte sitting on the couch watching T.V.

"Hey Keith. Hi Deonte" Crystal said

"Mmm. Hello" Denote said as if it was killing him to speak to her.

"I better be going" Deonte said as he got up and grabbed his coat

"Bye Denote" Crystal said

"Call me later Keith" Deonte said as he walked right past Crystal as if he didn't hear her say a word.

"I don't appreciate your friend treating me like that in my own home"

"Don't pay him any attention. Guess what?" Keith
said
"What?"
"I got a job today?"
"That's great where at?" Crystal asked
enthusiastically
"I'm going to be working construction"
"Oh that's' good"
"You don't sound happy for me" Keith said with an
attitude
"I am" Crystal said. *Maybe God is giving me a sign.
Keith had a job now and maybe I should have the
baby. I still have to think.* She totally blocked out
the possibility of it being Harold's baby. She
couldn't deal with that right now.
"I'm hungry" Keith said
"Me too"
"What are you cooking?" Keith asked
"Nothing. Let's go out and eat"
"You paying?"
"I guess I have no choice"
*I'm so tired of this shit! Thank God he has a job
now!* Crystal thought.
"Trish said she saw you yesterday"
"She didn't see me" Keith said nonchalantly
"She said she said "Hi" to you and you kept
walking"
"A lot of people keep telling me that. I must have a
twin out there" Keith said
"Yeah maybe" Crystal replied. But something still
didn't seem right.

...

"I'm going to order room service" Trish yelled out
to Jay in the bathroom
"Okay babe, order whatever you want"
"Do you want something?" Trish asked
"Yeah just order me whatever you get"
"Okay"

Trish placed their order and fell back on the bed
like a little child. The bed was covered with a least
10 fluffy pillows and she buried herself underneath
them. She never thought she could be this happy.
Not since Mike. Trish and Jay spent so much time
together and she never got tired of him. They had so
much in common. They both loved to shop, party,
and go to the best restaurants. They talked for hours
and the sex was amazing. She truly believed Jay
was her soul mate. When she thought about him she
smiled. She felt like she was falling in love. Then
she thought about last night and smiled even harder.

Jay sent a car to pick up Trish at 8pm sharp. By
8:15pm they were pulling up on Lexington Avenue
in front of the W Hotel. Trish walked over to the
front desk and gave the receptionist her name. He
gave her the room number and handed her a key.
Trish got on the elevator and pressed 4.   Trish got
off the elevator and walked to the end of the hall.
When she walked in the room Jay had the hotel
room covered with rose petals and there were
candles everywhere. It was so romantic.

"Hello beautiful" Jay said as he walked over and kissed her.

"Hello"

He slowly began to undress her and took her hand and led her to the bed. *Damn he's not wasting any time!*

"Trish I've never felt this way about a woman before in my life; not even my wife. I feel like you are my other half and I want to spend the rest of my life with you" Jay said

Trish was shocked but she was also happy because she felt the same exact way.

"What about your wife?"

"I'm going to leave her eventually. It's just been so hard because I love my daughters so much and they want to see their mommy and their daddy together. I don't want to hurt them. But my wife and I haven't been happy with each other for a long time. We are still cordial to each other for the kids. We hardly ever talk and we don't have sex"

"So why didn't you try to leave her before?"

"I told you because of my kids. Not to mention she is an excellent attorney and I was afraid that if I divorced her she would take everything I have. But I don't care about that anymore, I love you"

"I love you too" Trish said

That was the first time they said those words to each other and it meant so much to Trish. She couldn't remember the last time she said "I Love You" to someone and truly meant it. Trish had dealt with other married men and she heard the married man scenario a hundred times before but this seemed different. Jay really seemed genuine. She believed him and she wanted to spend the rest of her life with him too. They kissed again and made love for most of the night.

"So you are definitely going to be at my annual bash tomorrow, right?" Trish asked

"Of course. I wouldn't miss it for the world" Jay said

"I can introduce to all my friends tomorrow. They have been dying to meet you"

"I can't wait" Jay said

"Neither can I" Trish smiled as she thought of how much fun they would have at her party tomorrow.

...

"Ouch! Shit!" Nina screamed as she stubbed her toe on her dresser.

My hair is frizzed up and the zipper on my dress is stuck.

Nina was getting ready for Trish's party and everything was going wrong.

Her date cancelled on her 5 minutes ago, so now she was going alone and the zipper on her dress kept getting stuck.

"Yes!" She said as she finally got it zipped up.

I hope I don't have to pee tonight, Because I don't know how this shit is coming back down. Nina thought

She looked at herself in the mirror and smiled. She was wearing a silver metallic knee-length dress and strappy silver sandals. She spun around and she was pleased with how she looked. But she knew that all would change when she saw Trish. Trish always looked gorgeous for her annual bashes, she really went all out. *Why couldn't all eyes ever be on me instead of Trish for a change?* She thought Nina glanced over the invitation one more time it read:

Trish's annual bash Need I say more?
What happens here, stays here!
Come and create new memories!
Dress to Impress
Invitations only!
Smooches
Smooches! Who the fuck does she think she is?
Nina thought.
Nina picked up the phone and called Paulette and told her she was ready. Since her date cancelled on her she decided to go with Paulette. Paulette's mother, Marie ordered a limo from her and Phillip's car service for them because Nina and Paulette knew they had to pull up in style. Trish wouldn't have it any other way. Nina grabbed her purse and walked down the stairs.

...

"You look nice. Where did you get those shoes and that jacket from?" Crystal asked Keith.
Keith had on brown alligator shoes and tan slacks. He had on a tan shirt to match and a brown mink

vest to match his shoes. Crystal really didn't think
that he looked nice. He looked more like a pimp.
But she was wondering where he got all the
expensive clothes from.
"My cousin Shawn knows someone that works in a
store in Harlem with some of the hottest shit out. He
steals all the new shit and sells them cheap. I got a
good deal"
"Oh" Crystal said
"You look nice too" Keith said
"Thank you. We have to get out of here we're
running late" Crystal said
Crystal loved her dress. It was teal green and form
fitting. It matched her complexion perfectly. She
looked like a beautiful mermaid. She wore her hair
in an upsweep of curls and had a few tendrils
hanging down. She looked very elegant. She looked
like she was Keith's high-priced ho.
She looked at Keith again and shook her head.
...

"You sure you don't want a drink?" Keith asked
Crystal
"No I have to drive remember"
"Well it won't kill you to have one"
The truth was Crystal was still not sure about what
she wanted to do. So she definitely wasn't drinking
with a baby growing inside her.
"Bobby! Bobby!" A man called out in the crowd
"Keith is that man talking to you?"
"What man?"

"The man over there!" Crystal said as she pointed in his direction.

"I don't know him" Keith said as he bent down to tie is shoe

"Well he acts like he knows you"

"I told you I must have a twin somewhere out there. I'm going to the bathroom" Keith said

"Crystal, Nina, Paulette I want you all to meet Jay" Trish said as she introduced Jay to her friends

"Hello Jay" They all said at once

"We have heard so much about you" Paulette said

"I hope all good things" Jay replied

"Not all good" Nina said

Trish shot her a look. That said *you better shut up bitch!*

Nina had to admit they looked good together. Jay wasn't the cutest guy but there was something about him. He was sexy, in a Tyrese kind of way. As usual Trish looked flawless. She had on a black ankle dress that fit every curve perfectly. Her hair hung down in flowing curls and her makeup was perfect. Everyone kept telling Trish how beautiful she looked. Nina was tired of hearing it.

"Where is Keith?" Trish asked

"I'm not sure I guess he is around somewhere" Crystal answered

"Isn't that him over there talking to that guy" Nina said as she pointed to Keith talking to a man. They were talking like they were old friends.

That's the guy he said he didn't know. Crystal thought

Just then Keith saw them pointing and looking in his direction and he began to make his way over to them.

"Hello ladies"

"Hey Keith" Trish, Nina, and Paulette replied nonchalantly

"I thought you said you didn't know him" Crystal whispered to Keith

"Umm I didn't, he told me I look like someone named Bobby that he knows. I was telling him that I must have a twin out there"

"Oh" Crystal said. *She felt a little better.*

"Hi everyone" Trish's friend Karma said

"You still look beautiful Crystal. You haven't changed since the last time I saw you" Karma said

"Thank you. You do too" Crystal replied

Rude bitch! What about me? Nina thought

Crystal, Karma, and Trish hung out together all the time when they were in college. They had so much fun together. Trish and Karma looked so much alike it was scary. Karma looked like a light-skin version of Trish. They always told everybody they were sisters. Once they got of college they grew apart and they only hung out during some occasions.

"You look so familiar. What's your name?" Karma said to Keith

"Keith"

"I know I know you from somewhere. I can't think of it now but it will come to me" Karma said

As usual Trish went all out. The party was fabulous. They partied into the wee hours of the morning.

They popped champagne all night and had a ball.

...

"Hello" Crystal answered the phone half asleep
"Crys wake up" Trish said
"What happened?" Crystal asked worried
"Can you talk?"
"Yeah, about what?" Crystal asked
"Keith"
"Yeah, he went to work"
"On Sunday?" Trish asked
"I told you he does construction"
"Well anyway, remember Karma kept telling Keith
at the party how familiar he looked"
"Yeah and?"
"Well Karma remembered where she knew him
from" Trish said
"Where?"
"He is dating this girl in her building, she sees him
there all the time"
"What? Is she sure?"
"She said she is positive, call her yourself"
Crystal felt her stomach getting queasy. She felt like
she wanted to throw up.
"What's her number?"
"555-9453"
"Thanks. I'll call you back"
Crystal was usually not into the "he said, she said
mess" but she wanted to get to the bottom of this.
"Hello?"
"Hello, Karma. It's Crystal"

"Hey Crys"

"I'm calling you about what you told Trish, about seeing Keith in your building"

"Oh yeah, I knew I knew him from somewhere. He is dating this girl Christine that lives in my building. He is always over there"

"Really? Are you sure?"

"I'm positive. I see him at least 3 times a week. Christine's man is locked up and she has been dating Keith ever since"

"But when you asked Keith his name at Trish's party last night you didn't remember him" Crystal said

"I know. The guy Christine is dating has a different name. His name is something with a B. Bryan or something. But I know that's him"

"Is it Bobby?"

"Yeah. That's it. How did you know it was Bobby?"

"I just took a guess. Do you have Christine's number?"

"Yeah I do. Hold on let me go get it"

"Okay"

Crystal paced back and forth as she waited for Karma to come back to the phone. She couldn't believe this shit! *This had to be some kind of mistake! And if it wasn't she was going to kill Keith!*

"Its 555-9547"

"Thanks"

"No problem. I'm just looking out for you"

Crystal's hand shook as she dialed Christine's

number. She had no idea what she was going to say.
"Hello?"
Crystal was silent
"Hello?"
"Hi may I speak to Christine?"
"This is her. Whose calling?"
"You don't know me. My name is Crystal. You have been dating my boyfriend Keith"
"I don't know who the fuck this is or what game you are trying to play but I don't know a Keith"
"I mean Bobby"
Christine changed her tone instantly.
"How do you know Bobby?" Christine asked
"He is my boyfriend and he lives with me"
"What? Stop lying bitch! Bobby is at my house almost every day" Christine said with an attitude
"I have no reason to lie. I know it sounds crazy but he sleeps here every night. He lives with me"
"I don't believe you" Christine said
"Well since you don't believe me, where does he tell you he is going every night?" Crystal asked
"He told me his mother is sick and he doesn't feel comfortable leaving her alone all night. He has to go home and check on her"
  "Keith's, I mean Bobby's mother died 2 years ago"
"What? How do you know?" Christine asked surprised
"I was at the funeral. Like I said he sleeps here every night"
"What is Bobby's last name?" Christine asked
"Davis"

Well at least he kept the same last name. Crystal
thought.

"Well I want to meet you. Can you meet me at the
Diner on the corner of 61st and 2nd in an hour?"
Christine asked

"Okay" Crystal said but she still wasn't sure if she
wanted to. *This bitch sounds a little crazy.*

"Oh and bring a picture of him with you" Christine
said

"Okay" Crystal said and hung up the phone

Crystal was in a state of shock. She couldn't believe
she said yes but she wanted to meet her too. She had
to find out what was going on.

Crystal hung up the phone and looked for
something to wear. She didn't know why but she
wanted to look good.

An hour later, Crystal paid the cab driver and began
to walk into the diner. Christine hadn't described
herself so she didn't know who she was looking for.
She looked around for a while and then she saw a
light-skinned woman with wild flowing hair sitting
at a table all alone. She was reading a menu but she
looked uncomfortable. Crystal assumed that was her
and made her way over.

"Christine?" Crystal asked as she approached the
table

*That was Keith I saw the other day and he was with
Christine! That Bastard!* Crystal thought as she
looked at Christine.

"Yes. Crystal?" Christine asked

"Yes"

Crystal was amazed at how much they looked alike. They could pass for sisters. She could tell by the way Christine looked at her she was thinking the same thing.

Crystal sat down and said

"Did you bring the pictures?"

"Yes. Did you?" Christine asked

"Yeah"

"So where did you meet Keith?" Crystal asked

"I met him at a club about 8 months ago and we have been dating ever since"

"Wow. We have been together for 3 years"

"This is us on Christmas" Christine said as she showed Crystal a picture of her and Keith at Rockefeller Center.

I was with him on Christmas too but he did leave for a few hours to go by his brother's house. Crystal thought

Crystal looked at the picture and began to cry. It really was Keith in the picture and he and Christine were holding hands just like the day she saw them together. They looked so happy.

"This is us on New Year's last year" Crystal said as she showed Christine the picture of them.

Christine almost turned red when she saw the picture. Crystal could tell she was pissed.

"I love him" Christine said

"I do too" Crystal said

She never thought she would be having one of these conversations. These things only happened on T.V. or in books.

The waiter came over and they both ordered salads
and water with lemon. They sat in silence for a
while.

"I can't believe that bastard! I feel like chopping his
dick off! He told me he broke up with his girlfriend
right before we met and she wouldn't leave him
alone" Christine said

"What? Wow. He was playing us both" Crystal said
as she shook her head. This all seemed like a crazy
dream to her. *Somebody please wake me up!*

"He said he loves me and wants to marry me. I even
introduced him to my family"

"He told me that too" Crystal said

"I can't believe this shit! What am I supposed to do
now?" Christine asked

"I don't know but I'm putting his ass out" Crystal
said

"I'm pregnant" Christine said

"What?" Crystal screamed as she spit out her water

"I'm 3 months pregnant?"

"Does Keith know?"

"Yeah I called him and told him last night. He was
happy"

"He was?" Crystal asked shocked

Crystal was so hurt. She felt like she wanted to roll
over and die. The man she loved and had been
living with for three years had a whole separate life
that she knew nothing about and now she and
Christine were both pregnant.

What am I going to do?

"My man has been locked up for a year" Christine

blurted out

"What? Your man who?"

"The guy I was with before I met Keith. He has two more years to go. I didn't mean to cheat on him but I met Keith and fell in love. I have been letting Keith wear his clothes and shoes. I was going to leave him for Keith. I feel so stupid"

"You let Keith wear his clothes?" Crystal couldn't believe her ears

"Yeah. He asked me so I said okay" Christine said

How could Keith wear some man's clothes he doesn't even know? Why would he even ask to wear his clothes? What kind of man does that?

"I let him wear his mink and his alligator shoes. If he found out he would kill me"

He told me he bought that shit from his cousin. Lying bastard!

"Let's set him up" Christine said

"What?"

"Let's set him up"

"I don't know" Crystal shook her head

"I want him to see us both at the same time so he can't deny it. Ask him to go to dinner and then I can show up. That will surprise the shit out of him!" Christine said with a crazed look in her eyes

"I don't know" Crystal said unsure

"What's wrong? I know you're not scared? He's been playing us both"

"No I'm not scared" Crystal said

"Well then let's set him up tomorrow night. Ask him to go to dinner and I will hide in the backseat.

Talk to him a lot about your relationship and get
him to say I love you" Christine said
"Okay" Crystal said. She was still unsure
The two of them talked about the details of how
they were going to set Keith up. It seemed like a
good plan. Now Crystal seemed more confused than
ever. She knew that she had to break up with Keith
but now she was growing attached to the baby she
was carrying. She definitely didn't want to be a
single mother. And she damn sure wasn't telling
Harold about the baby.

Chapter 9

"Hello may I help you?" The receptionist asked
Nina.

"Yes. I have a 2 o'clock appointment with Ms.
Darwin" Nina replied

Nina was meeting with the lawyer that Michelle,
Paulette's mother recommended for the first time.
Michelle spoke so highly of her. Nina felt very
confident about her case.

"Mrs. Darwin is with a client, but she will be out in
one minute. Please have a seat"

"Sure" Nina said

Nina looked around the office. It was gorgeous.
Everything looked expensive. *She must be good.*

"Hello Ms. Franklin, Its nice to meet you"

"Hello Mrs. Darwin"

"Please call me Linda"

"Hi Linda, Call me Nina"

"Okay, Nina follow me"

Nina followed Linda into a huge office. The office
was decorated beautifully. There were nice
paintings and pictures everywhere.

"Is this your family?" Nina asked Linda about a
picture that sat on her desk.

"Yes that is my husband and my two daughters"

"They are gorgeous. You guys make a wonderful
family" Nina said

Nina looked at the picture a little longer

"He looks so familiar" Nina said

"You may know him, he's a producer"

"Oh maybe that's where I know him from" Nina said

I can't put my finger on it but I know him from somewhere.

"So let's talk about your case"

"Sure"

"I was reading over your file and I see that you have a copy of the bill of sale from when you purchased the automobile, correct?"

"Yes"

"I also did a background check on the couple you purchased the car from and they are not very creditable"

"Really?"

Never trust people in the church! Nina thought

"I think we will have no problem winning this case. Let me do a little more research and I will get back to you. Is this a good number to reach you at?" Linda asked as she pointed to Nina's cell phone number that she had written down in her file.

"Yes it is"

"Okay I will keep in touch. It was nice meeting you. Have a good day"

"You too" Nina said as she walked out of Linda's office.

That's Jay! In the picture! She must use her maiden name!

...

"I love you too, bye" Trish said as she hung up the phone. *I love that man.* She smiled as she thought about Jay. She couldn't wait until the Mr. Jay Hollis was all hers.

Trish walked into her building.

"Good Evening Ms. Grand" The doorman said "Hello Tommy" Trish said as she stopped at her mailbox to check her mail. *No mail? Great that means no bills.*

She waited by the elevator as she thought about how she was going to spend her night. Jay was going to be at the studio most of the night so she was spending a quiet evening all by herself. She was going to take a long bath and relax with some wine and a good book.

Trish walked off the elevator and three doors down to her apartment. When she reached her apartment there was a small white envelope lying on the floor in front of her door. She immediately thought of Jay. *He is always trying to surprise me.* She picked up the envelope and found a small note inside. She unfolded the paper and began to read the note. She was shocked when she read:

Find Your Own Husband Bitch!

Trish was so scared she dropped her keys and her purse. *Who the fuck sent this?* She had messed with so many women's husbands in the past that she wasn't sure who sent her the note. *How do they know where I live? Are they following me? Is it Jay's wife?*

Trish was so confused she didn't know what to

think. One thing she knew for sure was that she was not stepping foot inside her apartment alone. *They might be waiting inside to kill me.*

She turned around and walked right back down the hall and pressed the elevator button frantically. She was so scared she pressed the button over and over until the elevator came. As soon as she got downstairs she ran off the elevator.

"Tommy did you see anyone strange come into the building today?"

"No I didn't see any unfamiliar faces but I just came in at 5. Robert was here this morning, you can ask him tomorrow. Is everything okay?"

"Yeah everything is fine" Trish lied

Trish walked outside and down the street to her car. She looked over her left and her right shoulder to make sure no one was following her. She finally reached her car and pressed her alarm.

Once she got inside she locked the doors. *Calm down.* She told herself.

Maybe someone was playing some kind of sick joke on her. She started to dial Jay's number but then decided against that because she didn't want to worry him. *It can't be his wife because we are extra careful* She thought. But she still didn't want to stay in her apartment alone. Her first thought was to call Crystal, she always made her feel better but then she decided not to because Crystal always got too worried and she didn't want to stay the night with Crystal and her man.

I'll call Paulette. Trish dialed Paulette's number

and it went straight to the voicemail. *Paulette never answers her damn phone!*

Trish began to dial Nina's number.

"Hello?"

"Hey Nina"

"Hey, what you doing?"

"Nothing much. I'm grading some papers and making dinner. Why?" Nina asked

"Do you want some company?" Trish asked

"Is everything okay?"

"Yeah everything is fine" Trish lied. She did not feel like telling Nina what happened because she was not in the mood for her bullshit. She knew the first thing Nina would say was "I told you to stop messing with women's husbands, find your own man"

"Okay. Come over. I'll be here all night" Nina said

"I'll be there in 10 minutes"

"Okay"

Trish hung up the phone and turned on the car. She decided to take the long way to Nina's house because she needed to clear her head. She read the note one more time before she pulled off.

Find Your Own Husband Bitch!

Fuck you! She said to the note and balled it up and threw it out the window. She decided not to let it get to her. It wasn't her fault if a man was attracted to her and he happened to be married. *Don't be mad at me. Be mad at him.* She thought. She turned up the music, rolled down the windows, and let the wind blow through her hair.

...

"Hey baby" Keith said as Crystal walked in the house
"Hey" Crystal said
She didn't even want to look at his lying, cheating ass but she had to play it off if she wanted their plan to work. She had already called the office and taken the day off tomorrow. She planned on spending the whole day packing Keith's shit.
"Where were you?"
"Out"
"What?" Keith asked
"I was out with Trish" Crystal lied
"Where did you two go?" Keith asked with an attitude. *He got a lot of fucking nerve acting like he has attitude. Why doesn't he go freeload in Christine's fucking house tonight?* Crystal thought
"We went to eat. Look I'm tired. I'm getting in the shower and going to bed" She didn't even feel like talking to him. The more he talked the madder she got. If she didn't want to blurt everything out she knew it was best if she kept her mouth shut and did as least talking as possible.
Just then her phone rang. She grabbed it off the kitchen counter quickly. She looked at the caller id. It read Harold.
Damn! I don't need this shit right now.
She pressed the end button immediately.
"Who was that?"
"My mom" Crystal lied

187

"What's wrong with you?" Keith asked
"Nothing. I just have a headache"
"Yeah Whatever" Keith said as if he didn't believe
her.
Crystal walked in her bedroom and closed the door.
She walked over to her dresser and grabbed some
panties and a bra out of her drawer. Then she
walked in the closet and looked for her favorite pair
of old beat up pajamas. It was no sense in looking
cute. *He's not getting any.* She thought.
        She walked in the bathroom and closed the
door behind her. She undressed and thought about
the events of the day. She would have felt better if
Christine was ugly. She was mad as hell that
Christine was pretty- no- beautiful.   *What does she
have that I don't?* She thought. She got angrier
when she thought about men in general. *They are
always doing something stupid! I'm a good woman!
I have a good job! I'm in shape! I cook! I clean! I
don't have any kids!* Then she looked down at her
stomach and felt the small bump. She had to be at
least 2 ½ months now and she still hadn't made a
decision.
She turned on the water and stepped in the shower.
The hot water felt so good on her skin. She wished
she could stay in the shower all day and forget
about her life and her many problems.
The bathroom door slightly opened.
"Can I join you?" Keith called out.
"No!" Crystal screamed. *Shit! Why didn't I lock the
door!*

"Why not?"

"Because I'm about to get out" *He never wants to get in the shower with me any other time. I wish he would get the fuck out so I can finish taking my shower in peace.*

"Okay I'll leave" Keith said

"Thank you. I'll be out in a minute"

Crystal heard the door close and smiled. *Thank God. I am not in the mood for him.*

She closed her eyes and finished daydreaming.

"Ahh" Crystal screamed as she felt a hand on her shoulder.

"You thought I left? Didn't you?" Keith said as he stepped his naked body into the shower behind Crystal.

"Yes I did. You scared the shit out of me" Crystal said with an attitude

"What's wrong baby?" Keith asked as he rubbed her back

"Nothing! I told you I had a headache and I just wanted to take a shower alone and relax"

"Why? Are you fucking somebody else?"

"What?" Crystal couldn't believe what he was asking her.

"You heard me! Are you fucking somebody else?" Keith yelled

"No!" *I can't believe him! He is the one fucking somebody and has the nerve to question me!*

"So then what's your problem?"

"Nothing" Crystal said as she turned around and kissed him. She just decided to let it go. It was no

sense in talking to him because he never listened to
her anyway. She knew he just wanted to have sex
anyway. She just decided to give in because she
wanted their plan to work tomorrow. *This will be
the last time I have to fuck his nasty ass anyway!*

...

"What's up?" Nina said as she opened the door
"Nothing much, I was just a little bored" Trish lied
Nina knew something had to be up for Trish to stop
by her apartment in the middle of the week but she
let it go. *If she wants to tell me she will.*
"Come in, I made some chicken and mashed
potatoes"
"No, Thanks I ate already" Trish did not feel like
lying today and telling Nina her food was good.
Nina couldn't cook for shit!
Trish was shocked when she saw Nina. She looked
terrible. Her hair wasn't combed, she had bags
under her eyes and her clothes were a mess. When
Trish walked inside Nina's apartment it was even
worse. There were stacks of papers everywhere, like
she hadn't graded papers in six months. Newspapers
piled up on the floor. Clothes thrown everywhere
and dishes were piled up in the sink. Nina must
have seen the look on Trish's face because she tried
to adjust her hair and fix her robe as she said "I
know I have to clean up a little"

Clean up is not the word. Trish didn't even want to

sit down.

Trish was the one that needed to talk but judging by the way Nina looked she said "Are you okay Nina?"

"Yeah why?"

"You just don't look like yourself"

"Well we all can't be glamour girls 24 hours a day Trish!"

"What the hell is that supposed to mean?"

"What does it sound like? Sorry I didn't put on my best clothes because you were coming over" Nina said and took a bow

"What is wrong with you? I asked you a simple question because I care about you and you always have to take shit the wrong way"

"No you always have to say shit the wrong way!" Nina screamed

 "Whatever!"

"Whatever to you too!" Nina said as she walked to her bay window and sat on the ledge. She leaned back against the window sill and grabbed the ashtray. She picked up her lighter and her blunt, she lit the end and inhaled deeply as if Trish wasn't even there.

"Now you smoke again?" Trish asked. Trish remembered when she met Nina in college. Nina smoked all the time. She smoked morning, noon, and night. Trish tried it with Nina a few times but she never liked the way she felt. She felt like an asshole and she analyzed everything, it made her think too much. Trish preferred drinking on any day, that was her thing.

Trish wasn't one to knock anyone but she hated
how Nina acted when she smoked. She acted slow
and stupid and she hated being around her when she
smoked. Trish was so happy when they graduated
college Nina came out the blue and told her one day
"I quit". That was 4 years ago.
Nina rolled her eyes and said "What does it look
like?"
"What hasn't gotten into you?"
"Just leave me alone, I don't need a lecture right
now"
"I'm not trying to lecture you. You're bugging"
"And" Nina said nonchalantly and she took another
pull. Trish could see the stupidity coming and she
wasn't in the mood for it.
"I thought you had papers to grade?"
"If you are so concerned why don't you grade
them?"
"Maybe you should go lay down and get some rest,
you have to get up early"
"I'm not going to work tomorrow"
"Why?"
"Because I don't feel like it"
"Did you go to work today?"
"Nope"
"When was the last time you went to work?"
"A few days ago"
"Nina, what is going on? Do you want to talk about
something?"
"Nope" Nina said as she put her head back on the
window sill and closed her eyes.

They sat in silence for a few minutes. Trish decided to stop lecturing Nina, she had problems of her own and her own shit to deal with. Like who was leaving threatening notes at her door and trying to scare her ass. Besides Nina was grown if she wanted to smoke and call out of work that was her own damn business.

"So you still dating Mr. Al Bundy?" Nina asked as she started cracking up laughing like it was the funniest thing in the world.

"Mr. Al Bundy?" Trish asked confused *What the fuck is she talking about?*

"Yeah, Mr. Married with Children" Nina said as she laughed so hard she fell of the window sill.

Trish was really fed up with Nina now. She did not find anything funny.

"Yes we are still together"

"Excuse me. You guys are "together" now" Nina said as she did air quotes.

Trish ignored Nina's remarks.

"I have some pictures of all of us from the party" Trish said as she pulled them out of her purse.

"This is my favorite" Trish said about a picture of her and Jay arm and arm.

Nina looked at the pictures silently. She had no comments.

"Did you like any of them?" Trish asked

"Yeah, they were okay"

Nina placed the pictures down on the coffee table. Just then the phone rang. Nina sat there like she didn't hear anything.

"Your phone is ringing!" Trish yelled

"I know" Nina said as she rolled her eyes and got up and walked to the phone

Nina put on her nicest voice and said "Hello?" *If only they could see through the phone* Trish thought to herself.

"I'm great! Just grading some papers, how are you?" Nina lied

Trish sat there in amazement. *This bitch is crazy.*

"Sure I can meet in your office at 4 to talk about the case"

"Okay see you then?" Nina said and hung up the phone. She turned around and smiled.

"Who was that?" Trish asked

"No one" Nina said and walked to the bathroom

Nina was beginning to get on Trish's last nerve. *I don't care about a stupid note. I'm going home. I don't need this shit.* Trish said to herself. Trish grabbed her purse and walked to the door. She slammed it without saying goodbye.

...

Crystal's hands shook as she packed Keith's things. She was so nervous that he might come home and catch her and then their plan would be ruined. She was on her third box and she had about three more to go. It was killing her keeping everything inside. She hadn't told any of her friends what was going on, not even Trish. Christine called her early this morning to make sure everything was still on and she told her it was.

Crystal thought about last night and laughed to herself. *Men are so stupid.*

She thought about how her and Keith had sex in the shower last night. She moaned and groaned like it was the best sex she ever had in her life. Keith came in about three minutes. Crystal acted like she was upset, like she wanted to keep going, knowing damn well that she was elated because she didn't want him to touch her in the first place. Then he got in the bed and slept like a baby. *That was easy.* Crystal thought

While Crystal, on the other hand stayed up half the night like a kid on Christmas Eve.

"Knock. Knock"

Shit. Nobody knows I'm home today. Crystal thought.

She tip toed to the door and looked through the peephole.

It was Harold.

"Open up Crystal" Harold said as he knocked harder.

Crystal stood on the other side of the door quietly. A few minutes passed.

"Crystal I know you're in there, open the damn door" Harold said louder.

Crystal still didn't move.

"Knock. Knock"

"I'm not leaving until you open the door"

Just then Crystal flung the door open.

She hated her neighbors in her business and she
didn't want anyone to see Harold standing in the
hallway knocking at her door.
"What do you want?"
"What do you think?"
"Didn't I tell you don't ever come to my fucking
house"
"You should have returned my calls"
"I don't feel well, I'm sick. I'm gonna go lay down.
I'll call you tomorrow" Crystal said as she began to
close the door.
Harold put his hand up and blocked her from
closing the door.
"You look fine to me"
"Well I'm not"
"Look stop playing games with me"
"Why don't you just leave me the fuck alone"
"Why don't I just leave your fucking mother alone"
"You bastard"
Crystal hated how he blackmailed her. She also
hated that her mother was so fucking weak. She
knew her mother would fall apart all over again if
Harold left her and he knew it too.
"I'm not leaving until I get what I want. So we can
do this the hard way or the easy way"
Crystal opened the door and let him come in.
"I knew you would see it my way"
"Look lets just get this over with"
"You have a nice place here" Harold said as he
looked around. This was the first time he had ever
been in Crystal's apartment.

She had invited her mother over a few times but she always made sure Harold was at work. She didn't want him knowing where she lived.

"Thanks"

Harold walked over to her and kissed her on the lips. She moved her face away.

Even though she had sex with him, it was not intimate.

She just wanted it to be as quick as possible. No hugging, no touching, especially no kissing.

"Lets just get this over with"

Crystal was disgusted already.

"Whatever you say baby girl"

Crystal walked over to her couch and pulled her shorts off.

She bent over on the couch. She didn't even want to look at him.

He walked up behind her and unloosened his belt.

His pants fell to the floor.

She felt him go inside.

"Damn I missed you"

Crystal didn't say anything as tears streamed down her face. No matter how many times they did this she could never get used to it.

"I love you Crystal"

What?

She couldn't believe what he just said to her.

"Mmm.mmm" He moaned

She heard him moan and pump her hard one final time before he fell limp on her back.

She pushed him off of her and picked up her shorts

and ran in the bathroom.

She closed the door, turned on the hot water and wet a washcloth. She quickly wiped herself and put her shorts back on. She splashed some cold water on her face and walked back out into the living room.

Harold was dressed, sitting on the couch.

"I'm really tired and I want to lay down"

So get the fuck out!

"Okay I'm leaving. When can I see you again?" Harold said in a sweet voice. She didn't know who this man sitting there was. It was like he instantly changed.

"I don't know Harold. This really needs to stop. It's not right and you know its not right"

"Yes it is right, why stop now?"

"Because you are married to my mother and she loves you"

"Yeah, Yeah. I love her too, but what she doesn't know won't hurt her"

"Well I can't keep doing this"

"What the fuck is that supposed to mean?"

"That this was the last time" Crystal said with an attitude. She was truly fed up. She couldn't take it anymore.

"Its not the last time until I say it's the last time"

"Well I'm saying it"

"Well I guess I'm just going to have to tell your mother about the little affair we have been having all these years and I have pictures to prove it"

"What pictures? I don't believe you" Crystal asked shocked

"Don't believe me then, I bet your mother will, and you look real nice in the pictures. I wonder what she will think?"

Crystal didn't know if he was telling the truth or not. She never remembered him taking any pictures but he was a nasty pervert.

"No please don't tell her. Why do you want to hurt her?" Crystal begged

"I don't want to hurt her, you do"

"No I don't that's the only reason I put up with this shit, but I can't do this anymore!"

"Yes you can and you will"

"No I can't"

"Well I'll let you think about it. I also want you to think about how the rest of your life will be without a mother because she will hate your ass" Harold said as he walked to the door

"Fuck you"

"You just did"

Harold laughed as he walked out the door, looking like the happiest man in the world.

Crystal locked the door and walked into her bedroom. She started crying hysterically. She didn't know how she let this get so out of control.

Damn I wish he was dead.

Crystal never hated someone so much. She couldn't keep fucking him. It had to stop. She had to do something.

She looked at the clock 12:00pm. She only had a

few more hours to finish packing.
Shit!

...

"Hey this is Paulette I'm not available, leave a
message at the beep"
"Paulette, its your mother. This is my sixth or
seventh message. Is everything okay? I haven't
spoke to you in days. Please call me back"
Paulette sunk deeper into the bed and put a pillow
over her head. She hadn't spoke to anyone in two
weeks. All she did was go to work and come home.
The HPV thing was really getting to her. It had been
two months since she found out she was infected
and she still hadn't come to terms with it. Then to
make matters worse she had her first outbreak last
week. She didn't know what it was at first. She got
mad as she thought about it.

Last Monday Paulette walked into the bathroom
to take a quick shower. As usual she overslept so
she only had twenty minutes to get out of her
apartment. She took off her T-shirt and her shorts
and she was surprised when she looked and saw the
skin above and around her vagina was somewhat
dried out, it had a rash-like appearance. She sat on
the toilet and looked closer there were a few small
tiny red bumps all around the area. Paulette stared at
the bumps for a few minutes. She inspected them.
They didn't itch or irritate her so she decided not to
pay it any attention.

Maybe I'm irritated from shaving or I'm allergic to something Paulette thought. But deep down she knew the truth. Paulette took a shower and went to work as usual. She went to the bathroom every hour to see if there was any change in the bumps. They looked the same. She wished she could say the same now. Over the next few days the tiny bumps began to change. The bumps began to spread up her ass. They were in little clusters around her anus. She was surprised when she touched them they were very rough and raised, almost like they were hanging.

Paulette cried for hours.

She didn't know what to do.

She paged Dr. Patterson.

He called back in 2 minutes.

"Hello?"

"Hi. Did someone page me?"

"Yes. Hello Dr. Patterson. Its Paulette"

"What seems to be the problem Paulette? You don't sound so good"

"I'm not good Dr. Patterson. I don't know what's wrong with me. I have these bumps and things hanging" Paulette said as she sobbed.

"Okay calm down Paulette, remember we talked about the possibilities of this happening"

Paulette sat silently on the edge of her bed and cried.

"Paulette? Are you there?"

"Yes"

"I'm on my way to the office now. It will probably

take me about twenty minutes. Just meet me there
okay"
"Okay" Paulette said as she hung up the phone.
She stood up, put her cell phone in her back pocket
and put on her sneakers.
She grabbed a hoodie off the chair in her room and
a hat off the floor and put it on. Her hair looked
terrible but she didn't care. She stuffed her ID and
fifty dollars in her pocket and grabbed her keys and
walked out the door.
She walked outside and it was such a beautiful
today. Too bad she couldn't enjoy it. She was going
to take the train but decided against it because she
didn't want to be around a lot of people, she just
wasn't in the mood.
She stood on the corner and flagged a cab. About
six cabs passed before one finally stopped.
"Where you going?"
"57th and 3rd"
She sat in silence the whole ride. She was so happy
the cab driver didn't start a conversation because
she damn sure didn't feel like talking.
They pulled up twenty minutes later.
"You can let me out right here on the corner"
"Okay that's 14 dollars"
She handed the driver a twenty and got out. She
didn't even feel like waiting for any change.
She walked into the doctor's office and walked
straight to the front desk.
"Hello Ms. Jackson"
"Hello Tara"

Paulette was even more embarrassed because Tara
was the bitch that had to call her and give her the
bad news.

"Do you have an appointment?"

"No I'm here to see Dr. Patterson"

"Is she expecting you?"

"Yes"

"Okay have a seat and I'll let her know you're here"

"Okay thanks"

Paulette sat down and couldn't stop fidgeting. She
couldn't believe that this had happened to her. She
didn't feel the same about sex anymore and she
didn't think she ever would.

"You can go back Ms. Jackson"

"Okay"

Paulette stood up and walked back to Dr.
Patterson's office.

"Hi Paulette. How are you?"

"Okay I guess"

"Here take this robe and undress, you can leave
your bra on. Have a seat on the table and I'll be
back in a few minutes.

"Why do I have to undress? Can't you just give me
a prescription?"

"Well I need to see exactly what the problem is
before I can determine anything"

"Okay"

"I'll be right back"

Paulette was so ashamed of her body. She didn't
want to take off her clothes.

She didn't want anyone to see what she saw. She
undressed and quickly put the robe on. She sat on
the table and held the robe tight. As she sat there
she thought about all the people she had sex with in
the past and she wasn't really sure where she got it
from. But she had a gut feeling she got it from her
threesome with Gabriel and Jaime. Neither one of
them has called her since that night.
How could I be so stupid? She thought.
She constantly thought about Chris, her one night
stand. She cried even harder when she thought
about him.
She wanted to call him so badly but she knew she
couldn't. What if she gave him HPV?
What would he think of her?
She hoped and prayed that they used a condom.
"Okay Paulette I want you to slide back on the
table, lie back and place your feet in the stirrups.
Dr. Patterson put on a pair of latex gloves and sat on
a stool in front of Paulette.
"Paulette you have to open your legs"
"Sorry" Paulette said as she pulled her knees apart.
This had to be the most humiliating experience of
her life. She laid there and stood at the ceiling,
wondering what Dr. Patterson was thinking.
Dr. Patterson examined in silence.
"Okay Paulette it appears that you have external
genital warts, which means they are on the outside,
I haven't see any in the inside of your vagina,
although this may develop"

Paulette just listened.

"I am going to write you a prescription for a topical cream you can use, you will apply it at home. You are going to apply it to the genital warts three times a week before going to bed. You must wash your hands after applying the cream. Leave the cream on for 6 to 10 hours and then wash it off. You can use the cream until the warts disappear or for up to four months"

"Four months?"

"They are going to last for four months?"

"Probably not but I'm not sure exactly when they will go away, everyone is different. Honestly, they may not go away at all"

"What?"

Paulette began to cry again as she thought about how the warts looked.

"I am not trying to scare you Paulette. I am just trying to keep you informed of all the possibilities. In most cases the topical treatment works, but the warts may reappear. If this happens we will try the topical treatment again. If they re-appears again, they may have to be removed"

"Okay"

Dr. Patterson wrote Paulette the prescription and handed it to her.

"Have a good day"

That's easy for you to say.

"You too" Paulette said as she walked out the office and dialed Nina's number she had to talk to someone.

Chapter 10

"Hello Nina. It's good to see you again"
"You to Linda"
Nina had just walked into her attorney Linda
Darwin's office.
"It looks like everything is going in your favor for
this case. They are ready to settle, so this should be
over very shortly"
"Really? Already?"
Nina was happy that the case would be settled so
quickly but she also wanted to get to know Linda a
little better, she had an agenda of her own.
"Yes. I just need you to sign a few papers and that's
it for today"
"Okay. Well we should definitely go out and
celebrate sometime" Nina said
"That sounds like a good idea"
"I also may need your legal advice on another
matter I have, if you don't mind?" Nina lied
"Sure. Any friend of Michelle's is a friend of mine"
"Well are you busy now? Maybe we can grab a bite
to eat and talk a little"
"I just had a few more things to look over, then I
was leaving. If you don't mind waiting a few
minutes that's fine"
"I'll wait"
"Okay. Excuse me a second, let me just call my
husband and make sure he is picking up the girls"
Linda picked up the phone and dialed.
"Hey. I was just making sure you were picking up

Nia and Naomi"
"Okay. Thanks"
"I'll be in later"
"Goodbye"
Nina was surprised at how professional the phone call was.
She never would have guessed that Linda was talking to her husband.
"I'll be ready in a few minutes"
"Sure. Take your time"
"Hello ladies" The doorman at Da Silvano greeted them. The restaurant was very hip and chic, Nina had never been there but she could tell just by looking at Linda that she was used to the finer things in life. Linda had on a tan pants suit that was tailored to fit her perfectly. With tan and red snakeskin Stewart Weitzman pumps, with the briefcase to match, her pumps looked almost four inches high. Her hair was immaculate in a short Halle Berry style cut, it looked like she just walked out of the salon.
"Hello Pedro. How are you?" Linda said to the Hispanic hostess, who was clearly gay or very metro-sexual because his eyebrows were perfectly arched and there wasn't a hair out of place. He even looked like he had on a hint of eyeliner and mascara.
When the waitress walked over Linda asked
"Can we please have a bottle of Sauvignon Blanc, the California reserve"
Sure would you like anything else?

"Two bottles of Perrier" Linda added
The waitress turned to look at Nina.
"That will be fine" Nina said
She sat there and let Linda place the order, she seemed much better at it than her. Nina would have simply ordered a glass of ice water or maybe a coke.
"So where do you live?" Linda asked
"I live on the lower east side, what about you?" Nina said very proudly. Her apartment was her greatest accomplishment. Even though she spent almost every dime paying her rent, she was always trying to keep up with the Jones. She saw how most people reacted when she told them that she lived on the lower east side.

Her apartment was only a few blocks away from Trish's. She got angry just thinking about Trish. She remembered when she moved into her apartment, she was so happy, she had a house warming two weeks later. She went all out and hired a catering service, it was a nice party and everyone told her how gorgeous her place was. Three weeks later Trish bought a condo only a few blocks from Nina and she also had a housewarming. But Trish's housewarming wasn't your average "get together", it was wonderful. There were celebrities, free food, and champagne. It made Nina's place look like a dump.
"My husband and I live in Greenwich, I usually take the metro north in or hire a car service" Linda said

"Oh" Nina said.

Once again her place looked like shit. Nina knew how much the houses cost in Greenwich so Linda and her husband must be paid. *What does he want with Trish's gold-digging ass?*

"So do you have any children?"

"Yes. I have thirty" Nina joked

"What?"

"I'm only kidding. I'm a third grade teacher. I don't have any of my own yet"

"Oh. You scared me for a second. I have two little girls"

"How old are they?"

"Six and eight"

"Oh they must be adorable"

"They are really sweet little girls"

"So how long have you and your husband been married?"

"Nine years"

"Wow?"

"We got married really young. Right out of college"

"That is so sweet that you guys are still together, many marriages don't last"

"Well I love my husband and we are both really busy people, so truthfully we don't spend that much time together" It must have been the wine talking, because Linda was becoming really comfortable.

"Maybe you should plan a vacation, like a little weekend getaway for just the two of you"

"I don't know. We both are usually busy on the weekends, Jay is usually at the studio and we usually spend time with the girls"

"Are you sure he always at the studio?" Nina asked. She hoped she didn't say too much.

"What?" Linda asked with an attitude. *How dare she?*

"I'm sorry. I just think that maybe you guys need to take a little vacation and get your mind off of work"

"Maybe I will look into it, I do need a little break and Jay probably does too"

"He is a producer right?"

"Yeah, why?"

"I was trying to remember where I saw him before, but I think he was a party that a friend of mine had?"

"He probably was. What was your friend's name? I'll ask him"

"Trish, Trish Grand"

"Okay"

The women talked for a few more minutes until their main dishes came out. They ate in silence.

"I had a really nice time, we should do this again" Nina said

"I did too, we should"

"I would love to meet you girls one day"

"Well maybe one day when I get off early I'll cook dinner and you can come over"

"That sounds great"

Nina was going to make sure she kept her promise.

"Here's the check ladies, Its no rush" The waitress said

Nina glanced at the bill that read $256.00 she

almost spit her water out.

She was so happy when Linda pulled out an American Express Black card and said

"Don't worry about it, it's on me"

"Are you sure?"

"Yeah, no problem"

"Thanks"

Nina did a lot of thinking in the cab ride home. She was pleased with herself. She really liked Linda. She hoped that Linda was serious about them hanging out again. She was.

She's so much more classy than Trish. What does Jay see in her?

Just then she looked down at her phone and she had two new voicemails and one new text from Paulette. It said call me back ASAP!

She dialed Paulette's number

"Hello?"

"Yeah what's up?"

"Nothing can you meet me at my house? I need to talk"

"Is everything okay?"

"Yeah. I just need to talk, its important" Paulette said

"Okay I'm in a cab now, I'll tell him to turn around I'm on my way"

...

When Nina walked into Paulette's apartment she was surprised to see that Paulette's eyes were puffy like she'd been crying.

"What's wrong?"

"Nothing, I'm just having a bad day"

"What happened?"

"I found out that I have HPV?" Paulette cried

"What?" Nina asked shocked, she didn't expect Paulette to say that.

"Yes I have HPV" Paulette sobbed

"What exactly is that?"

"It's a form of genital warts?"

"So you have warts?" Nina whispered like there were other people in the apartment.

"Yeah"

"All the time?"

"No. I just have outbreaks"

"Well how did you get it?"

"From sex, what do you think?"

"I know that, but from who?"

"I think I got it from the guy Gabriel I was telling you about, the one that I met online"

"Mmm, well I told you about those online things" Nina said shaking her head.

She couldn't understand how Paulette could go online and talk to guys and actually meet them and go on dates. It was crazy.

Paulette was not in the mood for any I told you so's. Now she had second thoughts about even telling Nina her situation but she just felt like she needed to vent.

"Shut up" Paulette said with an attitude

"Ya'll didn't use a condom?"

"I'm not sure"

"You're not sure?" Nina screwed her face up

"Yeah I was drunk and I really don't remember"

"Well how do you know it was him that gave it you?"

"I really don't know but I told him and he won't return any of my calls, he was the last person I slept with"

"Well have you been to the doctor?"

"Yeah I went earlier today"

"How do you get rid of it?"

Nina was talking a mile a minute. She was asking Paulette a hundred questions. Paulette felt like she was on an interview. Now she felt like it was a bad idea telling Nina, she might have been better off keeping it to herself.

"I can't get rid of it. I can take medication, but it doesn't go away"

"So you have it forever?"

"Yes" Paulette started crying

"I'm sorry I didn't mean to make you feel bad, I didn't know"

"I know. I just feel so stupid! I can't believe this happened to me"

"Well have you slept with anybody else?"

"No" Paulette lied

She couldn't dare tell Nina that she slept with Chris and she wasn't sure if they used a condom either.

"Well if you meet someone new are you gonna tell them?"

"I don't know. I don't think so"

"What?" Nina asked shocked

"It's not something easy to tell Nina, I can't just walk up to someone and tell them I have warts, they probably won't have anything to do with me"
"Well you can't just go around sleeping with people and not telling them either, you wouldn't want somebody to do that to you"
"Somebody did do that to me!" Nina screamed
"Yeah and how do you feel?"
"Just shut up! Get out! It was a mistake even telling your ass. I should have kept my fucking mouth shut!"
"I'm sorry! I was just giving you my opinion"
"Well maybe I didn't want your opinion. I just wanted you to be a friend and listen"
"Well I thought I was being a friend by telling you the truth. I guess you don't want to hear the truth. So I'll leave" Nina said as she walked to the door
"Bye" Paulette said and slammed the door behind her.
...

"Knock-Knock"
Crystal's hands shook as she heard the knock at the door. She knew it was Christine but she just wasn't sure if she could go through with it.
"Knock Knock"
Crystal paced back and forth. *What if things didn't go right?*
"Open the door Crystal. I know you're in there!"
Crystal walked over to the door and opened it.
"What the hell were you doing in here?" Christine

asked with an attitude.

"I thought you backed out on me"

"I was in the bathroom" Crystal lied

She couldn't help but stare at Christine. They looked so much alike. Today they both had their hair pulled back in tight ponytails, it was even more noticeable. But Crystal was definitely the one with the class. Crystal sat on the couch and put on her 4 inch high black Christian Louboutin pumps, with the classic red bottom. She looked casual but classy in her blue J Brand skinny jeans and black cashmere sweater that fit her perfectly. Three carat diamond studs sat in her ears and a diamond heart pendant lay across her neck.

"Here are my cars keys, It's a silver Mercedes, just beep the alarm" Crystal said as she stood up and handed Christine her keys. She towered over Christine now who had on black leggings and black ballet flats, with a loose fitting floral shirt.

"I just called him, he said he'll be here in twenty minutes. That was about ten minutes ago, so hurry up"

"Okay I'll be in the back seat"

"Okay"

Crystal couldn't wait to see the look on Keith's face when he saw the both of them together. She laughed when she thought about it.

Crystal walked in the bathroom to put the finishing touches on her makeup when she heard a key turning in the door.

"Hey baby I'm in the bathroom. I'll be out in a minute" Crystal called out in her sweetest voice.
"Okay. I'm just gonna change my shirt"
When Crystal walked out of the bathroom Keith was sitting on the couch waiting for her.
"I'm ready"
"Me too. You got the tickets?"
"Yeah there in my purse"
Crystal had gotten them tickets to see the Nets, Keith's favorite basketball team. They were playing tonight at Madison Square Garden. The plan was to get out the car at Madison Square Garden and have him see the both of them. He will be so scared he won't know what to do, they would both tell him that they are leaving his sorry ass and go to the game together.
Crystal checked her black Gucci bag and made sure they were there. "Yeah I got them, let's go, so we don't run into any traffic"
Crystal began to walk down to the parking garage where her car was parked.
"Why don't we just take a cab, then we don't have to worry about parking"
Shit!
"Well what if we want to go to dinner after or something, I'd rather drive"
"Okay"
When they reached the car Crystal searched her bag for the keys, she couldn't find them.
Shit! I gave Christine my keys, what was I thinking!

"I can't find my keys, I think I left them upstairs"
Crystal said as she thought about the spare set that
she had in her top drawer. Keith bent over and
looked in the driver's side window.
Crystal got so nervous.
"What are you looking at?"
"You left your keys' right there in the ignition"
"What?"
"Look they are in the ignition" Keith pointed
"Oh. I think I was on the phone. I probably wasn't
paying attention" Crystal lied.
Good thinking Christine.
They got in the car and Keith turned on the radio.
"Shawty is a ten, a ten, Shawty is ten" Keith sang
along with the Dream on the radio
Crystal turned down the radio.
"What are you doing, that's my shit!"
"I'm sorry I just wanted to talk to you" Crystal said
in a sweet voice
"About what? You always want to talk" Keith said
with an attitude
"About us"
"What about us?"
"Well we have been together for a while now and
you know I Love you, I was just thinking that
maybe we could take things to the next level"
"I was thinking the same thing baby"
Crystal was shocked.
"You were?"
She thought it was going to be much harder getting
him to express his feelings.

"Yeah. I love you so much and I want to make you
my wife. You are the only girl I ever loved the way
I do"
Crystal was shocked. She searched his eyes to see if
he looked genuine and he really did.
"What the fuck did you just say?" Christine
popped up off the floor in the backseat. Keith
almost had a heart attack.
"What? Who is that?" He didn't recognize Christine
at first.
Crystal was so scared she didn't know what to do.
This wasn't part of the plan.
"You heard me motherfucker. Did you just say that
you love her and want to marry her?" "Christine?
What are you doing here? What the fuck is going
on?" Keith asked. He looked like he just saw a
ghost.
"Oh now you remember my fucking name? You
had no problem remembering the shit last week!"
Christine picked up an umbrella off the floor in the
backseat and started swinging it at Keith. She was
banging him on top of the head over and over.
"I loved you! How could you do this to me?"
Crystal was swerving in out of traffic trying to
avoid being hit with the swinging umbrella.
This bitch is crazy.
"I'm sorry Christine you know I love you too"
What? Crystal thought.
"No you don't! You love that bitch!"
She began swinging the umbrella even more.
"Please calm down Christine" Crystal said

"Don't tell me to calm down you booshie bitch!"
She banged Crystal on top of the head with the umbrella.
Crystal tried to grab the umbrella with one hand and drive with the other.
"I hate you! I hate you! How could you do this to me? I'm gonna kill you" Christine screamed at Keith at the top of her lungs.
Crystal managed to get the umbrella out of Christine hands and then Christine really went crazy. She started pulling Crystal's ponytail and tried to grab her face.
"Get the fuck off of me. You crazy bitch!"
"Fuck you! I'm gonna kill you too. You're not taking my man"
"You can have his ass! Just get the fuck off of me"
"Fuck you bitch!"
Christine said as she smacked Crystal in the back of the head.
Keith just sat there and stared in amazement.
"Get your crazy bitch off of me!" Crystal screamed at Keith
Keith just sat there.
"If I wasn't driving I would fuck you up" Crystal yelled.
"Watch out Crystal! Keep your eyes on the road!" Keith yelled but it was too late, they crashed head on into a tow truck.

. . .

Chapter 11

"Paulette? Paulette?"

Paulette turned around to see who was calling her name.

"Hey stranger how you been?"

"Hey Chris how are you?"

Shit! Paulette thought. She hoped she never ran into him again.

"I'm doing good. I left you my number and you never called"

"I am so sorry I misplaced it"

"Well how about you give me yours this time and I'll make sure I call you" Chris said

Paulette hesitated.

"Unless you don't want to" Chris said a little unsure of himself because of the look on Paulette's face.

"Yeah, I do" Paulette played it off and gave him the number.

She couldn't help but look at him again, he was so damn fine. Paulette couldn't believe how much he resembled the actor Boris Kodjoe, only a dark skinned version. He had perfect white teeth and his three piece Armani suit hugged every muscle perfectly.

My mother would love him.

"How about we get together and have dinner one night this week"

"I don't know I've been real busy" Paulette lied. The truth was she was afraid to go on any dates because she was afraid to take her clothes off.

Nina's words constantly stuck out in her mind. She
didn't want to put anybody in jeopardy, but she
didn't have the nerve to tell anybody either. Paulette
hadn't had many relationships in her life that were
not sexual. She didn't know how to just have a
friendly dinner or just be herself. She also knew that
since her and Chris had already had sex if they went
out again he would be expecting sex again and she
would look like an asshole if she said no. She just
couldn't do that to him. She couldn't put him at
risk. Even though, the warts had cleared up. *Thank
God.*
She was still scared.
I can't go out with him.
"I gotta run back to the office, I'll call you" Chris
looked down at his Tourneau watch and then gave
her a dazzling smile.
Damn he's fine.
"Okay"
...

"One missed call" Nina read across the screen on
her blackberry.
She glanced at the number and it was Linda. She
was so happy.
*Maybe she wants to get together for drinks and
dinner, or maybe she wants me to come over to her
place for dinner.*
Nina anxiously dialed Linda's number.
"Hello?"
"Hey girl?" Nina said like they were old girlfriends

"Who is this?" Linda asked in a very professional tone.

Nina immediately changed her tone as well.

"It's Nina Franklin"

"Oh, Hi Nina, How are you?"

Linda asked, much more relaxed when she discovered it was Nina.

"I'm doing good, How are you?"

"I'm okay, I need you to come by when you have a chance and sign some final documents for the settlement"

"Okay. I can come over now, I just got out of work"

"Okay I'll see you when you get here"

"Okay" Nina said and hung up the phone. She was disappointed. She expected Linda to be much friendlier and want to hang out with her.

I'll get her to like me. I don't care what I have to do.

Nina pulled up to Linda's office twenty minutes later. She adjusted her black DKNY pencil skirt and her white Cashmere sweater. She took off her Nine West flats and slid her feet into a brand new pair of black Jimmy Choo pumps. She had just bought them specifically for the next time she saw Linda. She wanted to look her best.

Nina cringed when she looked at the price on the box. $535.00.

I spent half my paycheck on these damn shoes!

She got out the car and slammed the door.

She felt like a million bucks.

It's amazing what a new pair of shoes could do.

Nina walked with so much confidence. She walked through the heavy set of glass double doors and stopped at the receptionist's desk.

"Good afternoon? How may I help you" A blonde perky girl with even perkier breasts asked Nina. Nina immediately looked down at her breasts that were now a B-cup with her extreme push-up bra on. *Bitch.*

"I'm here to see Mrs. Linda Darwin"

"And your name?"

"Nina Franklin"

"Mrs. Darwin. Ms. Franklin is here to see you" The receptionist buzzed

"Okay send her in"

"Sure Mrs. Darwin" the perky receptionist responded

"You can head back Ms. Franklin"

"Thank you" Nina said as she rolled her eyes.

Nina adjusted her skirt one more time and took a deep breath before she opened the door to Linda's office.

"Hi Nina"

"Hey Linda"

"Its good to see you"

"You too"

"I love those shoes. Are those Jimmy Choo?"

"Yeah" Nina said nonchalantly, like they were no big deal.

"I have a similar pair in red"

"Oh" Nina responded as if she didn't notice them the last time she saw her.

Nina couldn't help but notice that Linda looked great as usual. Linda had on a Navy blue pants suit that hugged every curve perfectly without looking to unprofessional.

She had on a crispy white button down shirt and a pair of red, white, and blue Marc Jacobs pumps that went perfectly.

Nina immediately felt insecure.

"I can't seem to find the documents that I need you to sign"

"Go ahead take your time, I'm not in a rush"

Nina lied. She had stacks of papers to grade, that she hadn't even touched.

"I remember looking them over last night at the dining room table and then I was going to put them in my briefcase when the phone rang. Shit!"

"What's wrong?" Nina asked

"I left them on the table. I am so sorry for making you take a wasted trip. I can have a delivery service deliver the papers to you tomorrow and you can send them back to me"

"Do you want to stop by your house and I can sign them there" Nina asked, hoping she would say yes. She was dying to see what her and Jay's house looked like.

"Well if you don't mind the drive"

"You live in Greenwich right?" Nina asked as if she wasn't sure.

"Yes"

"No, that's not a problem"

"Okay, let me just grab my keys and you can follow me"

"You drove today?"

"Yeah. I had a few things to take care of today so I drove in, instead of taking the train"

When they got downstairs Nina's mouth almost fell open when Linda beeped the alarm to a pearly white Bentley.

"This is your car?" Nina asked trying not to sound too surprised

"Actually it's my husband's car. I was having some maintenance done on mine"

"Oh. It's beautiful"

"Thank you. So where are you parked?"

"It's over there" Nina waved in no particular direction. She didn't want to show Linda her new Jetta. She had just got it a few days ago, thanks to her insurance. They covered the down payment for a new car. She was pleased with it until she saw Linda's Bentley, now it looked like a piece of shit.

"I'll pull up behind you" Nina said

"Okay" Linda said

Nina walked briskly to her car.

What am I doing wrong? Why can't I have the finer things in life?

Nina couldn't believe her eyes when they pulled up in front of one of the most beautiful homes she had ever seen in her life. She followed Linda up a brick winding drive way that led them directly into a five car garage.

The house was three stories high with two large marble pillars in the front. The pillars stood in front of a set of glass double doors with two gold handles in the middle. Nina parked behind Linda and got out. She stared at the house. This was something straight out of *The Lifestyles of the Rich and Famous.*

"Come this way. We can go through the garage" Linda led Nina through the garage and up a set of stairs.

She opened the door to the living room.

Nina quickly scanned the place.

Linda took her shoes off at the door. Nina followed her.

Nina's feet sunk into the plushest, softest carpet she had ever felt. This was much better than the carpet she had in her apartment. The carpet was beige and Nina understood why she wouldn't want to get it dirty. She looked at the cinnamon brown suede couch and matching love seat. They were huge. She had never seen that color in the store.

They must be custom made.

She noticed the 60" inch plasma screen TV that was mounted on the wall, outlined in deep cherry wood. It made her think about her 42" in her own living room that she had saved up to buy. She didn't know plasma's came in colors besides black and silver.

I guess you can get whatever you want when you have money. Nina thought bitterly.

Nina looked around at the African art and paintings that were on the walls. She couldn't help

but notice the breathtaking family portrait that
rested on top of the marble fireplace. It was an oil
painting that looked like it was done a few years
ago because Linda was holding a baby girl and
another toddler was sitting on Jay's lap. The
painting was beautiful.
They looked perfect.

Nina couldn't help but wish that she had her own
perfect little family, and her own perfect house, and
her own perfect Bentley. Then she thought about
Trish.
That home-wrecking bitch!
"Make yourself comfortable while I go get the
papers" Linda said
"Thanks"
Nina inspected the place some more.
The kitchen was gorgeous.
It resembled a chef's kitchen and it was big enough
to sit a family of eight. There was a huge marble top
island that sat in the middle, beneath a circular
stainless steel rack that hung from the ceiling, it
held every kind of cooking utensil you could
imagine. On the black and white marble counter
tops rested all the latest appliances you could think
of from, a food processor to the magic bullet, all
stainless steel. The matching stainless steel double
door refrigerator and dishwasher looked spotless. In
fact the entire house looked spotless. Nina was
afraid to touch anything.

Linda walked back in the room with a small stack of papers.

"Can I get you anything to drink?"

"Yeah, some water please"

"Sure"

Linda walked over to the refrigerator and handed Nina a bottle of Fiji water.

"Thanks"

"Here are the papers I need you to sign"

"Okay" Nina took the papers and had a seat at one of the bar stools in front of the island.

Just then two of the cutest little girls Nina had ever seen came running through the door.

"Mommy, Mommy!" They both screamed

"Hi girls"

"You're home early" The oldest girl said

"I know I missed you guys" Linda smiled.

She bent down to give each of the girls a kiss on the cheek. They both looked like two brown skinned dolls. They each had long jet black hair that was neatly styled in two ponytails. They had long eye lashes and the older girl had deep dimples.

They were both dressed alike in jean skirts and navy blue Ralph Lauren sweaters with a brown teddy bear on the front. They had on blue thick tights and tan Ugg boots. Nina couldn't help but notice that each of the girls had on Burberry jackets. *Their clothes probably cost more than I make in a week.*

"Girls I want you to say hi to Ms. Nina"

"Hi Ms. Nina" both of the girls said and Nina

couldn't help but smile when the youngest girl was missing her two front teeth.

"Introduce yourselves" Linda said

"I am Nia" said the youngest sister

"And I am Naomi" Said the older sister.

"Those are such pretty names for pretty girls" Nina said

"Thank you" Both of the girls giggled.

"Are you guys hungry?" Linda asked the girls

"No daddy took us to Mc Donald's on the way home" Naomi said

"Oh he did, did he?" Linda asked

Jay knew how she felt about him giving the girls McDonalds.

She didn't like them eating too much junk food.

"Where is your dad, anyway?"

"He said he had to finish an important phone call and he would be right in" Nia said imitating her dad.

"Oh okay" Linda giggled

"Well then go upstairs and start your homework"

"Okay" both girls said and ran upstairs.

Nina couldn't help but be envious. They seemed perfect.

"Nina you can get started on signing those papers, I don't want to keep you all night"

"No it's fine I'm not in a rush"

Nina was in no rush to get back to her boring life. Linda's perfect life seemed so much better. Just then Jay walked through the side door that led to the garage.

He was wearing a white fitted T-shirt and a black vest. He had dark blue True Religion Jeans and Black Louis Vuitton loafers, he carried a black Louis Vuitton book bag in his hand. He looked cool and casual, Nina couldn't help but notice how sexy he was.

"Hey Lin"

"Hey Jay"

"This is Nina, a client of mine"

A client? Not a friend? Do you bring all your clients to your house?

"Nice to meet you Nina" Jay said barely looking up. He was too busy reading a piece of mail from the stack he grabbed out of the mailbox on his way in.

"You have a beautiful home and such beautiful daughters" Nina commented

"Thank you" Jay said this time looking up. When he looked up he stared at Nina for a moment.

Where do I know her from?

"Is there something wrong?" Linda asked

"No, you just look familiar" Jay said to Nina

"That's funny she said the same thing when she saw your picture. Nina said she saw you at one of her friend's party, what was the name?" Linda asked Nina

"Oh excuse me, I have to take this" Linda interrupted as her blackberry vibrated on her hip. Nina didn't expect to be put on the spot like that.

"I think I was mistaken" Nina said to Jay once Linda left the room

"Yeah maybe you were" Jay said and walked out

the room

...

Trish stopped at Starbuck's on her way home. It was her fourth cup of coffee all day.
It had been keeping her up, she hadn't slept in two days. Not since she got the latest note.
She was on her way home from a long day of shopping at Bergdorf's and Bloomingdales and all she wanted to do was drink a glass of wine and read a good book. She had just picked up Lolita File's latest book and she couldn't wait to get started.

She handed the cab driver a twenty and got out the cab in front of her building.
She walked inside. She was so happy because she picked up a sexy La Perla lingerie set that she couldn't wait to show Jay. She walked in her building.
"Hi Tommy"
"Hi Ms. Grand"
"How are you?"
"I'm good and yourself?"
"I'm great" Trish responded with a smile.
She couldn't help but think about how far she had come. She was grateful for all the things she had. She still missed Mike sometimes but she also saw it as God's way of putting her in a better situation. It took her a long time to realize it, but she did now.
She checked her mailbox and pressed the elevator.

She got off the elevator, made a right and headed to her door. Trish froze when she saw a

white piece of paper folded up in front of her door.
She stared at it for a moment before she decided to
pick it up. She slowly bent down and picked it up.
She unfolded the note and read

**I'm not playing! This is not a game! If I have to
warn you again you will regret it!**

Trish folded the note and put in her back pocket.
She frantically pressed the elevator. She had to get
out of there. She didn't know where she was going,
but she had to get the hell out of there.
She got in the elevator and pressed G.

She got off the elevator and ran straight to her car.
When she reached her car she screamed and fell on
the floor. Her beautiful black, BMW 745 was a
wreck. All four tired were flat and the word
BITCH!
Was keyed across the driver's side of the car.
She walked around to the front of the car and in red
lipstick it said

"I'M NOT PLAYING!"

Who is doing this to me?
She immediately called Jay.
"Hello?"
"Hello?" Trish sobbed on the other end of the
phone.
"What's wrong baby? What happened?"

"Just get here please!"

"Where are you?"

"I'm at the garage in my building"

"Okay I'm on my way" Jay said

"Please hurry"

"I will"

...

"What the fuck is wrong with you? You stupid bitch!" A white greasy man with long stringy hair pulled into a ponytail yelled at Crystal.

"Fuck you" Crystal yelled back

She looked over at Keith whose forehead was bleeding. Then she looked in the backseat at crazy ass Christine who was knocked out.

Thank God. I hope she's dead.

Crystal looked down at her stomach and felt it. She was glad she was okay. She hit the tow truck pretty hard but nobody was badly hurt. She took out her blackberry and called 911. Keith reached over and placed his hand on Crystal's thigh.

"Get the fuck off me, all this shit is your fault!"

"No it's not! You wanna go and try to be that bitch on murder she wrote!" Keith spat back

"Fuck you Keith! I'm just glad I found out about you now. You sorry ass motherfucker"

"Fuck you, you stuck up bitch!"

"Fuck me? Fuck me? I'm the one that's been there for you all this time. While you're sorry ass didn't have a job. I was paying all the fucking the bills"

Crystal screamed
I can't believe him.
"There you go trying to throw that shit in my face"
"Look I'm done. Your shit will be at Christine's"
"What?"
"You heard me. I packed your shit and it will be at Christine's"
"I'm not going nowhere. I will be home tonight"
"We'll see about that"
"We will"
...

"Are you sure she hasn't found out about us?" Trish asked Jay
"I'm positive. She doesn't know anything"
"Well then who is doing this to me? You're the only person I am seeing"
"I don't know but it's not Linda, that's not even her style, besides she's always at work and she hasn't been acting strange"
"Well how is everything going with the divorce? Do you think she found out about that?"
"Everything is going good. I'm trying to get some more things finalized and I'm going to talk to her about it in a few weeks"
"Okay"
Trish said as they waited for the cops to arrive.
Jay convinced her to file a police report and tell the police about the letters she had been receiving.
But she was too embarrassed to tell them that she was sleeping with someone's husband.

...

Nina checked her voicemail for the eighth time today. She hadn't spoke to Paulette since she left her house that day. She wasn't mad at her though, she hoped that Paulette would see it her way. It was wrong for her to go around infecting innocent people.

It had been four days since Nina left Linda's house and Linda still hadn't called her.
Weren't they friends. Why hadn't she called?
Nina had left her two messages and she hadn't returned any of her calls. She was getting angrier by the minute. She thought they had a nice time when she was at her house. They ordered Chinese and talked for a while before Linda told her she had to put the girls to bed and finish up some work.
What went wrong?
Nina walked over to her purse and took out a small silver change purse. She opened it and took out her stash of weed. She walked over to the kitchen and opened the top drawer and took out a fresh box of Dutches. She grabbed a knife out of the dish rack and slid the Dutch down the center and emptied the contents into the trash can. She walked over to her favorite spot on the window sill and began to empty her stash into the Dutch. Four minutes later she was inhaling and relaxing.
She needed that.
It allowed her to think.

All she could think about was Linda and Trish, Trish and Linda.

She didn't know why but she couldn't think about anything else. She hadn't spoke to Trish since the day she dropped by.

Fuck her!

She couldn't stand Trish sometimes. She didn't know where their friendship went wrong, they started out as such good friends in college.

She's always trying to put me down!

She thinks she's so damn cute!

Fuck her!

And I bet she thought it was real funny setting me up on that date with that crippled motherfucker! We'll see who gets the last laugh!

And that goddamn Linda. She's just like Trish. Those stuck up bitches. They always want to look down on people, they think their better than everybody. Fuck Linda too!

Nina took another puff. She was feeling it.

I tried to be nice to her but I'm not being nice anymore.

...

"I miss you"

"I miss you too" Paulette said

"I'll see you later, at seven, don't be late"

"Okay. See you later"

Paulette hung up the phone and smiled. She knew she wasn't supposed to get involved with Chris but she couldn't help it. He looked so damn good and

he was so sweet. He called her six times before she
finally answered any of his calls. They had been
going out for two weeks now and they still hadn't
had sex again. Paulette thought that was going to be
the first thing he wanted but surprisingly it wasn't.
Chris told her that he knew she was drunk when
they met and he apologized for taking advantage of
her.
"You didn't take advantage of me. I knew what I
was doing" Paulette responded
Now she really felt like shit because she took
advantage of him. She wanted to ask him so bad
Did we use a condom?
But she didn't.
"Let's just start over getting to know each other"
Chris said
"That sounds nice"
And it was nice. Paulette wasn't used to having a
relationship with no sex, but Chris was a real
gentleman. He took her to the nicest restaurants and
pulled out her chair and constantly complimented
her and he was funny too. She couldn't stop smiling
whenever she was around Chris. She wanted to
have sex with him so bad but she was so afraid to
tell him about the HPV, she didn't know how he
would react. She didn't want to lose him. She
thought about keeping it to herself. She hadn't had
any more outbreaks and she contemplated having
sex with him just making sure they were protected.
She knew it was wrong but she wanted him so bad.
Is that selfish?

Chapter 12

Trish got up and searched her closet for something to wear. She wasn't in the mood to do anything. She hadn't left the house in days. Not since the incident with her car. The auto body shop had just left a message telling Trish that her car was ready and she could come pick it up before 5pm. She finally picked out an olive green Juicy sweat suit and laid it on her bed. She grabbed her towel and walked into the bathroom to take a long hot shower.

"I feel so much better" Trish said to herself as she stepped out the shower. She tried to forget about the events that happened in the last few days and she hoped they would stop.
Trish moisturized her skin with some Almond Spice Body Butter from the Body Shop and put on a brand new Victoria Secret black lace bra and panty set. She felt so much better when she had on something new. She pulled her hair into a loose ponytail and put on an olive green tank top and then put on her sweat suit. She reached in her drawer for a pair of socks and put on some new Nike's that matched perfectly. She quickly sprayed herself with some Burberry Brit and smiled at her reflection in the mirror.
She felt good.

Trish grabbed her Gucci purse and walked to the door. She looked for her keys and then she

remembered that auto body shop had them.
"Duh" she said to herself.

She was heading out the door when she looked
down and screamed. There was a white piece of
paper folded up in on the floor as if someone had
slipped underneath her door. Trish began to shake.
She was so scared. She was in her apartment all
alone.

Who is doing this to me?

She bent down and picked up the note. Before she
could read what it said small pieces of a picture
started to fall out of the note.

She sat on the floor and tried to put the pieces of the
picture together. There were 13 little pieces. She
carefully pieced the picture together and she
screamed when she saw it was a picture of herself.
But it wasn't a new picture, it was an older picture,
maybe 6 or 7 years ago. Trish stared at the picture.
She couldn't remember taking the picture.

She picked up the note and read it

You still haven't learned your lesson!

What are they talking about? What lesson? Trish
thought.

Should she stop seeing Jay? It hurt her to think
about it because she loved him so much.

This has to be his wife! The only person that came
to mind was Jay's wife that could have been doing
these crazy things to her. As much as she hated to,
her and Jay had to stop seeing each other for a
while.

She sat on the floor with her back to the wall and cried. She didn't know what to do. She hadn't told anybody besides Jay what had been going on. She needed to talk to someone. She dialed Crystal.

"Hello?"
"Crys"
"Trish what's up?" Crystal asked concerned
"I need to talk"
"Me too"
"Meet me at Houston's in an hour"
"Okay"
Trish got there twenty minutes early and sat at the bar.
"Can I get a Grand Marnier and Pineapple Juice" She told the bartender.
"Sure pretty lady"
Trish drank the drink in a matter of seconds and ordered another one. Four drinks later her sidekick vibrated on her hip. She looked down and saw Crystal's number.
"Hello?"
"Yeah where you at?" Crystal said sounding like a true ghetto girl. Trish smiled when she thought about her friend who was a true diva. She knew how to be ghetto when she had to and in the courtroom she was nothing but classy and professional.
"I'm at the bar"
"Oh I see you I'm coming over" Crystal said as she put away her blackberry and met Trish at the bar.

"Hey stranger" Trish said
"Hey boo I missed you" Crystal said as she gave Trish a kiss on the cheek
"I can't tell. You haven't called me" Trish joked
"I know. I've had so much shit going on you wouldn't believe"
"Me too"
"For real? What's up?"
"First of all Jay is leaving his wife and wants to get married"
"What?"
"Yeah. I love him" Trish smiled
"Well I'm happy for you but how is his wife taking it?"
"That's another story. I have been getting all these crazy ass letters at my apartment telling me to find my own husband and if I don't I'm gonna be sorry"
"What? Are you serious?"
"Hell yeah. It scared the shit out of me" Trish said as she shook her head
"So his wife is doing this?"
"I asked him about it and he said no, it's not her style. But who else could it be?"
"I don't know. It's probably is her, people are crazy when their in love"
"But that's the thing. They're not in love anymore"
"How you know?"
"Because he tells me"
Crystal busted out laughing
"He could be lying" Crystal said
"I believe him" Trish said with an attitude

"Well that's all that matters"

"That's not the worst part"

"There's more?" Crystal asked surprised

"Yes. My car was fucked up. I just picked it up today. My tires were flat and it was all keyed up"

"What?"

"I know I can't believe it. This shit seems crazy"

"Well you need to leave his ass alone"

"I thought about that, but I love him"

"Well maybe you need to wait until the divorce is final"

"I know I thought about that too"

"You should come stay with me until this shit cools down" Crystal said

"Thank you, but I don't want to stay with you and your man, you know I'm not crazy about his ass"

"I put him out"

"What?" Trish screamed

"Yes I did. It was so much drama going on that's why I haven't called you"

"Tell me everything"

"Remember when you called me and gave me Christine's number after your party?"

"Yeah"

"Well it turns out she has been fucking with Keith for almost a year"

"You're lying"

"No I'm not and she's pregnant"

"What?' Trish screamed

"Yes were both pregnant" Crystal whispered

"So what are you gonna do about that?"

"I think I'm gonna keep it"

"Are you sure?"

"No I'm not sure"

"Why because of Keith? I'll help you"

"No because I'm not sure who the father is"

"What? You were fucking somebody else?"

Crystal looked down at her feet and didn't answer.
Trish had seen that look before and she knew what
that meant.

Please tell me you your not still fucking Harold's
nasty ass.

A tear slid down Crystal's cheek.

"It's not what you think"

"Then what is it?"

"I told you I don't want to hurt my mother"

"Yeah but that was ten years ago. How long are you
gonna let this go on"

"I know Trish. I feel like I can't take it anymore. I
hate him. I want him dead"

"Be quiet" Trish reminded Crystal that they were at
a crowded bar with a lot of ears around. They never
knew who was listening to their conversation.

Crystal looked around.

"Sorry"

"Why don't you just tell your mother?"

"What am I supposed to say? Mom I've been
fucking your husband for the past ten years, she will
hate me"

"No you tell her the truth that he's been raping you
for the past ten years"

Crystal cried harder when Trish said it out loud. She

felt like such an idiot for letting it go on for so long.
"She won't believe me"
"You have to try"
"You don't know my mother she won't believe me
trust me"
"Okay" Trish let it go.
She wished her friend would come to her senses but
she had her own problems to deal with.
"So you staying at my place tonight?" Crystal asked
"Yeah"

...

"Hi I'm here to see Mrs. Darwin" Nina said
"I think she's in a meeting, do you have an
appointment?" The perky blonde receptionist asked
"No I don't have an appointment. I just had a few
things to ask her about my case" Nina lied
"Well Mrs. Darwin is a very busy woman, would
you like to make an appointment for another day or
leave your number and she can call you back?"
How dare she act like I'm not busy too. Fuck her.
"No I'll wait until she gets out of the meeting"
"Okay you can have a seat it may be about 30
minutes. Are you sure you want to wait?"
"Yes I'm sure" Nina said with an attitude
Nina took a seat in the burgundy leather chair and
picked up the latest issue of Essence magazine that
sat on the Mahogany coffee table.
Beyonce was on the cover.
She looked beautiful.
Stuck up prissy bitches. They were everywhere.

Nina skimmed through the Essence, not really looking at any article in particular. She tapped her Marc Jacob pump on the floor. She had went out and bought the same exact pumps that Linda had on the last time she saw her. They were sold out in Bloomingdale's so she had to order them online, they just came yesterday. Nina looked down at her foot and smiled.Exactly thirty minutes later. Linda's office door opened.

"Thank you so much Mrs. Darwin, it was a pleasure" An older petite Hispanic woman said.

"It was my pleasure Mrs. Lopez. I will keep in touch"

"Okay" Mrs. Lopez said as she smiled.

Linda looked at Nina surprised.

"Hi Nina is something wrong?"

"Hey Linda. I was just in the neighborhood and I wanted to stop by and say hello" Nina said as she put the magazine down and walked into Linda's office.

"Oh that was nice of you. How are you?" Linda asked as she walked back around to her desk.

"I'm okay. I called you a few times"

Why haven't you called me back?

"I have been so busy I'm sorry I didn't get back to you. Was there something in particular that you wanted to talk about?"

"No I just thought maybe we could hang out"

"Oh" Linda said and gave her a strange look.

Why the fuck is she looking at me like that? I'm not

good enough to hang out with her? Nina thought.

"Well are you busy now? Maybe we could go get a drink"
"Actually I am. I'm on my way out right now, maybe another time. I'll call you" Linda said as she picked up her Louis Vuitton purse and walked by her office door and stood by it.
"Yeah maybe another time" Nina said as she walked out the door.
Bitch! I can't fucking believe her. She practically threw me out of her fucking office and she didn't even look at my shoes!!
…

"Trish, make sure you lock the door I'm leaving" Crystal called out to Trish. She was on her way to work.
"Mmm hmm" Trish said with a pillow over her head.
Trish looked over at the digital clock on the night stand.
7:35 am. "Please. I'm not getting out this bed for at least 2 more hours" Trish said to herself and put the pillow back over her head.
Crystal closed her front door to her apartment and felt her Blackberry vibrating on her hip. She placed her brand new red and black patent leather Gucci briefcase on the floor in front of her apartment and read the latest email.
"Work" she said to herself as she placed her

Blackberry back on her hip. She bent down and picked up her briefcase. When she turned around she was surprised when out of nowhere she felt a fist come right to her jaw. Crystal fell flat on the cold hallway floor. She felt a swift kick on her left side and another one on her right.

What the fuck is going on?

She was curled up in a fetal position trying to protect herself.

"Get up bitch!"

Crystal looked up and saw a young dark skinned girl in a black sweat suit and black Nike's. She had her hair in a pulled into a short ponytail and she looked no older than nineteen.

"Look at her she's crying" Another girl laughed

The other girl looked about the same age. She was Puerto Rican with a long curly hair. She also had her hair pulled into a ponytail. Crystal could see a tattoo on the right side of her neck that read "Jealous One's Envy" in script.   She sported the same outfit as the other girl.

"Fuck you" Crystal yelled back.

"Fuck me?" The dark skinned girl yelled back and kicked twice Crystal in her stomach.

"Ahhhh" Crystal screamed from the pain as tears rolled down her face.

"Stupid Bitch! You should just shut the fuck up" The Puerto Rican girl said to Crystal.

"Chrissy was right this bitch is stuck up! Look at her shoes and that bag"
"Shut the fuck up" The Puerto Rican one said.
"Oh my bad" The dark skinned girl said realizing she had said too much.
"Lets get the fuck outta here. She ain't getting up" The Puerto Rican girl said
"Wait get her bag. I'm a get her shoes"
"Aight"
The Puerto Rican girl bent down and grabbed Crystal's brand new Gucci purse, she left the briefcase. The black girl bent down and tried to take Crystal shoes off and she kicked and screamed.
"You still trying to fight bitch!" The black girl laughed and held Crystal legs down and pulled her shoes off. Both of the girls ran down the steps while crystal laid there with blood soaking through her black silk shirt.
...

"Are you sure your ready for this I'm not trying to rush you"
"Yes I'm sure. Now stop talking and kiss me" Paulette said
She had made up her mind that she was going to have sex with Chris. She wanted to. She needed too. He looked so damn good and she was so drunk the last time they had sex she couldn't remember how it was. She had decided that she wasn't going to tell him. She just couldn't.

She couldn't risk losing him.

We're going to use a condom, and everything is going to be okay. Paulette told herself.

"I have been waiting for this for a while" Chris said as he softly kissed Paulette on her neck

"Me too"

"I just want it to be right. Don't rush it. I really care about you Paulette" Chris said as he looked in her eyes and stroked the side of her face.

Damn. He here goes, being sweet. Making me feel guilty.

"I care about you too and it is going to be right. Now shhh" Paulette said as she placed her finger on Chris's lips and unbuttoned his shirt and started kissing his chest.

Paulette admired Chris's chest. It was cut and smooth, he was so fine.

She kissed all over his chest and down his stomach. She stopped at his belt and unbuckled it. Chris's pants fell down to his ankles. Paulette grabbed at his boxers, she was feigning.

"Slow down baby, let me please you" Chris said as he grabbed Paulette's hands and pushed her back on the bed.

He slowly pulled her Lucky T-Shirt over her head and then unbuttoned her Citizens of Humanity Jeans.

He tugged at her jeans and they didn't budge.

"Damn are these painted on?" Chris joked

"Shut up" Paulette said as she wiggled out of the tight jeans

Next she took off her boy shorts and she laid naked on the bed.

"C'mon baby. I can't wait no more" Paulette begged as she pulled Chris close to her.

"Yes you can" Chris said as he bent down and spread Crystal's legs open.

"What are you doing?" Paulette asked nervously. She wanted to have sex with him but she wasn't sure she wanted him to eat her pussy, she didn't want to risk anything.

"What does it look like I'm doing baby?" Chris began to lick in all the right places and Paulette couldn't say anything she was in heaven. All her guilty thoughts went out her head, it felt so good.

An hour later they laid sweaty in each other's arms.

"Damn baby that was real good" Chris joked

"Yeah it was" Paulette said as she drifted off to sleep.

But now all the guilty thoughts came back.

...

"Who the fuck is knocking at the door at 8:00 o'clock in the damn morning?" Trish said to herself. She attempted to put the pillow back over her head but whoever it was had been knocking for a while so she figured she would answer it. She got out the bed and stomped all the way to the door.

"This better be fucking important!"

Trish pulled the door open and screamed when she

saw Crystal bloody body laying in the hallway .

"Oh my God!! Oh my God! Crys what happened?"
Trish got down on her knees to get a better look at
her.
Crystal didn't respond she just cried from the pain.
"Who did this to you?"
Crystal still didn't respond
"Its gonna be okay, let me call somebody, its gonna
be okay"
Trish was panicking as she ran in the apartment.
"Where the fuck is the phone?"
She couldn't find it anywhere.
She frantically pressed the page button.
"Please lord let her be okay, please"
Trish found the phone on the couch and dialed
9-1-1.
"Hello?"
"Please come, my friend she's hurt, she's hurt bad,
please hurry"
"What happened ma'am?"
"I don't know! Just fucking hurry"
"Okay ma'am, were on our way"
Trish hung up the phone and ran back over to
Crystal.
"They're on their way. Hang in there Crys it's
gonna be okay"
"We're gonna get whoever did this to you. I
promise"
Trish held Crystal like a baby in her arms.
She broke down and cried when she looked at her.

"Please God let her be okay. Please"
Trish said as she rocked Crystal back and forth.
...

Trish paced back and forth in the emergency room
while she waited for the doctors to tell her how
Crystal was doing. It brought back so many
memories. And she remembered how Crystal was
there with her. She cried when she thought about it.

She called Crystal's mom, Nina and Paulette and
told them what happened. Nina didn't answer the
phone so she left a message on her voicemail.
She must still be bugging. Trish thought
She was waiting for them to come. Marie, Crystal's
mother came running through the door.

"Where's is she? Is she okay?"
"I'm still waiting for the doctors to come out, they
haven't told me anything yet"
"Well what happened to her?"
"I don't know"
"Were you with her?" Marie asked
"No, not really, yeah, I was sleep" Trish said
confused
She felt so guilty that she had been sleep. She didn't
hear what went on.
"Do you know anything?" Marie asked meanly
*Do you know your husband has been molesting your
daughter for years?*

Trish wanted to say but she didn't.

She ignored the comment, she was not in the mood for any of Marie's shit.

Just then Paulette walked in the emergency room doors followed by Harold.

I can't stand his ass.

Paulette walked over to Trish and they hugged and kissed on the cheek.

"Hi Marie"

"Hello Paulette"

"How is she? Can we see her?" Paulette asked.

"I just got here and apparently Trish doesn't know anything"

This bitch got one more time. Trish thought

"The doctors haven't said anything yet, we're just waiting"

Harold walked over to Marie and hugged her.

"Everything is gonna be okay, our little girl is gonna be fine" Harold said to Marie

Trish looked at him in disgust. He reminded her of all the nasty ass men that her mother used to have running in and out of their apartment, all the men that used to touch her.

"Is Nina here?"

"No I left her a message, she didn't call me back"

"Me too"

"She's really been bugging lately" Trish said

"Really? I haven't spoke to her"

"Well she hasn't been acting like herself, I think she's depressed"

253

"Excuse me Ms. Grand I have some good news and bad news. Your friend is stable and-" The nurse said to Trish

"Hello, I'm her mother" Marie cut her off

"Oh, hello. I'm Michelle. The good news is Ms. Dawson is stabilized now, but the bad news is she lost a lot of blood and she lost the baby, but she is going to be okay"

"Baby?" Marie asked shocked

"Yes she was 12 weeks pregnant"

"Are you sure?"

"Yes ma'am. The doctor is going to come out and speak with you and then you can go and see Ms. Dawson in a few minutes"

"Okay" Marie said

Trish and Paulette smiled, they were so relieved that Crystal was going to be okay.

"I can't believe she wouldn't tell me she was pregnant, especially if she was three months pregnant and who was she pregnant by, that low-life Keith? I'm glad she lost it" Marie said with very much attitude

Paulette was shocked at Marie's response. Trish wasn't surprised. *Marie was such a bitch.*

"It may not have been Keith" Trish said as she stared at Harold

Harold looked as if he had seen a ghost.

"Well then who?" Marie asked confused

"I don't know, do you know Harold?" Trish asked

"Why the hell would I know?" Harold asked. He was scared at this point.

"I don't know. I thought maybe she would have told you" Trish said nonchalantly

"Don't be stupid why the hell would she tell me?"

"Yeah what the hell are you talking about Trish? Why would my husband know, and I don't?" Marie asked

"I don't know maybe you should ask your husband!" Trish said matching Marie's attitude Paulette stood there confused she had no idea what was going on.

"What is she talking about Harold?"

"I don't know she's crazy"

"No I'm not crazy why don't you tell your wife the truth"

"Why don't you shut the fuck up!" Harold screamed

"No! tell Marie what's been going on"

"I don't know what you're talking about"

"I think you do"

"Fuck you"

"Its seems like that's what you do best"

"What the hell is she talking about Harold?" Marie screamed

"I don't know" Harold said as he looked at the ground.

"Tell Marie who Crystal was really pregnant by"

"What are you talking about?"

"You heard me! Tell Marie how you have been raping Crystal since she was fifteen years old. You fucking bastard!"

"What?" Marie screamed

"You're a fucking liar, you don't know what the

hell you're talking about" Harold screamed at Trish
"She's lying baby" Harold said to Marie
"Yeah your lying Trish, there is no way that Harold
has been raping Crystal, that's just crazy. He's like
a father to her!" Marie screamed
"I'm not lying. Ask your husband, ask him who
Crystal was pregnant by"
"Just shut up Trish, she was pregnant by Keith her
boyfriend" Marie said
"Just ask him" Trish said as she walked away when
she saw the doctor approaching them.
"Excuse me everyone you can go in and see Crystal
now, she's very tired so don't make too much noise.
We usually only allow two, but you all can go in"
The doctor said
"Thanks" Paulette and Trish replied at the same
time.

They all walked down the hall to Crystal's room in
silence. When they entered the room Crystal looked
like sleeping beauty. She laid there with her hands
folded on top of her stomach. Trish walked over to
the bed and kissed Crystal on the cheek.
Paulette held her hand. Marie walked over to the
other side of the bed and just looked at Crystal.
She didn't have any emotion. She still looked a little
shook up from the conversation they had in the
hallway.

Harold just stood in the doorway silently.

Trish stroked Crystal's hair
"I'm so glad your okay, you scared me"
Crystal opened her eyes and
"Thanks" she whispered
"Hey girl, we didn't mean to wake you up" Paulette
said as she smiled
"Its okay, I feel like I been sleeping forever"
She turned to the other side of the bed
"Hi ma"
"Hey Crystal" Marie said as if she was preoccupied
with something else.
Crystal looked around and saw Harold standing at
the door and she rolled her eyes the best she could,
it took so much energy.
"Where's Nina?"
"She's not here. We couldn't get in touch with her,
we tried" Trish answered
"I hope she's alright" Crystal said
"Look at you always worried about other people.
You're the one in the hospital. Let us worry about
you for a change" Paulette said
Crystal tried to laugh but it hurt so bad.
"Okay"
"Can you try to remember what happened?" Trish
asked
"I've been trying hard and I don't remember much"
"Well don't try too hard, you'll remember. Just try
and relax for now" Paulette said
"Okay"
They sat in silence for a few minutes

"Have you been sleeping with my husband?" Marie broke the silence.

Harold, Trish, and Paulette stared in amazement.

"What?" Crystal asked confused

"You heard me! Have you been sleeping with my damn husband?"

"What are you talking about mommy?"

Crystal didn't know where all this was coming from all of sudden.

"Just answer the goddamn question!" Marie screamed

"Leave her alone Marie, let her sleep" Harold jumped in

"Be quiet Harold" Marie snapped

Crystal began to cry.

"Were you pregnant by Harold?"

Crystal cried even harder.

"Were you pregnant by Harold?"

Crystal shrugged her shoulders as if to say "I don't know"

"What do you mean you don't know?" Marie screamed

"Leave her alone Marie" Trish said

"Shut the fuck up bitch! You started this shit!" Marie snapped back

"Mom I wanted to tell you but-"

Smack!

Marie smacked Crystal so hard she thought she chipped a tooth.

Marie jumped on the hospital bed on top of Crystal

and started choking her.

"You little bitch! How could you do this to me? You fucking bitch!" She choked her.

Trish and Paulette jumped on Marie's back and tried to pull her off Crystal.

"Get the fuck off me!" Marie screamed as she turned around and punched Trish in her face. Trish immediately grabbed her jaw and felt her lip that was bleeding.

Paulette and Trish were amazed at Marie's strength. "What the fuck is wrong with you? You crazy bitch!" Trish screamed as she pulled Marie by her hair.

"You little ho! I see the way you always looked at my husband ever since you were a little girl, always wearing those tight clothes and short skirts. Fast ass little bitch! I should have fucked you up then!" Marie shouted back.

Marie turned back around to Crystal and started hitting her and choking her again. She was trying to kill Crystal. She looked like she was on steroids. Paulette and Trish were struggling to get her off of Crystal and they couldn't.

Harold finally walked over to help them.

Crystal was choking and gasping for air.

Marie had a strong grip around Crystal's neck.

"Marie stop it! You're going to kill her" He screamed

"She's better off dead! The nasty bitch!" Marie screamed

"Help! Help! Please help!" Paulette yelled out for

one of the nurses to help.

Harold began pulling and he finally pulled Marie off Crystal and she fell to the floor and sobbed like a baby.

Two male guards ran in the room and asked "What's going on?" One of the guards asked

"She's over their on the floor. She was trying to kill her" Paulette pointed to Marie on the floor

"Both of the guards walked over to Marie and picked her up off the floor.

"Get off of me"

"We're going to have to escort you out of here ma'am"

"You should have died last night, because you're not my daughter anymore"

Marie yelled to Crystal

Tears rolled down Crystal's cheeks. She felt like shit.

"Would you like to press charges?" The other guard asked Crystal

Crystal just shook her head no.

"You should, she tried to kill you" Trish said

"No!" Crystal said as she shot Trish a look that said shut the fuck up.

"Well fuck that! I am! the bitch punched me in the face" Trish said with very much attitude.

"Follow us ma'am, so we can get a statement" The guard said to Trish

...

Chapter 13

"I'm not available leave a message after the beep"
"Hey Nina! Where are you? Pick up the phone if
you're there. I've been trying to call you for days
now. I'm out the hospital. I got home a few days
ago. Let me know that you're okay" Crystal said
Nina listened to the message from her favorite spot
on the window sill. Weed had become her best
friend these days. She felt bad.
She got Trish's and Paulette's messages about
Crystal being in the hospital but she really
didn't feel like seeing Trish, she didn't feel like
doing shit.

She figured that if Crystal would have gotten worse
Paulette or Trish would have called her again and
they didn't so she must have been okay. Lately all
she did was smoke and think. She was called into
the Principal's office a few days ago and they
requested that she take some time off. Now she was
on a two week leave of absence. Linda hadn't called
her since she left her office last week and she
couldn't understand why.

Why didn't she like me?
Who the fuck does she think she is?
I bet her husband would like me.

Nina smiled.
Shit! She looked down at her stash and realized she

was almost out. She had been spending so much money lately and her high was getting weaker and weaker, she needed something stronger.

She walked over to her dining room table and shuffled through some papers until she found a small piece of paper with a name and number scribbled on it.

She got the number from the guy she bought weed from. He told her if she ever needed something stronger she should get in touch with Jason, he just moved to the city, but he had that good shit for a real good price.

Nina wasn't sure if she wanted to go that route but she scribbled the number down anyway.

Right now she needed to speak to Jason. She needed something to take her away from her life if only for a little while.

She walked over to the phone and dialed the number.

"Yo"

"Can I speak to Jason?"

"Who is this?"

"Its Nina, Mark gave me your number"

"What's up? What you need?"

"I need something stronger than weed"

"What you want?"

Nina wasn't sure what to ask for because she had never done any other type of drugs before.

"I'm not sure"

"Okay I got something for you. Where you at?"

"95th and Broadway"

"Aight. Give me a few minutes. I'll hit you back when I'm on my way"
"Okay"
Nina said and hung up the phone.
She smiled and smoked the rest of her blunt. She hoped whatever he had did the trick.
...

"Knock Knock"
"Who is it?"
"Open the fucking door!" Crystal yelled
"Who is it?" Trish yelled on the other side of the door
"It's me!"
Trish looked through the peephole and saw Crystal standing on the other side of the door.
Trish swung the door open.
"What the fuck is wrong with you? Why are you at my house yelling like you lost your goddamn mind?"
"I should fuck you up!" Crystal screamed
"Excuse me? What the fuck are you talkin' about?"
"You heard me! You put my fucking mother in jail! How could you do that?"
"Your fucking mother punched me in my face. Did you forget that?" Trish yelled back
"Yeah, but that's still my mother Trish!"
"That's your fucking problem! You're always worried about your mother and she don't give a shit about you!"
"Fuck you! She cares more about me than your

fucking mother!"

"She might! But I'd put my mother's ass in jail if she punched me in my face too!"

"That's your fucking business! You're a bitch!"

"Don't come in my house calling me a bitch! You're just mad 'cause you let everybody walk all over your ass!"

"Fuck you Trish! And please don't tell me that my mother found out about Harold and me because of you!"

"Well he came to the hospital looking all arrogant, talking about our little girl is gonna be okay and shit and I couldn't stand it. I wanted to punch him in his fucking face"

"Well you should have kept your fucking mouth shut! It wasn't your place"

"You're right! You should have said something! I shouldn't have to speak up for you!" Trish screamed

"You didn't have to speak up for me. I would have eventually told her myself in my own way. Mind your damn business"

"When? When you got pregnant a few more times?"

Tears welled up in Crystal's eyes and Trish knew she went too far.

Crystal punched Trish right in the mouth.

"Get the fuck outta my house!" Trish screamed holding her mouth

"Fine! You don't ever have to worry about me speaking to your ass again! Bitch!"

"Whatever! Fuck you!" Trish yelled as she

slammed the door behind Crystal.

...

Crystal was furious when she left Trish's apartment. She couldn't believe what her life had become in a few months. She felt like a child all over again. She had called her mother about hundred times since she left the hospital and she hadn't returned any of her calls. Harold told her that Trish had gotten her locked up and she had to spend a night in jail.

She tried to call her mom again today and the number had been changed. She was so hurt. How could her mom do this to her? *How could she choose him over me?*
She wasn't surprised but she was hurt. She thought that after all these years her mother would have gotten a little stronger and maybe she would leave Harold. She was wrong.
Keith had stopped calling her. He never showed up at her apartment like he said he would. He must be happy with Christine.
Even though she didn't want him anymore it hurt her that he could just move on and forget about her that fast. He could start a new family, like she was a piece of shit.

Crystal got madder when she thought about that bitch, Christine. She still couldn't completely remember what happened that day but she did remember one of the girls saying "Chrissy said she was a stuck up bitch" when they were beating her up.

Chrissy had to be Christine. She didn't know what
she was gonna do yet but she was gonna get
Christine, she was gonna make her pay for what she
did. She looked down and felt her stomach and
cried. She had such mixed feelings about losing the
baby. Part of her was relieved because if it was
Harold baby she didn't know how she would look at
it every day. But it was still her baby and she would
love it regardless.It wasn't Christine's choice or
anyone else's, it was her choice and Christine
robbed her of making that choice and Crystal was
gonna make that bitch pay.

...

"Hey baby"
"Hey" Paulette said as she walked through the door
on her way in from work.
"I missed you, give me some suga" Chris pulled
Paulette close to him
"I missed you too"
Paulette said as she put her arms around Chris's
neck and kissed him.
"Mmm. I'm a lucky man"
"No I'm the lucky one" Paulette said
And she truly meant it. She loved Chris from the
bottom of her heart. He made her so happy.
She loved hanging out with him. It was like he was
one of her girls except she could have sex with him
too, he was perfect.
Over four short months he had become her best

friend. He was so open and honest with her. He told
her everything. They had no secrets, all except one.
As many times as she tried to tell him she just
couldn't. She couldn't risk losing him, especially
not now, she loved him too much. She never
imagined a one night stand would become the love
of her life. She had so many in the past that were
just one night stands and nothing more.

"Remember we're having dinner at my parent's
house tonight" Chris said
"I know. I'm gonna take a quick shower and change
my clothes"
"Oooh. Can I join you?"
"Let me think about it" Paulette joked
"What did you say?" Chris asked as he started
chasing her
"I said let me think about it" Paulette said as he ran
in the bedroom, she was laughing so hard she fell
on the floor. Chris jumped on top of her and started
tickling her.
"Stop! Stop I gotta pee!" Paulette screamed
"Too Bad!" Chris said as he tickled her some more
Paulette was laughing so hard tears were coming
down her cheeks.
"Now can I join you?"
"I don't know" Paulette managed to say through
laughs
"Oh you still want to be tough? Huh?" Chris said as
he ticked her under her arms
"Okay! Okay!"

"Okay what?"

"You can get in with me!"

"I thought so punk!" Chris said as he kissed her on the forehead

"You big bully" Paulette said as she pushed him off of her

"You love this big bully" Chris said as he punched his chest like King Kong.

"Unfortunately I do"

Paulette said as she shook her head and walked into the bathroom. She smiled when she thought about him. He was so damn silly. They spent so much time together she couldn't imagine her life without him.

...

"Brring Brring"

"Hello?"

"Yo. I'm downstairs. You coming down? Or you want me to come up?"

"You can come up"

Nina said as she gave him her building and apartment number.

Nina ran in the bathroom and threw some water on her face and rinsed her mouth out with some mouthwash. She brushed her hair into a decent ponytail. She was moving as fast as she could even though she felt like she was doing everything in slow motion, she was still high. She had on a t-shirt and a pair of shorts, that made her already big butt look even bigger. She put on some slippers and sat back on the window sill. A few seconds later she heard a knock at the door. She walked over to the door and opened it.

"Hi"

"What's up?"

"You can come in" Nina said as she walked to the couch and sat down. She knew he was looking at her ass, most guys did.

"I don't know what you really wanted but I got something here that you might like. I'll let you sample it first"

"Okay" Nina said.

She looked him up and down. He looked good. He looked kind of young but he still looked good. He was a nice caramel brown complexion and he had neat corn rolls that reached his shoulders. He had on some dark blue jeans that were baggy, but not too baggy with a green leather jacket and green, tan and white Air Force one's to match. She licked her lips and looked at him. She was horny. He sat down on the couch next to her and pulled a small bag out of his pocket. He poured some of the white contents out on the table. He took a business card out of his pocket and made a little white line.

"Here hit that"

He said to Nina.

She looked at him for a second. She wasn't sure if she wanted to.

"Go ahead"

She bent down to the table and sniffed the line. Immediately her heart began racing. She felt good. It was different from smoking weed. She liked it; it

was exactly what she needed.
"How you like that?"
Nina looked at him and smiled.
"Its good"
"I thought you would like it"
Nina licked her lips again.

He could tell what was up. He poured some
more of the contents on to the table. He made two
lines this time. He bent down and sniffed one and
then he told Nina to do the other line. After she
sniffed the other line she felt real good. He leaned
over and kissed her. She started kissing him back.
She straddled him and began kissing him harder and
feeling all over his chest. She helped him take off
his jacket and threw it on the floor. They were both
breathing heavy and she started to unzip his pants
and reached inside his boxers and found what she
was looking for. He started reaching for her shorts
and she stood up and let him pull them down. She
stepped out of them and sat back on his lap. He
reached in his pocket and pulled out a condom. He
ripped it open with his teeth and threw the wrapper
on the floor. Nina took it out of his hand and put it
on him and then she sat on top of him. She started
riding him wild and crazy. Ten minutes later she got
off him and laid on the couch.
"Damn baby that was crazy"
"Yeah. I know"
"What's your name again?" He asked
"Nina. What's yours?"
"Jason"

"Oh yeah"

"Where's your bathroom?"

Nina pointed down the hall

A few minutes later Jason came out the bathroom. He stopped and stared at a picture on her entertainment center.

"These are your friends?"

"Yeah" Nina said about a picture of Her, Trish, Crystal, and Paulette they had taken a few years back in Atlanta at All-star weekend.

Jason stared at the picture for a few seconds.

"What's wrong?" Nina asked

"Nothing, she looks familiar. What's her name?" He asked as he pointed to the picture

"Who Trish?"

I fucking knew it! I just finished fucking him! And he's asking me about Trish! That bitch!

"Yeah Trish" He said as he nodded his head

"You know her?"

"Umm. No I thought I did" He said as if he was thinking about something

"Oh" Nina said

"I gotta get outta here I got some more running around to do. Hit me if you need anything" He said as he left a small bag on her table and grabbed his coat and walked out the door. He didn't ask her for any money. I guess he thought they were even.

Nina thought he was gonna stay longer, she was ready for round two. But after he saw that picture he was ready to go.

What the fuck was that about? She thought.

271

Chapter 14

Trish had been so miserable the last couple of days.
Her and Jay could only talk on the phone. She
hadn't seen him and she missed him like crazy.
They decided it was for the best until the divorce
was final.
She figured that it must be working because she
hadn't gotten any letters in a while.
She wanted to call Crystal and tell her she was sorry
but she had too much pride for that.
Fuck her!
Trish still didn't really feel like she was wrong for
what she did but she knew she hurt Crystal and that
was what she was sorry for.
Her I-phone vibrated, snapping her out of her daze.
She looked down and it said one new text.
She opened the text and it was from Nina.
"Hey what's up?"
*What the fuck does she want? Now she decides she
wants to speak to me?*
"Nothin'. What's up with u? Trish texted back
"I'm off today. What r u doin'?"
"Nothin' I'm in the house now. I want to go buy
some shoes for this party on Saturday"
"I'm a call u" Nina texted
"K"
One minute later Trish's phone rang.
"What's up stranger?"
"Nothin'"
"Where you been at? You know Crys was in the

hospital?"

"Yeah. I got you and Paulette's messages. But I didn't feel good" Nina lied

"Mmm" Trish said like she didn't believe her

"How is she?" Nina asked trying to sound concerned

"She's good now"

"So what time you tryin' to go get some shoes?"

"I gotta hop in the shower and get dressed. Gimme an hour"

"Okay. I'll call you when I'm down stairs"

"Okay"

Trish hung up the phone. She didn't know what was up with Nina. One minute she was buggin' and the next she was fine.

I hope she's don't start acting like she was last time.

Trish said to herself as she thought about the last time she went by Nina's house.

I might have to slap the shit outta her today.

Trish laughed to herself.

She wasn't in the mood for no bullshit, but she could use some company today. She was bored as hell. So Nina would have to do.

...

Nina hung up the phone and smiled.

Damn that was easier than I thought.

She's such a dumb bitch!

...

"Brring Brring Brring"
Crystal looked at the phone ringing.
She didn't recognize the number so she didn't answer.
"Brring –Bring Bring" The phone rang again.
She looked at the caller id again, it was the same number.
Who the fuck is this?
She decided to answer.
"Hello?" Crystal answered annoyed
"Hey baby?"
"Hello?"
"Its been that long you don't know me anymore?"
"Keith?"
"Yeah. Keith "
"What the fuck do you want?"
"Why are you being so mean?"
"Are you really serious calling me after all the shit that happened?"
"Lets put all that behind us. We have history baby. You can't just forget me and I can't just forget you"
This motherfucker got a lot of nerve.
Crystal was quiet for a while. She wanted to just hang up the phone. But then she thought about Christine. She didn't know who she hated more. Her or Keith. This might be her only chance to get that bitch back. So she decided to play along with Keith.
"You're right baby I missed you so much. I was waiting for you to call" Crystal lied
"See that's what I'm talking about baby. Stop

fightin' your feelings. You know you love me"
"I do"
"So when can I see you?"
"Are you sure you can get out the house?" Crystal
asked. Trying to make sure that he was still living
with Christine.
"I got this under control don't worry about me
baby" Keith said arrogantly
Crystal was getting madder by the minute. He was
such a nasty bastard. That's probably the same shit
he said to Christine when he was staying with her.
Lying bastard.
"I got some things to take care of but I'll call you
and let you know when we can get together"
"Aight. Don't take too long"
"I won't" Crystal smiled and hung up the phone.
...

Nina looked at her cell phone while she stood
downstairs waiting for Trish. It had already been 6
minutes.
What the fuck is she doing?
Nina was very impatient and she did not feel like
waiting on Trish.
Five minutes later Trish came strolling out the door.
"Hey sorry I took so long. The phone rang when I
was on my way out"
"Its cool" Nina lied
Nina looked Trish up and down quickly. As usual
she looked great. She had on a pair of black skinny
jeans that fit her perfectly with a snug graphic tee

and a large red Balencia Bag with matching red
pumps. Her huge black Christian Dior shades
covered half her face and her hair was pulled back
into a loose ponytail. Nina looked down at her worn
blue seven jeans and her flat black nine west slides
and immediately felt insecure.
"I thought we were just going shoe shopping not
going to a party?" Nina said with an attitude
"What are you talking about?" Trish asked confused
"I just threw something on and look at you! If I
would have known you were gonna get all dressed I
would have too"
"You look fine. I figured we could stop and get
lunch or something, you never know who you might
see" Trish joked
"Mmm" Nina mumbled
Nina was already getting on Trish's last nerve.
I'm not in the mood for her bullshit today.
It's not my fault she looks like she just rolled out the
bed.
"So where do you want to go?"
"I was thinking Macy's on 34th. I'm not sure what I
want to get"
"Macy's is always so packed" Nina said twisting
her face up.
"I know but I'm not in a rush" Trish said ignoring
her.
"So are you still seeing your friend?"
"Who Jay?"
"Yeah"
"Yes we're still together. But we decided to stop

seeing each other until the divorce is final"
"Divorce?" Nina screamed. Her eyes almost
popping out of her head.
What the hell is wrong with her? Trish thought
"Yes divorce. We are really happy" Trish was
glowing.
"So he is divorcing his wife because of you?" Nina
asked like Trish was a piece of gum on the bottom
of her shoe.
"Well him and his wife have not been happy for a
long time. And yeah I think it has a little to do with
me. I make him happy" Trish smiled like a little girl
"I wonder how his wife and daughters are going to
take it?" Nina asked
"Why are you worried about them? And how do
you know he has daughters I never told you that?"
Trish asked all attitude
"Yes you did"
"No I didn't"
"Yes you did. Maybe you don't remember" Nina
said with just as much attitude
"Well I don't remember"
"Maybe I guessed it. Its not that serious" Nina lied
"Anyway. What's going on with you? Who are you
talking to now?" Trish asked changing the subject
"I met this guy. He seems cool"
"What's his name?"
"Jason?"
"Where did you meet him?"
"Through a friend" Nina lied
She couldn't tell her that he was her drug dealer and

now she was fucking him.

"How long have you been seeing him?"

"Only about a week"

"What does he do?"

"Damn! what's up with all the questions?" Nina joked. But she was really serious.

"I was just making conversation. Just forget it"

Nina was happy Trish dropped it because she didn't know what she was gonna say.

...

Today was Crystal's 27th birthday and her first day back at work and she was nervous. So much had happened in her time off and she hoped that no one at work had found out about all her drama, as far as they knew she had a family emergency. No one knew that her boyfriend left her, his girlfriend had someone beat her ass and she was pregnant by her mother's husband, and now she lost the baby and her mother. Damn that was a lot!

Crystal rested her head on her steering wheel and took a deep breath. She grabbed her briefcase out of the backseat and got out the car. She beeped her alarm and walked out of the company parking lot to the elevator. She waited for the elevator with butterflies in her stomach. It felt like her first day all over again. She stepped on the elevator.

"Good Morning"

She said to the random strangers in the elevator. They all worked in the building together but she didn't know any of them personally.

Thank God.

She rode the elevator in silence to the 18th floor. She stepped out the elevator and walked down the hall. The first person she saw was her personal assistant/receptionist Alice.

"Good Morning Alice"

"Good Morning Ms. Dawson. It's good to have you back. How have you been?"

"I've been good. Thanks for asking" Crystal lied

"Is everything okay with your family?"

"Yeah, everything is fine"

"That's good. Well since you've been gone a lot has been going on. There are three new cases that you need to review. I left everything on your desk. I also left all your phone calls, messages, and memo's on your desk as well. I told everyone that you would be back tomorrow. So you have today to get caught up. I didn't know if you wanted your phone ringing off the hook" Alice joked

"Thank you so much. I really appreciate it" Crystal smiled

Crystal truly did appreciate Alice. She was always so together and on top of everything. She was a cute petite black woman in her early thirties. Alice had been working at the company since she was 23 years old. She knew all the ins and outs and Crystal never understood why she didn't go to law school. She was much too qualified to be just a receptionist.

"No problem. Let me know if you need anything"

"I will thanks"

Crystal walked in her office and took a deep breath.

She didn't realize how much she missed her office
until she stepped inside. She walked over to her
window and looked at the view of central park. It
was beautiful. She sat down and sunk into her
custom made Mobili Italian Chair. She closed her
eyes and wished that all her problems could go
away. She wished everything could go back to
normal. Then she remembered that her life hadn't
been "normal" since she was thirteen years old.

Crystal looked at the stack of folders and papers
piled on her desk. She didn't feel like dealing with
those at the moment, she decided to call her father.
She spoke to him every now and then and usually
she was the one that had to pick up the phone and
call. She hoped for a while that him and her mother
would get back together and her mother would
leave that bastard Harold but they never did. Crystal
hardly ever remembered her father even asking
about her mother, its like they weren't ever married
at all, like they never had a family. Like the first
thirteen years of Crystal's life was all a dream and
now she woke up. She hadn't spoke to her father in
about a year and she hadn't seen him in about 4
years, since he moved to Atlanta, but suddenly she
had the urge to call him. She still knew his number
by heart.

"Hello?" a little girl answered

"Hi may I speak to Luke?" Crystal said

"Hold on" The little girl said

"Daddy! Daddy! It's the phone!" The little girl
screamed

Daddy? Crystal thought.

"Who is it baby?"

"I don't know, some lady"

"Hello?" Luke's deep voice boomed through the phone

"Hi Daddy, its me" Crystal said

"Who is this?"

"It's me Crystal"

"Oh hey Crystal" He said like they were old friends instead of father and daughter.

There was silence for a minute.

"Was that your daughter that answered the phone?" Crystal asked

"Yeah. That was Misa" Luke said

"She sounds grown. How old is she?" Crystal joked

"She's only three but she's so smart. I just love that little girl. " Luke said enthusiastically

Crystal was silent for a minute.

How can men just do that?

How can they start new families and forget about the old ones?

"Yeah. She sounded older than that"

Crystal remembered when her dad used to feel that way about her. She remembered all their family vacations and all the surprise gifts her father would bring home for her from work. *How could he forget about all that?*

"So how are you?" Luke asked

"I'm okay. You know today's my birthday" Crystal said hoping that maybe he would remember and tell her that he was just about to call her or maybe he

281

sent her a gift or card and it was in the mail.
She was so embarrassed that she had to remind her
own father of her birthday. He used to call her on
her birthday every year until she was nineteen. Until
he married Nikki, wife number three.
"It sure is. How old are you now? I lost track"
"I'm 27 Dad"
"Wow. You're a grown woman"
"Yeah I am. Look, I'm real busy at work. I just
wanted to say hi. I gotta go" Crystal said as she
hung up the phone and wiped the tears from her
cheeks. She hung up before she could hear his
response.

...

Four pair of shoes and two dresses later Trish was
tired of shopping and she could tell by the look on
Nina's face that she was tired too.
"Are you ready yet?" Nina asked with an attitude
"Yeah I'm done. I'm ready to get something to eat
and go home. You sure you not buying nothing?"
Trish asked
"Yeah I'm sure. I did a little shopping last week"
Nina lied. The truth was she didn't have any money
to go shopping, She had $87 dollars in her bank
account and she didn't get another check until next
week.
*That bitch could have offered to buy me something.
I know she got the money. Fuck her!*
"Oh okay"
"Well it's about time you're ass is ready to go.

We've been here for four hours" Nina said annoyed
"Did you have somewhere to be?" Trish asked
sarcastically
"Shut up"
"What do you want to eat? I'm starving"
"Whatever you want it doesn't matter"
"Lets go to Houston's on 53rd . I love their ribs and
their jazz band"
Damn why didn't I pick a place? Nina thought
"If that's what you want I'm not that hungry" Nina
lied.
Houston's was a little on the pricey side and her
meal would probably overdraw her account.
*That stuck up bitch! What? She's too good for
Fridays?*
Trish saw the look on Crystal's face.
"My treat" Trish said
"Okay" Nina smiled
...

Paulette sat at her desk and smiled as she
daydreamed about her night with Chris later. It had
been almost six months and she still got butterflies
in her stomach when she saw him and they still
talked on the phone for hours. Chris called at
8:00am, his daily wakeup call and told Paulette to
be ready at 7:30 tonight. He wouldn't tell her where
they were going he just told her to be dressed and
ready. He told her he had something really
important that he wanted to talk about and he
wanted tonight to be special. Paulette thought back

on the conversation

"What do you want to talk about?"

"I can't tell you that. Then it wouldn't be a surprise"

"Just give me a little hint"

"No"

"Please?"

"No"

"Okay. I'll call you later"

"Okay. I love you"

"I love you too"'

Paulette smiled when she thought about those three words.

They had just recently starting saying I love you. They had only been saying it for about a week, but Paulette felt it much earlier, she was just too scared to say it first. Chris said it first and once he did Paulette said it right back. Now every time they said it Paulette got butterflies in her stomach. She felt like she was fifteen all over again.

I wonder what he wants to talk to about?

Paulette was a little scared she hoped he didn't have any bad news.

She felt terrible when she thought about her secret. She still couldn't find the right time to tell Chris. Every time she tried to tell him. She got so scared. She didn't know how she would say it?

What will he think of me?

Now that he told her he loved her she felt a little more secure about their relationship.

Maybe if I tell him now he won't leave me.

But what if he does?
Paulette couldn't stand the thought of Chris leaving her.
She decided that depending on how their conversation went tonight she would just tell him the truth.
If he loves me. He won't care.
Or will he?
...

"You sure you want another drink?" Trish asked Nina after she got the waiter's attention.
"Look, I'm grown"
"I know. But you already had three and you look a little tipsy"
"I'm okay"
"Whatever" Trish waved her hand.
She had enough of Nina. She did not miss hangin' out with her at all.
I know her cheap ass wouldn't be getting four drinks if she was paying for this shit! This is her last drink!
"Can I have another Long Island Ice Tea" Nina told the waiter
"Sure. Would you like anything else?" The waiter asked Trish
"No I'm still working on my drink. Can you just bring me a box and the check please" Trish smiled as she pointed to her usual Grand Marnier and pineapple juice.
"Sure"

"Now you're ready to go? After I spent all day shopping with your ass?" Nina asked with an attitude

I know she must be drunk. Who the hell is she talking to?

"I know you're tipsy, but you better lower your fucking voice" Trish said so only Nina could hear her. Trish was very concerned with appearances and she hated to be even slightly embarrassed in public.

"Fuck you" Nina said as she stuck up her middle finger

"I'm not playing with you Nina"

"Don't fucking tell me what to do. I'm grown! I'll talk loud if I want to! Who the fuck are you?" Nina yelled

A few heads turned in their direction and Trish wanted to jump across the table and slap the shit out of Nina.

"You're acting real stupid right now! I told you not to order all those fucking drinks"

"I don't give a shit what you told me. Fuck you!" Just then the waiter walked over and Trish was lucky she was brown skinned because if not she would have been bright red from embarrassment.

"Here is the check ladies, there's no rush"

Trish glanced at the bill and gave it back to the waiter.

"I'm sorry but can you split the bill. Put my items on one and hers on the other. Sorry about the inconvenience"

"No problem" The waiter said as he took the bill

back and disappeared.

"Oh so now you're not paying? You're such a bitch!"

"You damn right I'm not paying! Pay for your own fucking food. You drunk bitch"

The waiter brought the bill back over and placed it on the table.

Trish looked at the two bills and realized that hers was the cheaper bill. It was $58.00. She only had two drinks and a rib platter.

Nina bill was $89.00. She had four drinks an appetizer and a roasted chicken meal.

Nina looked at the bill and began fidgeting. She looked in her purse and pulled out her Bank of America Debit Card. When the waiter came back over Trish handed him her American Express Card and Nina handed him her debit card. They both sat in silence until he came back. The waiter came back over and handed Trish her card and a slip to sign and then he turned to Nina and said.

"I'm sorry Miss. Do you have another form of payment? Your card was declined"

Nina looked like she seen a ghost.

"What? Are you sure? Can you try again?"

"I tried twice Miss. Do you have another card or maybe cash?"

Trish signed the slip and put her card back in her purse. She wanted to bust out laughing but she held it in.

"Yeah let me check" Nina said

She knew damn well she only had $87 in her
account. Or at least she did the last time she
checked.

That fucking Trish! Dumb Bitch! She could have
just paid for the fucking meal.
I can't stand her ass!

Nina looked over at Trish she swallowed all her
Pride and said

"Trish can you please-"

But before she could finish Trish said

"No I can't. I'm a fucking bitch! Right? Have a
good night"

She said as she put on her shades, grabbed her purse
and walked out the door.

...

Paulette walked through the door to the restaurant at
exactly 7:45pm. She knew she was late but fifteen
minutes was on time as far as she was concerned.
She walked over to the hostess and told her that she
was there for Chris Jones, party of two. The hostess
told her that Chris had already arrived and began to
escort her over to the table. Paulette adjusted her
black tube top dress and looked down at her black
pumps and took a deep breath. She was still a little
nervous about what Chris wanted to talk to her
about. But the two Grey Goose and orange juice
cocktails she made herself while she was getting
dressed helped to calm her nerves.

She followed the hostess towards the back of
the restaurant. They passed many tables and

Paulette wondered where she was taking her. When they reached a set of black double doors the hostess stopped and turned to Paulette
"Here we are. I hope you enjoy your evening" The hostess said as she smiled.
She opened the door and Paulette walked through and couldn't believe her eyes.

It was a wonderful vision of red and gold. Paulette's favorite colors. The room was dimly lit with what looked like hundreds of gold candles. There were dozens of red roses in tall, slender gold vases all around the room. Paulette looked at the bronze colored walls and down at the plush red carpet and she couldn't believe how beautiful everything was. She glanced over to a round table in the corner that was covered with a gold table cloth with two tall red candles, one on each side of the table. She figured that was where she was supposed to sit.

Just as she was about to make her way to the table when Chris came out of another door. He looked scrumptious in a black three piece suit, that fit him perfectly. Paulette smiled at him with tears in her eyes. He walked over to her and kissed her lightly on the cheek.
"Do you like everything?"
"Yes" was all Paulette could say; she was speechless.
"I knew you would" Chris smiled pleased with himself
"Why are you crying? What's wrong?"

Paulette wiped her eyes and nodded
"Nothing's wrong. I'm happy, silly"
"Oh you scared me for a minute" Chris joked.
Chris held her hand and walked her over to the
table. He pulled her chair out for her and let her sit
down. Paulette smiled again because she couldn't
believe how lucky she was to find a man like him.
Once they were seated a waiter dressed in black and
white came over to the table with a chilled bottle of
wine.
"Your starters will be out shortly"
"Thank you" Chris said to the waiter
"You ordered everything already?"
"I got this under control just relax and enjoy the
evening, okay"
"Okay" Paulette smiled
"So what did you want to talk about?"
"Didn't I tell you it was a surprise?"
"I know but I'm here now so you can tell me"
"You are so impatient"
"I know. So what is it?"
"Okay since you can't wait any longer I guess I'll
tell you"
Paulette's heart stopped for a second.
"Tell me what?" Paulette could barely catch her
breath.
Please lord don't let him be Gay.
"That I love you and"
"And?"
"And you mean the world to me and"
"And?"

"Would you be quiet and let me finish"

"Okay sorry go ahead"

"And I knew from the first day that I met you that you were something special. Even though you were drunk as hell, I still knew you were the one"

Paulette busted out laughing

"Oh you had to bring that up" Paulette joked

"I have never been this happy in my life. You make me a better man. I am a different person when I am with you. I love you Paulette. You make me happy in every way. You are my friend and my lover. I love you so much and I want to spend the rest of my life with you"

What?

Paulette couldn't believe it. That was the last thing she thought he was gonna say.

She couldn't wipe the tears from her eyes fast enough. They just kept coming.

She loved him so much. She felt the same exact way.

"Paulette will you marry me?" Chris asked as he pulled out a red velvet box with a 3.5 carat pear shaped diamond engagement ring inside.

Paulette cried even harder when she saw the ring.

She couldn't believe it.

It was real!

He really loves me!

She couldn't stop crying.

"Well? " Chris asked nervously

"Yes! Yes! I'm sorry. I just can't believe it! Yes I will marry you!"

"Thank you! You better stop scaring me!" Chris smiled.

Paulette was so happy. This had to be the happiest day of her life. She couldn't wait to get home and rip that suit right off Chris, her fiancé. She smiled at the thought of it.

Then she thought about her secret.

I can't tell him now. It will spoil everything. The time is not right.

I may not even tell him at all, it will be my little secret. Forever.

"What's the matter baby?"

"Nothing" Paulette lied.

...

Chapter 15

Trish walked outside and flagged a cab. She looked back at the restaurant a couple of times and contemplated going back inside then she decided against it.

Fuck that bitch! I'm tired of her ass. For real! I don't know who the fuck she thought she was talking to. She's lucky I didn't jump across the table and beat the shit out of her. I know her cheap ass got to have $90 dollars on her anyway. She's a grown ass woman, with a job.

Yeah, I don't feel bad.   Trish reassured herself. Trish finally flagged a cab and headed uptown towards her apartment.

Trish laughed when she thought about the crazy day she had with Nina.

That bitch is really crazy!

The cab driver looked back at her to see what she laughing at.

Trish wanted to pick up the phone and call Crystal and tell her about her crazy day but then she remembered they weren't speaking. Trish picked up the phone and dialed Paulette instead and her phone went straight to voicemail.

Ever since she met Chris I hardly ever speak to her ass.

Trish smiled when she thought about it. That's how her and Jay use to be.

She dialed Jay's number and his phone went straight to voicemail too. She hadn't spoke to him all day.

She missed him so much. She hated not seeing him, but so far it had been for the best.

She couldn't wait until they could be together every day, so she figured it was worth it.

"Right here this building on the right" Trish said to the cab driver

"That's $12"

Trish handed him $15 and grabbed her bags and got out the cab.

She walked inside her building and was greeted by Tommy her doorman.

"How are you today Ms. Grand"

"I'm good Tommy. How are you?"

"I'm good thanks for asking"

Trish kept meaning to tell him to call her Trish instead of Ms. Grand but every time he said it she smiled. She still couldn't believe how her life had turned out sometimes. If only her mother and sister could see her now. *I should send those bitches a post card.* Trish laughed when she thought about them. She hadn't seen either one of them since she left home eight years ago.As far as everyone was concerned she was an only child and her parents were dead. They died in a car crash when Trish was 15 and she inherited money from their insurance policies. She was raised by her grandparents that sent her to the finest schools and she had a wonderful childhood. Nobody knew the truth except Crystal and even she didn't know how ugly it was sometimes. She kept up this façade for everyone at

all times. She couldn't imagine anybody knowing
the truth about where she came from. She knew she
wouldn't have made half of the acquaintances she
made or been invited to any of the parties she was
invited to if people knew the truth.

She checked her mail and pressed the elevator.
She got on the elevator and pressed her floor.
On the ride up she thought about Nina again and she
felt a little guilty. *I should have just paid for the
damn food.* She walked off the elevator to her door.
She put the key inside and she was surprised when
it turned so easily.

I must have not locked the door on the way out.
She pushed the door open and almost fainted at
what she saw. Her apartment was wrecked, it was
really fucked up.

"Ahhhh!" She screamed
Trish didn't know what to do.
She looked around at her things.
She walked straight into the kitchen. Her kitchen
drawers were on the floor, dishes and glasses were
broken everywhere. Spoons and forks were
sprawled all over the floor. Papers were everywhere
as if somebody was looking for something. Trish
couldn't believe her eyes. All she could do was cry.
Her glass dining room table was flipped over and
broken and her chairs were lying across the floor.
Trish tiptoed into the living room, trying not to step
on any glass. She didn't know that it could get any
worse until she saw the living room.

Her suede brown couch had long scars like it

was stabbed with a knife repeatedly. The cushions were hanging out. Her plasma screen T.V. was on the floor and the screen was cracked in several places. Trish held her head, she felt like she couldn't take anymore. She walked into her bedroom and saw some of her favorite dresses and outfits cut up into pieces. She picked up the pieces and cried.

Who is doing this to me?

Her bed had got the same treatment as her couch and her comforter was shredded in several places. The nightstands that were once by her bed were both turned sideways and all the contents of the drawers were emptied out onto her bedroom floor. Trish sat on the floor and cried. She didn't know what to do.

She dialed 911 and waited. She dialed Jay still no answer. She dialed Paulette still no answer. She wanted to call Crystal but she still didn't feel bad enough to swallow her pride. She decided to call Nina and apologize, she had to talk to somebody. She wasn't surprised when Nina ended her call and sent her to voicemail.

Trish had nobody to talk to. At times like this she wished she had a mother that she could call for advice and would tell her she loved her and that everything would be okay. Just when she thought it stopped. It wasn't over. Just then Trish got up and started looking all over apartment. She was looking for a piece of paper or a note or something, the usual and she was surprised when she didn't find

anything.
That's strange.
...

"Excuse me Miss but do you have another form of payment?" The waiter asked again. This time he seemed a little annoyed
"Yes I do. Can you give me a few minutes" Nina snapped
"Okay Miss but its been a half an hour and I'm going to have to seat another party at this table"
"Well I'm sure you can wait a few fucking minutes!"
The waiter rolled his eyes and walked away.

Nina searched through her purse and all she could find was nineteen dollars in cash and some loose change. Nina frantically dialed Bank of America's automated service. She knew the number by heart but she was so tipsy she kept misdialing the number. Finally after four attempts at dialing she went to her phonebook and found the number and pressed send. She entered her account information and almost fell off the stool when the voice on the automated service said "your account is currently overdrawn by $458.00"
What the fuck?

Nina couldn't understand what happened. The last time she checked she had $87.00 in her account. Then she remembered she had automatic bill pay set up on her account and the bank must have paid her bills.

She usually had enough money to cover everything but her weed habit now turned coke habit was a bill she didn't factor into the equation.

What the fuck am I gonna do?

Nina was scared and embarrassed but she was even more mad at Trish. She literally wanted to kill her. If she was in front of her right now she would choke the shit out of her.

How could she do this to me? That fucking bitch!

Nina looked around to see if she saw the waiter in sight. She didn't see him anywhere. Then she looked towards the door and she saw a few hostesses standing by the door she decided she couldn't go that way. She grabbed her purse and walked to the bathroom.

She figured she would wait in there for a while. Maybe they would think she left.

She found an empty stall and went inside and sat down. She wanted to cry. She couldn't think of anyone to call. She couldn't call Crystal because she didn't even go see her ass in the hospital. She decided to call Paulette.

Damn!

Her phone went to the voicemail.

She looked at her phone and decided to call Linda. She dialed Linda's office number.

"Hello?" Linda answered on the first ring.

"Hi Linda its' me Nina"

She sobered up real quick.

"Oh, Hi Nina"

"I'm so glad I still caught you at the office. I know

this is a lot to ask Linda, but I had dinner at
Houston's in the city and I forgot my cash at home.
I was wondering if you could loan me some cash
until I get home and I'll pay you back"
There was dead silence.
Nina thought Linda hung up the phone.
"Hello?" Nina asked
"Yes, I'm still here. Am I the only person that you
could think of to call? Actually I'm in a rush. I'm
going to meet my husband for dinner. I really don't
have the time, sorry" Linda said
"Oh don't worry about it. Thanks anyway" Nina
forced a giggle
She hung up the phone and she was pissed.
How dare that bitch act like that?
She only works a few blocks from here!
Those stuck up bitches!
Fuck them all!
Just then she saw Trish's number come across the
screen.
She immediately pressed end.
Fuck that bitch!
What the fuck am I gonna do now?
She punched the door.
　　Nina wished she would have just stayed at
home and smoked a blunt and called Jason to bring
her some coke. She would have been high right now
instead of mad as hell. Then she reached in her
purse and found a small white bag. She smiled
when she realized she had a little coke left from the
last time she'd seen Jason. She took a mirror out of

her bag and poured the coke on to it.

She used a business card to make a straight line and she brought her face down and sniffed a line. She instantly felt a rush. That's just what she needed. She threw everything back in her bag and opened the stall door. She glanced at herself in the mirror and walked out the bathroom. She walked back out into the crowded restaurant and proceeded to make her way to the door. She wanted to get out of the restaurant as quickly as possible.
She looked around and she didn't see the waiter in sight. She picked up her pace and walked quickly towards the door.
Damn! Where the fuck did all these people come from?
Nina thought as she tried to push through the crowd. She was almost at the door when she heard someone yell across the room
"Stop her! Stop that woman!"
"Nina acted like she didn't hear anything and kept walking"
"Stop her! Michelle don't let her leave!" She heard the voice yell at a hostess that was near the door. Nina looked back and saw her waiter yelling across the room and running towards her.
Why can't he mind his fucking business?
Nina turned back around and walked towards the door but Michelle stood in her way. Michelle should have been named Michael because she was about six feet tall with broad shoulders and a slight mustache.

"Excuse me Miss but I can't let you leave" She said
in a deep voice

"You better get the fuck out of my way"

"I'm sorry I can't do that"

"Bitch! I'm not playing with you, you better move"
Michelle did not budge. So Nina punched her right
in the gut. Michelle didn't expect that and bent over
holding her stomach while she gasped for air. While
she bent over Nina punched her in the face.
Michelle yelled and fell to the ground.
Her ass is big for nothing.

A few people around them started to scream and
one woman yelled out for security. Nina jumped
right over Michelle and pushed the door open. She
ran out the restaurant and straight down the block.
She turned around and saw the waiter with two big
body guards behind her chasing her.
What the fuck?

She was out of breath. She wanted to stop but she
kept going. They were catching up to her.
All this shit for $89.00?

And now she assaulted the woman. She had to keep
going she didn't want them to call the cops. Nina
kept running. She felt like she was running a
marathon.
All of this shit is Trish's fault.
And that fucking Linda.

Nina couldn't take it anymore she had to stop. She
had to catch her breath. She stopped and bent over
and tried to catch her breath. Nina looked up and
she saw that she had ran six blocks. *Damn!*

She looked behind her and she didn't see them.
They had given up on chasing her.
Thank God.
But now she was more pissed than before and her
high was gone.
...

"Hello?" Trish answered half asleep
It was 9' o'clock in the morning but she had just fell
asleep from the night before. When the police
finally got to her apartment they asked her hundreds
of questions and took pictures of her apartment.
They kept asking her who could have done this to
her apartment and she told them she didn't know.
The truth was she knew it had to be Jay's wife. Who
else could it be? She couldn't think of anyone that
hated her this much. Then she went down to the
police station and made a statement. After all of the
questioning was done an officer escorted Trish back
to her apartment to get a few belongings so she
could check into a hotel. They didn't think that it
was safe for her to stay the night there alone and she
didn't think it was either.
Shit! She was scared as hell.

She decided to check into the Marriot Marquis
in Times Square. By the time she was settled in her
room and took a shower she was ready to go to bed
it was damn near 6'oclock in the morning and the
sun was coming up. She laid in the bed and tried to
go to sleep, but with the sun shining in her eyes she
just couldn't. She started to think of all the things

that happened to her and she ended up crying herself to sleep.

...

"How the fuck could you do this?"

"Hello?" Trish answered the phone confused.

She tried sat up in the bed and wiped the cold out of her eyes.

"You fucking heard me. How the fuck could you do this?" Jay's voice boomed through the phone

"What are you talking about?"

"Don't act like you don't know what the fuck I'm talking about. My wife's car is fucked up. My house is fucked up"

Trish had never heard Jay this mad before and he never talked to her in this tone. She instantly started crying.

"What? Why do you think I would do something like that?"

"Because the word bitch was keyed across her car and there was a picture of me and you on the windshield. That's why! And there was a little note attached saying "he's my man" That's why!" Jay yelled

"Jay I don't know what you're talking about. I didn't do anything" Trish sobbed

"There were rocks, no fucking boulders thrown through my window! My little girls were in there! They could have been hurt! How could you do that? Are you fucking crazy? All I asked you was to give me some time!"

"Jay please believe me. I wouldn't do anything like that! I wouldn't want to hurt your kids"

"Whatever! I don't know what the fuck I was thinking leaving my family for your crazy ass"

"Jay don't talk like that. I love you"

"I thought I loved you too. Just keep your crazy ass away from me and my fucking family"

"Jay?"

"Leave me alone!"

"Jay? Wait"

The phone went dead.

Trish dialed Jay's number back. It rang and rang he didn't answer.

She dialed it over and over and he still wouldn't answer.

She needed to talk to him.

How could he not believe me?

How could he not love me anymore?

She dialed it again. He turned the phone off it went straight to voicemail.

"Ahhh!" She screamed

She threw her blackberry across the room.

She didn't want to talk to anybody.

What is going on?

She felt like she was in the twilight zone.

Who is doing this to me?

Who is trying to make my life miserable?

...

"Ms. Dawson you have a visitor" Alice buzzed through the intercom

"Who is it?"

"A Mr. Harold Nelson"

What the fuck does he want?

"Okay. Send him in Alice"

"Sure"

Crystal instantly felt sick to her stomach when she saw Harold standing in the doorway of her office.

"Close the door behind you please"

Harold did as he was told and turned his attention back to Crystal.

She looked at him with disgust.

"Is everything okay? Is something wrong with my mother?" Crystal asked nervously

She couldn't think of any other reason Harold would show up at her job.

"No. She's fine"

"Well then what the fuck do you want? And why are you coming to my job?"

"Well Hello to you too"

"What do you want Harold?"

"I wanted to see you"

"How dare you come to my fucking job with this bullshit! I want you to leave now! I have a lot of work to do"

"Don't act like that baby girl I know you missed daddy"

"Get the fuck out now!" Crystal said raising her voice.

"Look, just calm down, don't you want to do a little favor for me before I go" Harold asked as she walked towards her

"What?!"

Crystal couldn't believe that he would still ask her this even after her mother found out.

"You heard me. I missed you and I have needs baby girl" Harold said as he stroked the side of her face.

Crystal flinched and moved back.

"Please leave Harold"

"I'll leave as soon as I get what I came for"

Crystal didn't want anyone to hear her yelling; she didn't want to cause a scene.

"Please, Harold leave, this is my job" Crystal pleaded

"I wouldn't have to come to your job if you would have been returning my calls"

Crystal started to cry.

She couldn't understand why he kept doing this to her. She wished he was dead.

"What about my mother? She knows now. I don't have to put up with this shit anymore!"

"What about your mother? She ain't going nowhere. She don't know shit! She believes what I tell her to believe. When are you gonna learn that this is gonna stop when I want it to stop and right now I don't"

"Harold I'm at work. Please go. I'm begging you"

"I'll go as soon as you do a little something for me" Harold said unbuckling his belt

"Get the fuck out before I call security!" Crystal screamed

"And what are you gonna tell them when I show them these?" Harold asked as he pulled out three pictures of him and her having sex out of his jacket pocket

Where the fuck did those come from?

Crystal tried to hold it together but she couldn't, she broke down and started crying harder.

"Just get out!"

"Stop making this difficult and just do what the fuck I ask!"

"No Harold, please go I told you before that I can't keep-

"Ms. Dawson you're 11 o'clock is here. I will send them in the conference room" Alice said over the intercom

"Okay thank you so much Alice. I'm on my way"

"Okay"

Thank God.

"Harold look I have to go. I know you don't give a shit but this a really important meeting"

"You're damn right I don't. If you would have stopped fucking playing games we would have been finished now. This is not over" Harold said as he started unbuckling his belt

"Yes it is Harold I gotta go" Crystal said as she pulled herself together and walked out of the office

"We'll see"

...

Nina sat on the floor of her living room at the coffee table doing line after line of coke.

Jason was in the shower and she was ready to have sex again when he got out. It would be round three. She felt like she had the best sex when she was

high. Nina still smoked weed but it couldn't
compare to how she felt now.
She felt wild and crazy, like she could do anything.
She laid her back against the couch and closed her
eyes and started daydreaming.
"Shit!" Nina said as she jumped
   The sound of Jason's phone vibrating on the
table snapped her out of her daze. She didn't want
to answer his phone so she let it vibrate. The same
number called again. Whoever was calling must
have wanted to speak to him really bad because
Jason's other phone started ringing right after.
It was annoying the hell out of Nina. She was trying
to relax and enjoy her high.
*That's what the fuck they have voicemail for. Leave
a fucking message.*
So she reached over and answered the phone.
"Hello?" she asked with an attitude
"Yo can I speak to Jr.?"
"Who?"
"Jr."
She figured Jr. must have been a nickname for
Jason.
"He's a little busy I'll tell him to call you back"
"Aight. Tell him to call Biggs. Its important"
"Okay" Nina said and hung up the phone.
She put the phone back on the table just as Jason
was walking out of the shower in only his boxers
with a towel hanging over his right shoulder.
Damn he looks good.
"You answered my phone?"

"Yeah, they kept calling"

"Who was that?"

"Somebody named Biggs said call him, its important"

"Aight" Jason said as he reached for the phone.

"This is important too" Nina said as she crawled on all fours over to Jason. She took his phone out of his hand and placed it back on the coffee table and pulled his boxers down.

Once Jason realized what was going on he immediately got hard and Nina let her lips work magic. Jason didn't put up a fight, he just stood there and enjoyed himself. Biggs could wait. After the third time this morning Nina was tired as hell. They laid across her bed, she rested her head on Jason's chest.

"I gotta get outta here baby, I got some runs to make. Messing with you I already missed half the morning" Jason said as he lifted Nina's head off his chest and got out of bed

"Why you gotta go right now?" She whined

Nina didn't want to be alone and she was beginning to feel like they were almost in a real relationship. She liked having him around. She also liked the fact that he supplied her with free coke as long as she was fucking him and she didn't mind that. She didn't have a steady paycheck coming in now, so money was tight.

"I told you I got things to do. I'll come through later"

Jason said as he picked up his clothes off the floor

and got dressed. Nina was starting to get on his nerves. She was cool and she had some good pussy but he wasn't the relationship type. He didn't like explaining where he was going or when he was coming back. He liked to come and go as he pleased. She was getting too damn clingy. But he needed to keep her around for a while.

"Yeah whatever"

Nina knew that he probably wouldn't come by later. He was so unpredictable. She knew she probably wouldn't see him until tomorrow or the day after that.

"Why you got an attitude? Why don't you go hang with your girls or something?"

"What girls?"

"Aren't those your girls in the picture in your living room?"

"Whatever. If that's' what you want to call them"

"What about Trish weren't you with her the other day?"

"What about that stuck up bitch?"

How did he know I was with her?

Nina was pissed that he kept asking about her. *Why is it always about her?*

"Stuck up?" Jason asked surprised

"Yeah that stuck up bitch! With all her money and her apartment and fancy clothes and cars"

"Word?!"

"Yeah I can't stand that bitch!"

"So she's paid?"

"Yeah. Her parents died in a car crash way back and

she got a lot of money from the insurance policies"

"Yeah? That's what she said?"

"What you mean?"

"Forget it. That's crazy" Jason said dropping the subject

"I gotta go. I'll call you later"

He grabbed his phones and headed towards the door.

"Bye" Nina said and turned back over in her bed.

Chapter 16

"Jay. Please pick up the phone. This is like my
hundredth time calling you. Please call me back. I
love you"
Trish hung up the phone and sunk into her bed. She
didn't care how desperate she sounded she just
hoped that Jay would call her back. It had been
three weeks and he hadn't returned any of her calls.
She was in so much pain. She felt like her heart had
been ripped out of her chest. All she wanted was for
him to believe her and call her back and tell her he
loved her. She cried every time she thought about
the last conversation they had. She couldn't believe
he could be so mean to her. She still couldn't
understand who was doing all this shit to her.
She thought it was Jay's wife but if his wife's car
was fucked up too then it couldn't be her.
Who was it?
        Every time she thought about it, it drove her
crazy. Trish looked around her apartment and put
the covers back over her head. She had been back at
her apartment for a week and she hadn't cleaned up
anything. All she did was order takeout, watch T.V.
and call Jay. Her apartment still looked like shit but
she didn't feel like doing anything and she didn't
know where to start. She needed some advice and
some kind words. She wanted to call Crystal, but
she didn't. She didn't feel like apologizing.
        ...

It was Friday night and Crystal sat on her couch eating a big bowl of her favorite ice cream, Chocolate Chip cookie Dough. She was relaxing in her favorite pair of black velour Juicy sweat pants and a black tank top watching the last season of the Sex and the City on HBO on demand. It was unusually hot for a spring night in April. She could hear all the New Yorkers outside having a good time through her living room window. She wished she was out too.But lately she spent almost all her free time at home.

It had been almost a month since Harold showed up at her job but she couldn't get that day out of her mind. She replayed it over and over. He called her a few times since then but she hadn't answered or returned any of his calls. She knew he was going to show up again soon, he always did. He never left her alone. She hated him with a passion. She never hated anybody that much in her life. Crystal truly wished he was dead.

She didn't realize how much she would miss her mother until she didn't speak to her, it had been about three months since that day in the hospital and she missed her so much, she was so hurt. Part of her hated her mother too, how could she not believe her only daughter. Crystal just wished that Harold was out of their life. She had to think of way to get rid of him.

She picked up the phone and dialed Keith.

"Hello?"

"Hey what's up?" He answered on the first ring

"Nothing much I was calling to see when we could get together" Crystal said getting right to the point
"I was wondering what the hell took you so long"
"I'm sorry I've been so busy at work" Crystal said in her sweetest voice
"So what about tomorrow night? I'm going out tonight"
"Tomorrow is cool around 7. Meet me in front of my building" Crystal said
"Aight"
"Okay" Crystal said as she hung up the phone. She smiled hoping maybe something good would come out of this crazy situation.
...

Paulette couldn't stop smiling as she looked down at her ring. She got so many compliments on it. It was gorgeous. She didn't think Chris could make her any happier but she was wrong. Ever since they got engaged they were both happy all the time. She hadn't told Trish, Nina, or Crystal anything yet. She had called them all but none of them returned her calls and she didn't feel like leaving a message. She hoped everything was okay with them. She missed them. But she was so happy in her own world she really didn't stop to worry about anyone else.

Paulette and Chris had just told her mother the news yesterday at a surprise visit to her house. Paulette's mother was happier than she was. You would have thought she was the one getting married. Like she hadn't got married four times before.

Michelle loved Chris from the moment she met him. Paulette knew that she would because he fit her mother's criteria, he looked the part. She even caught her mother drooling over him sometimes. All she did was shake her head and laugh. She was just happy that her mother actually approved of someone she dated. Chris was charming, good looking, educated, had a great job, a nice car and nice clothes. How could anyone not like him? According to Michelle he was perfect. And she reminded Paulette of that every chance she got.

"You know that's a good man, you better not let him go"

"You need to start dressing better and keeping yourself up if you want to keep him"

"I don't know how you got such a good man like him. Do you know how lucky you are?" Michelle would tell Paulette over and over. She didn't care how he treated Paulette or if they got along that was a minor detail to Michelle.

Michelle couldn't wait to start planning the wedding. She was ecstatic. As soon as Paulette showed her the ring she began talking about wedding colors, flowers, ice sculptures, and wedding planners. Paulette didn't even stop her mother because she was happy that they finally had something in common for a change. They usually had nothing to talk about, they were complete opposites.

As far as Paulette was concerned she and Chris could have a small wedding in one of their parent's backyard with their closest friends and family. They didn't need anything big and fancy. As long as she was marrying Chris she didn't care about anything else. But not Michelle, small was not in her vocabulary. She wanted at least 250 people, with all the works. Money was not an object because she planned on putting the whole wedding on Phillip's tab. Chris insisted on paying for the entire wedding but Michelle told him that she and Phillip were paying for it and she wouldn't have it any other way. Paulette and Chris said okay and decided to let Michelle have her fun with planning the wedding. She told Paulette and Chris all they had to do was show up.

"So have you picked your bridesmaids and maid of honor?" Michelle asked

"Well you know I definitely want Nina, Trish, and Crystal to be in the wedding, but I haven't even told them yet. I'm going to tell them everything this weekend"

"Well you need to hurry if you plan on having a September wedding, they need to be fitted for dresses and get on any diets if necessary, fat bridesmaids aren't cute"

"Okay mom"

Paulette laughed, shaking her head. Her mother was a trip.

She decided to call them all and invite them to

breakfast on Sunday.

She dialed Trish, no answer.

So she left a message.

The same thing with Nina.

She was beginning to get frustrated.

Where are your friends when you need them?

She hoped they all showed up on Sunday.

She dialed Crystal.

"Hello?"

"Hey Crys. What's up?"

"Paulette?"

"Yeah"

"Hey girl. How you been?"

"I've been good. How are you? I haven't spoke to you in so long. Are your fingers broke. You don't know how to dial my number no more?"

Paulette joked but she knew she was just as guilty because she hadn't called Crystal either.

"I know girl. I'm sorry. I just haven't really been in the mood to talk to anybody"

"I understand. But I have something to tell you"

"What?"

"I can't tell you now but I want you to come to breakfast on Sunday and then I can tell you all"

"All?"

"Yes all. Me, you, Nina, and Trish. Duh!"

"Mmm" Crystal said

Crystal hadn't spoke to Trish since the day they had that argument and really didn't care to see her. As far as Nina went she didn't care if she spoke to her or saw her either. She had called Nina several times and she never returned any of her calls. She didn't even come see her in the hospital. *I could have been dead.*

"What is mmm about?"

"Nothing" Crystal lied

She didn't want to spoil Paulette's good news so she would just suck up her attitude and go to breakfast, even if she only stayed for a little while. *I'm still not speaking to those bitches.*

"I know its something but you don't have to tell me. I just expect to see you at Norma's in the Parker Meridian at 10am on Sunday"

"Ooh you know I love Norma's. I'll be there" Crystal said as her mouth watered thinking about their famous scrambled egg and bacon quesadilla. At least if she had to look at Trish and Nina's face she would be getting some good food.

"Okay I'll call you later. I'm about to go out" Crystal said

"Okay" Paulette said and hung up the phone

One down and two to go. Paulette said to herself hoping that Trish and Nina showed up.

...

Crystal hung up the phone and walked into her bedroom. She looked at herself in her full length mirror and she was pleased.

She wanted to make sure she looked extra sexy tonight. She wore a black off the shoulder mini dress with matching black stilettos. It was simple and sexy.

She had just got a complete wax earlier from head to toe and her legs looked great. She sprayed on some of her favorite perfume, Burberry Weekend and put on her favorite shade of Mac lip glass, Prize Petal. Crystal glanced at the clock. It was 7:02pm. She grabbed her jacket and silver clutch, turned off her lights and headed downstairs. It was a nice night so she didn't mind waiting outside for Keith for a few minutes. She had made dinner reservations for them at 8pm at Tao, a new Chic Asian restaurant on 58th street. Crystal had ate there once before and she loved the food. She also loved that it was close and she could hop in a cab instead of driving.

Five minutes later Keith strolled up the block. He must have taken the train because she didn't see a car anywhere in sight. She shook her head when looked at him. Looking at him now she didn't know what she ever saw in him before. He had on a colorful sweater, it looked like a Coogi knock off with Baggy jeans and some tan timberlands boots. *He looks hot and tacky* she thought to herself. But she didn't care they only had to be together for one night.

"What's up baby? You look good" he said as he kissed her on the cheek

"Thank you. You do too" she lied

"So where we going?"

"I made reservations for us at this restaurant Tao"

"Tao? What kind of food is that?" Keith asked twisting up his face

If it's not fried chicken and French fries then he

doesn't like it. Ghetto ass.

"It's Asian food. Its good"

"Well as long as they have shrimp fried rice. I'm cool" Keith said

Crystal ignored his last comment and walked in the street to hail a cab.

Once they were in the cab Keith started rubbing on Crystals' thigh. She wanted to move his hand but she didn't. She wanted everything to go well tonight.

"So what's up baby? How you been" he asked as he moved closer to her

"I'm okay. I missed you so much" Crystal lied

"Me too baby. What took you so long to call?"

"It was too long but I promise I'll make it up to you later" Crystal said with a sexy smile

"Mmm. I can't wait"

Crystal smiled because everything was going good.

...

"You sure you don't want another drink?" Crystal asked Keith

She had been pushing drinks on him all night. He was working on his fifth or sixth and he looked fucked up.

"Nah baby. I'm good. I want to put it on you later so I can't be too drunk" He slurred

"Yeah baby I can't wait. So hurry up and finish that one"

Crystal said as she smiled. She had one drink and had been drinking cranberry juice the rest of the night. She didn't want anything to impair her judgment. After Keith finished his drink Crystal flagged the waitress over and asked for the bill. Keith didn't even budge when the waitress placed the bill on the table, like he had no intentions on paying for anything.

Crystal looked at him in disgust.

Some things never change.

She was used to paying for dinner when she went out with his sorry ass. She pulled out her American Express card and handed it to the waitress. When the waitress returned Crystal left her a tip and put her card away.

Keith was trying to stand up but he looked like he was having some trouble.

Crystal started laughing to herself.

She walked over to his side of the table and helped him up.

"You okay baby?" Crystal asked

"Yeah I'm cool" He lied

Once they were outside Crystal flagged them a cab. Inside the cab Keith couldn't keep his hands off Crystal. He rubbed all over her breasts and her legs. He started kissing her rough and sloppy. Crystal went along with everything, so far everything was going like she planned.

She kissed Keith back and started jerking him off. He was going crazy. She was surprised when he came in her hand before they even got to her apartment. When they pulled up in front of her apartment she paid the cab driver and they got out

the cab. Keith stumbled out the cab and almost fell
on his face. Crystal helped in up the steps and once
they were inside he started stripping. He was buck
naked except for his socks in one minute flat.
Crystal wanted to bust out laughing. She kissed him
and led him into the bedroom. She stepped out of
her dress and she stood in front of him in her black
lace strapless bra which matching panties. She left
on her pumps.

"Damn baby I missed you" Keith said like he was
seeing her without clothes on for the very first time
"Hold on I'll be right back" Crystal said as she
walked to the bathroom to pee. When she walked
back into the room. Keith was laying on her bed
knocked out. She walked over to him and kissed
him on the cheek to see if he would wake up. He
didn't move he just snored.
She smiled.
The night went better than she thought. She thought
she was at least gonna have to fuck him before he
was knocked out. She tiptoed out the room and went
back into the living room and picked up his pants.
She searched in his pockets. She found a key ring
with two keys on it.
Jack pot!
Crystal found what she was looking for.
She went in her purse and found the business card
for Advantage Locksmith, Advantage Locksmith
was a 24hour locksmith on 25th and 3rd avenue. She
grabbed her phone and walked into the bathroom.

"Advantage Locksmith. How may I help you?"
"I need a key made. Its and emergency" Crystal whispered
"I can't hear you. Speak up"
"I need a key made. It's an emergency'
"A house key or a car key?"
"A house key"
"Okay what's your address?"
"1413 E. 82nd Street"
"Okay I'll send someone out. Give me about 20 minutes. I'll call you when they're on their way"
"Okay. I'll be outside"
Crystal hung up the phone and smiled.
It was 4' o'clock in the morning and Nina lay across her bed snoring loudly.
Jason got out of bed and walked in the kitchen to get something to drink. He shook his head in disgust when he looked at the dishes piled up high in the sink.
Damn she's a nasty bitch.
All she cares about is getting high and fucking.
He peeked back in Nina's bedroom, she was knocked out. Jason laughed when he thought about earlier. He got her so high on some new shit that she was bugging.
He called his man Biggs over and they both took turns fucking her. Now she finally crashed.
I know her ass is tired as hell.
He had to cut his ties with her pretty soon. Her habit was getting out of control and he couldn't keep giving her no freebies. Plus she was getting so

skinny she was losing her ass.

He finished his cup of Minute Maid Fruit Punch and put the cup in the sink on top of all the other dishes. He walked over to her coffee table and found a photo album. He sat down on the couch and started flipping through the pictures. It was Nina and her friends, the same girls in the picture on her entertainment center.

He recognized Trish instantly.

She looked like a million bucks in all the pictures.

She outshined all the other girls.

I guess my money is treating you right.

He closed the photo album and put it back on the coffee table. He looked around the apartment for Nina's cell phone. He couldn't find it anywhere.

Damn. Where the fuck is it?

He picked up his cell phone and called hers.

He heard it ringing but he still couldn't find it.

It was coming from her bedroom.

It was getting louder. Nina started moving on the bed and he hung up the phone. He didn't want her to wake up. He tiptoed around the room and looked down on the floor and found it under a pile of clothes.

He played with her phone for awhile until he found what he was looking for and he put it back on the floor where he found it.

He got dressed and left Nina's apartment without even saying goodbye.

...

Chapter 17

When Crystal walked through the doors of Norma's she took off her white Christian Dior Shades and she saw Paulette and Trish already sitting down.
Damn why the fuck did she have to show up?
Crystal put her shades in her green Fendi bag and adjusted the belt on her white linen dress.
She walked over to the table
"Good Morning" She said to them both
"Good Morning" Paulette said cheerfully
"Good Morning" Trish whispered so barely nobody could hear.
Crystal could tell by the shocked look on Trish's face that she didn't know that she was coming. She must have thought it was just a breakfast for her and Paulette.
"We ordered some scrambled egg and bacon quesadillas, crunchy French toast, blueberry pancakes, and banana pancakes. We can all share everything. If you want anything else just order it"
"No that's fine" Crystal lied
She wanted her own food and she didn't feel like sharing
"I guess Nina's not coming" Paulette said like she was sad
"I guess not' Crystal said
She could care less if she showed up or not.
"Well let's wait a little while and if she's not here then I will tell ya'll my good news"
"Okay' Trish said

"So what up? I haven't spoke to neither one of you in so long. What's new?" Paulette asked excitedly. She really missed hanging out with her girls. She had been spending so much time with Chris lately.
"Nothing much" Trish lied.
When she thought about her life she wanted to cry. She didn't feel like talking about all that drama right now.
"What about you Crys? What's up?"
"Nothing I just been working like crazy"
"Well me and Chris are getting married!" Paulette screamed as she took the ring out of her purse and put it on her ring finger. She didn't want to give it away earlier so she didn't wear it.
"Congratulations" Both Trish and Crystal said unenthusiastically
They knew that would happen sooner or later. They had never seen Paulette that happy before.
"Well damn! Ya'll don't seem happy for me"
"I'm sorry. I am really happy for you Paulette. I just got a lot of things on my mind" Crystal said
"Yeah me too" Trish added
"Well when is the wedding?" Crystal asked trying to sound more enthusiastic
"It's in September and I want you both to be my bridesmaids"
"Wow that's soon. Only a few months away"
"I know. I wanted to do it sooner but then Chris decided on September.   I am so happy. I love him so much" Paulette beamed
"I'm really happy for you" Crystal said

She really was. She just had so much on her mind
right now that she couldn't show it like she wanted
to.

"Yeah me too" Trish managed to say but her mind
was somewhere else. She remembered when she felt
like that about Jay and when they were talking
about getting married, now he wouldn't even return
her calls. She wanted to break down but she held
herself together.

Paulette was so happy when the food arrived so
they could eat more and talk less.

They weren't giving her the reaction she expected.
They didn't even seem happy for her.
Fuck them!

Breakfast went better than Crystal expected.
After the food came they all loosened up a little.
Her and Trish even said a few words to each other
but not too much, most of their conversation was
with Paulette. They were all interrupted when they
heard a loud commotion coming from the hostess
area in the front. They heard yelling, cursing, and
screaming.

"Some people have no class" Trish laughed as she
shook her head

"I know. I bet they're black too. Always one to
make us look bad" Paulette joked

They all almost fell out their chairs when they
realized that the loud skinny woman in the baggy
clothes and the red scarf on her head causing all the
fuss was Nina.

...

"I have a fucking reservation!" Nina screamed at the hostess.

"Are you sure ma'am?" The frightened white woman in her mid forties asked Nina. She was clearly embarrassed and wanted to get Nina out of the restaurant as quickly as possible.

"Yes I'm fucking sure my friends are here!" Nina answered scratching her head

"Please watch your language ma'am or we are going to have to ask you to leave. Who are you friends?"

"Paulette and Crystal"

"I'm sorry but we don't have any guests by that name" The hostess said as she checked a large black leather book which held several names of customers on a tall black podium.

"Well check again I know they're here!" Nina screamed

Her high was gone and she needed another hit. In a few short weeks her habit had escalated out of control. She was out of money and Jason hadn't returned any of her calls. She was hoping she could borrow a few dollars from one of them. The hostess quickly did as she was told

"I'm sorry ma'am I don't see those names"

Nina knocked the black book on the floor and tried to knock the podium to the ground.

"Stop fucking playing with me!"

The hostess backed up and stood against the wall.

"I am going to have to ask you please leave"

"Fuck you! I'll find them myself"
Nina said as she walked passed the hostess and into
the restaurant. She searched the crowd and didn't
see them anywhere. She saw many stares and
disapproving faces looking back at her but she
didn't give a shit. She just wanted to get the money
and get the fuck outta there.
"Paulette! Crystal!" She started to yell before she
was lifted off the ground by two tall men.
"Put me down! Get the fuck off me!' Nina kicked
and screamed
"Please keep your voice down ma'am. We tried to
ask you to leave nicely and you wouldn't listen"
"We can't just let her get dragged out of here"
Paulette said to Crystal and Trish as she looked and
shook her head at the two men escorting Nina out of
the restaurant. Paulette and Nina hadn't spoke since
that incident at her house but she didn't hate her,
Nina was entitled to her opinion, and she was still
her friend.
"Then you go over there and say something"
Crystal said.
A part of her felt bad but then another part of her
didn't care what the fuck happened to Nina, she still
wasn't speaking to her.
"One of you come with me" Paulette said to Crystal
and Trish. Even though Nina was her girl she did
look crazy right now. Paulette was embarrassed as
hell and she didn't want to go over there alone.
"I'm not going nowhere! I'm tired of that bitch
going out and acting a fool. Let them carry her

329

crazy ass outta here!" Trish said

"What?" Paulette and Crystal both looked at Trish. They didn't know what Trish was talking about

"Nothing. I'm not going nowhere" Trish said with an attitude. She sat there and folded her arms across her chest.

"Well look at her. Something must be wrong with her. We're her friends. Fuck it! I'm going over there" Paulette stood up

Crystal thought about it for a moment and Paulette was right. Nina did look like shit. Maybe something was wrong with her and she was their friend.

"C'mon I'll go with you" Crystal said as she took her napkin of her lap and put it on the table and dusted the crumbs off her dress.

Crystal took a deep breath and prayed that nobody she knew was in the restaurant. She had a reputation to maintain.

...

"Excuse me sir she's with us can you please let her go" Paulette said to one of the men holding Nina's arm

"Are you sure?" The bouncer asked looking at Paulette and Crystal and then back at Nina who clearly looked like a crackhead.

"Yes I'm sure. She's part of the Jackson party"

"Yeah I told you motherfuckers to get off me" Nina yelled

Crystal looked at Nina like she'd lost her mind. She couldn't believe how she was acting.

"Okay but if there are any more outbursts we are going to have to ask her to leave"
The man said like Nina wasn't standing right there.
"Everything will be fine" Crystal assured the men
The men let Nina go and the three of them walked back over towards the table. Trish had went to the bathroom so the table was empty.
"What's up Nina?" Paulette asked once they were seated at the table.
"Nothing. What's up with you?" Nina asked like everything was fine
"I'm okay, Me and Chris are getting married. But you don't look so good. Is everything okay?"
"I'm okay don't worry about me" Nina snapped
"You don't look okay" Crystal butted in
"I didn't ask for either one of your fucking opinions, can you pass the fucking pancakes please"
Nina was starving. She hadn't eaten a good meal in a while and seeing all the food on the table made her mouth water. She just wanted to eat and get some money so she could go get high.
"Look, you're our friend and we're concerned about you"
"I appreciate the concern, and if ya'll are so concerned can you lend me a couple of dollars?"
"For what?" Crystal asked. She knew a crackhead when she saw one and she knew damn well that Nina was doing some type of drugs. *I'll be damn if I give her money to get high.*
"Because I need it! Fuck you! Can you loan me something Paulette?"

"I only have about $40 dollars on me, but I'm with Crystal, what do you need it for?'

"Because I fucking need it! Look I didn't come here for ya'll to judge me!"

"I'm worried about you Nina. Are you doing drugs?"

"Look mind you're fucking business!" Nina said raising her voice

Just then Trish walked back over to the table from the bathroom.

"Oh this bitch is here too! I'm out!" Nina said as she got up.

"Wait Nina don't leave. Let me drive you home. You really don't look good" Paulette pleaded

"I don't need you to drive me home. Just give me that $40 dollars"

"I'm not giving it to you if you don't let me drive you home"

Paulette figured she would try to talk to Nina when they were alone and try to convince her to get some help.

"Fuck you! Don't worry about me and my problems, handle your own shit!"

"What are you talking about?"

"Did you tell you're fucking boyfriend about your nasty little secret?"

"Fuck you! You bitch!"

Paulette said as she started to cry. She couldn't believe Nina would say something like that to her. Crystal and Trish just stared at them because neither one of them knew what was going on.

"Don't be mad at me! You sitting here trying to preach to me and you need to deal with your own shit"
"I was just trying to be your friend"
"I don't need no fucking friend, I need that $40"
"I don't have it!"
"Okay you want to play with me, we'll see how Chris feels about what I have to tell him"
"Fuck you Nina!"
"Fuck you too!" Nina said and got up from the table and walked out
…

Brr-ring- Brr-ring
"Hello?"
"Hey Patty what's up?"
Trish's heart dropped into her stomach. She hadn't heard anybody call her Patty since she was 13 years old.
"I think you have the wrong number" Trish said and hung up the phone.
"Brr-Brring"
The phone rang again.
"Hello?"
"I know you didn't hang up on me Patty?" The voice on the other end chuckled
"Who is this?"
Trish was terrified.
"An old friend"
"An old friend who?"
"An old friend of the family"

Trish was scared as hell. She had no idea who it was. She damn sure didn't need anybody from her past trying to mess up the new life she made for herself.

"What do you want?"

"I want what's mine. I want what you owe me"

"What are you talking about?" Trish asked as she paced back and forth in her bedroom.

"I know you remember what you did, don't play dumb"

"I don't know what you're talking about" Trish said and hung up the phone

The phone rang again.

"Leave me alone!" She screamed into the receiver

"I'll leave you alone when I get what I want!"

"What the fuck do you want?!" She screamed`

"Look bitch! Stop playing with me or I'll fuck up more than your apartment next time"

Trish slammed the phone down and pulled the cord out the wall.

She was scared as hell. She didn't know what to do but she couldn't stay there. She ran to her closet and grabbed a pair of Nike's then grabbed her I-phone and car keys off the kitchen counter and ran out the door. She didn't know where she was going.

...

Paulette couldn't stop thinking about that day at breakfast. She felt like everything was going so good in her life and then Nina had to bring that shit up.

I wish I would have never told that bitch shit!
She looked over at Chris sleeping so peacefully next
to her. Part of her wanted to tell him so bad but the
other part of her just couldn't. She couldn't think of
how to say it to him. It never seemed like the right
time. She loved him so much and she couldn't live
with herself if she infected him but she also
couldn't live if he left her. It was so hard for her.

She wished she could go back in time and erase
the night she slept with Gabriel and Jaime. Deep
down she knew that's where she got it from.
The wedding was getting closer and closer. Her
mother's plans looked so beautiful and she even
found the wedding dress of her dreams a few days
ago. It was perfect. She looked over at Chris again
and she felt like crying. She was so blessed to have
him, he truly was an angel.

Just recently they started having unprotected
sex. Chris felt like since they were going to be
married soon they could start working on starting a
family. They had only had unprotected sex a few
times and each time Paulette felt worse and worse,
but she still couldn't tell him. *He hasn't gotten it so
far, so everything will be fine.* Paulette told herself
to make herself feel better about what she was
doing. She knew it was wrong but she couldn't lose
him.
Am I a terrible person?
…

Crystal sat in her room staring at the blank television screen. She was so bored.
Even though her and Trish had exchanged a few words at Paulette's breakfast, things still weren't the same between them. As far as Crystal was concerned if Trish didn't apologize for what she did she didn't have shit to say to her. So they hadn't spoken since. Crystal called Paulette a few times but she was so busy with the wedding plans that they hardly ever talked. Nina was a whole 'nother story. She tried to call Nina a few times since the breakfast and her phone was disconnected. She even stopped by her apartment three times and she never got an answer. She just prayed that Nina was okay. She had never seen her look that bad, it was scary. Lately Crystal had so much time to think. Tomorrow was her mother's birthday and they still weren't speaking. Usually Crystal took her to dinner and spent the day with her. She knew this year would be different.

Even though she knew her mother wasn't going to answer she was going to call her tomorrow anyway. She couldn't help but think about Harold. She hated him so much. She held him responsible for her and her mother not speaking. Crystal's phone rang snapping her out of her daze. She stared at the caller id in amazement as she looked at Harold's number, it was like he knew that she was thinking about him. She didn't want to answer but she knew if she didn't he would call over and over again and if she still didn't answer he would just

show up. She didn't want to look at his fucking face
so she picked up.

"Hello?"

"Hey baby girl"

"What do you want?"

"Why you gotta talk to me like that?"
Harold said trying to be nice.

"What do you want?"

"You know what I want, why you even gotta ask?"
Crystal sat on the other end of the phone in silence.
She decided that now was the perfect time to put her
plan into action. She had been thinking about it for
a couple of days now and she was scared, she just
didn't want anything to go wrong.

She weighed the pros and cons of the situation over
and over. Her job and her possible freedom vs.
constantly being raped until God knows when and
never speaking to her mother again.

It was worth it.

"Yeah I know I'm sorry, I don't know what I was
thinking " Crystal said sweetly

"Crystal?" Harold asked confused. In all the years
he knew Crystal she had never welcomed any of his
calls or visits and he had become used to her
attitude.

He smiled when he figured that finally she came to
her senses and decided to be with him.

"Yeah its me Harold" She giggled

"Its about time you stop playing with me"

"I always felt this way, I was just scared I didn't
want to hurt my mother, but I don't care anymore"

Crystal lied

"I knew you would come around baby girl" Harold couldn't stop smiling, she had made his day.

"Sorry it took so long" Crystal was saying whatever bullshit she could think of, she couldn't believe it was working so good.

"So when can I see you?"

"Well I got something else in mind"

"Like what?"

"Well its kind of freaky" Crystal said like she was embarrassed

"I like freaky, what is it?" Harold was getting excited

"You know I've been thinking about you a lot lately and I know I am supposed to keep our business between us but I told one of my friends how good it is and she wants to see for herself"

"For real?" Harold was almost jumping up and down

"Yeah. She looks a lot like me, but she's freaky"

"I told you I like freaky"

"Okay good, I want you to do this for me and if you like it then maybe we can do some things with all three of us"

"Okay when?"

"Tomorrow night. She likes to role play, so I want you to come in her house like a burglar and take it, she's gonna act like she doesn't know you but that's all part of the plan"

"I never did nothing like that before, ya'll are freaky" Harold said as he licked his lips just thinking about it

"Since you're role playing you're name is not Harold and you can't mention my name either"

"Okay, how am I gonna get in?"

"I'm gonna give you the key, don't worry"

"Okay baby girl. I can't wait"

"Okay I'll call you tomorrow and we can discuss all the details, goodnight"

"Good night"

And that's exactly what it was for Harold he was so excited, he wasn't sure if was going to be able to sleep. He couldn't stop thinking about tomorrow night.

Crystal hung up the phone and smiled.

She couldn't believe how easy that was.

She prayed that soon enough Harold would be out her life and things would go back to normal.

Whatever normal was

...

Chapter 18

"Knock! Knock! Knock!"
"Open up Nina! I know you're in there" Mr.
Gladsberg screamed on the other side of the door.
Mr. Gladsberg was Nina's landlord. Nina was three
months behind on her rent and he had been stopping
by at least twice a week to try and collect. She had
been ducking each time, but today he was knocking
for a half an hour, she didn't think he was going
away. Nina sat in the dark on the floor in the corner
of her living room. She tried to be quiet and hoped
that Mr. Gladsberg would go away. Tears streamed
down her face as she pulled her knees to her chest
and buried her face.

She hated times like this when her high was
gone and she had to face reality and her fucked up
life, that's why she constantly chased that high, real
life had become too much for her. She tried to run
her fingers through her hair that were matted up
almost forming dreadlocks. He lips were white, dry
and ashy like she hadn't seen chapstick in years.
Her body looked just as bad. Nina's once plump ass
was completely flat and her barely there titties we
now invisible. Now Nina weighed about 95 lbs, and
that was stretching it.

She looked around at her dirty apartment. There
was garbage, food and dirty clothes everywhere.
"Í got to get the fuck outta here" She said to herself
She tiptoed in her room and grabbed some worn out
jeans from a pile of clothes on the floor. She slipped

her ashy feet into a pair of beat up Nike's and but a baseball cap on her head. Nina tiptoed to the door and placed her ear against it. She listened and she didn't hear anything. She got down on her knees and looked under the crack on the door to see if she saw any feet, she didn't. She slowly turned the door knob and opened the door. She looked left and then right she didn't see Mr. Gladsberg. Nina ran to the stairway and ran down the four flights of steps as fast as she could.

　　She didn't have a dollar in her pocket. She needed some money, she needed to get high, that was all she was thinking about. She had borrowed from everybody she knew and everyone was tired of her. She decided to pay Paulette and Chris a little visit. Nina was sure that Paulette would pay her to keep her mouth shut and if that didn't work she knew Chris would pay her tell her little secret. She was guaranteed some money and she wasn't leaving there without it.

...

Trish pressed the elevator button frantically. It was taking forever and she couldn't wait. She decided to just take the stairs. She always avoided the stairs since she was on the 11th floor but today was an emergency. She rushed down the stairs skipping steps, two at a time. By the time she reached the ground level she was sweating. She opened the garage door and saw her car on the other side of the parking lot.

"Thank God its in one piece" She said out loud.
She started to run towards her car when a black
BMW came out of now where and slammed right
into her. Trish was thrown to the ground. She
looked in front of her and the car was backing up
and coming forward like it was going to hit her
again.
"Aaaaah" She screamed
She tried to get up but her legs felt like noodles. She
couldn't move.
She tried to roll but she wasn't fast enough the car
was coming towards her.
All she could do was scream, she put her arms up in
front of her as if that was going to block her from
the impact of the car, but it was a reflex.
She looked up to the sky and said a quick prayer as
she saw her life flash before her eyes

...

Nina got off the train at 125th street in Harlem. She
managed to get some change from passing strangers
to buy her $2.25 train fare. She didn't remember
what apartment Paulette lived in but she
remembered the building, she figured it would come
to her when she got there. She walked the 9 blocks
to Paulette's building on 116th and 7th Ave. Paulette
lived in a brownstone in Harlem, there were only
four floors so Nina buzzed each intercom asking for
Paulette. She got no answer on the first two and the
third said"Nobody lives here by that name"
So she buzzed the fourth intercom and man with a

deep voice said

"She's not here right now"

"It's me Nina, can I come up for a second?" Nina said in her sweetest voice

The intercom buzzed and Nina pushed the door open. She walked up the four flights of steps and tried to adjust her tattered clothing as best she could. When she reached the door it was cracked and she walked inside the apartment. Chris was in the refrigerator pouring a glass of juice when Nina walked in. When he turned around and saw her he dropped the glass on the floor and it shattered into little pieces.

She could tell by the look on his face that she looked like shit, but she didn't give a shit she only came there for one thing and one thing only. Nina and Chris had only met one time before but he remembered thinking to himself that she was a cutie, but today she looked like walking death, he wanted to throw up. He bent down and started picking up the pieces of glass.

"So Paulette's not here?" Nina asked ignoring Chris' stares

"Umm no she won't be back until late tonight her and her mother are doing some more planning for the wedding, but I'll tell her you stopped by" Chris said as normal as possible

"Well I need a little favor"

"What is that?" Chris asked

"I need a little cash"

Chris could tell by the way she looked what she

needed the money for but he didn't feel comfortable
giving it to her, he knew Paulette would be upset if
she found out.

"I don't have any money on me" Chris lied

"Look don't fucking lie to me I know you got
money in here" Nina said looking around their
apartment.

"I really don't maybe you should come back
tomorrow when Paulette is here"

Nina thought about what Chris said for a second
and only a second, she needed to get high and she
wasn't taking no for an answer.

"No I'm here now and I need the money now, how
about I give you a little something for it"

Chris looked at her in disgust. He hoped she wasn't
talking about fucking because she couldn't pay him
to fuck her.

"Nah I'm good" Chris said

"Well I have a little information that I think you
might be interested in, its about Paulette"

"What?" Chris asked confused. He didn't expect
Nina to say that

"I said I have a little info on Paulette that I think
you might wanna know"

"What is it?" Chris couldn't help it, he was curious

"It's gonna cost $150 dollars" Nina said

"I don't have $150"

"You got $100?"

"Yeah" Chris nodded

Nina shook her head, she knew the bastard was
lying when she first asked him.

"Well give it to me and then I'll tell you what you need to know"

Chris went in his pocket and counted out 5 twenty dollar bills.

He laid them on the counter.

"No you tell me what you have to say and then you take your money. I'll leave it right here on the table"

"Okay" Nina smiled, she felt like doing a cartwheel when she saw that money on the table

"Paulette has warts, HPV, something like that, I thought you should know before you married her nasty ass"

"What? You're lying"

"I'm not fucking lying ask her"

"I don't believe you , you fucking crackhead, get out!"

"Fuck you! At least I ain't got no warts all over my coochie! I was trying to help your stupid ass out, just gimme my fucking money"

Chris grabbed the money off the table and shoved it back in his pocket.

"I ain't giving you shit, get the fuck outta my apartment!"

"What? We had a deal! You bastard!"

Chris walked over to her and grabbed her by the arm and started dragging her out of the apartment. Nina started begging she really needed the money.

"Look I'm sorry. I really don't have any money to get home or to get anything to eat. I just need the money to buy some food, please"

"I'm not fucking stupid you wasn't gonna buy no
food with that money"
"Look please, just give me $40, I'm begging"
Chris pulled 2 twenty's out of his pocket and
handed them to her as he pushed her out the door.
"Don't ever come back here"
"Okay but I'm telling the truth"
Chris just slammed the door in her face.
...

"Here's the key and make sure you are real quiet
when you go in. After you open the door throw the
key in the garbage chute right next to her apartment,
don't forget.   She's gonna act scared like she
doesn't know you but that's all part of the plan, she
wants you to take it. Don't stop, even if she asks
you to. Remember don't say your real name and
don't say mine. Your name is Joe and her name is
Cindy" Crystal laid out the details
"Okay I'm gonna go tonight when I get off work, I
don't get off until midnight so I'm gonna go around
1 in the morning" Harold smiled
"That's good, she should be sleep by that time, so
she will be real surprised"
"She don't live with nobody?" Harold asked like he
was getting nervous
"No she lives alone, everything will be fine" Crystal
lied.
But she wasn't worried she had that part under
control as well.
"Okay. I'll call you tomorrow"

"Okay. Tell my mom I said Happy Birthday"
"Yeah whatever"
Marie was the last thing on Harold's mind at this
moment. He couldn't wait until tonight.
Crystal got up and walked out of the diner.
She made the meeting as quick as possible. She
didn't want anyone seeing them together.
She quickly dialed Keith's cell phone.
"Hello?" He answered on the first ring
"Hey what's up? I was just making sure that we're
still on for tonight?"
"Of course. 8:30 right?"
"Yeah in front of my apartment"
"Aight I'll see you later"
"Okay bye"
"Bye"
Crystal hung up and smiled, so far everything was
going as planned.
...

Chapter 19

Trish's heart was in her throat when the car stopped an inch before her nose. The tires came to a screeching halt and Trish couldn't help but scream. She tried to move but she still couldn't.
A man got out of the driver side door and she couldn't make out who it was because it was too dark.
"You still think I'm playing bitch?" The man moved closer to Trish so she could get a better look at him. She immediately noticed the man as Jr., Mike's old friend.
"Jr.?"
"Yeah bitch it's me Jr."
"What do you want?"
"What the fuck do you think I want?"
"Why are you doing this to me?" Trish cried
"Doing this to you? You always think some shit is all about you, you always did. You took my fucking money"
"What are you talking about?"
"Stop fucking playing with me!" Jr. screamed, he was getting frustrated with Trish
"I'm not playing I don't know what you're talking about" Trish cried
She didn't want to admit to taking the money, she didn't know what he might do to her.
"Do you know I could have just killed your fucking ass and you still want to play games with me?"
"I'm not playing please let me go" Trish begged

"Let you go? I know Mike told you about that stash, I know you took that shit! And I want my fucking money bitch!"

"I don't have any money"

"Stop fucking lying. You live in this fancy ass building, driving a fancy ass car, I'm not fucking stupid"

"I really don't have any money"

"Well that's not what your lying ass told my brother"

"Your brother?"

"Yeah my fucking brother!"

"Get out the car" Jr. said to someone sitting in the passenger side of the car.

Just then Jay stepped out of the car. Trish couldn't believe her eyes. She rubbed her eyes to make sure she wasn't seeing things.

"Jay?"

"Shut up!" Jay answered nastily

All Trish could do was cry. She felt like her world was crumbling right before her eyes. The one man that she loved since Mike, didn't give a shit about her.

"Jay you knew about this?"

"What? You mean about all your fucking lies? Your parents dying in a car crash? Your money from investments? Your grandparents taking care of you?"

Trish put her head down. There was nothing she could say, she was so embarrassed.

"You don't have shit to say now do you? And what

about my fucking house? Jay asked
"Jay I really didn't do that. Please believe me. I'm
sorry about everything else. I really am. I love you"
"Shut up! I don't believe you. You don't love me. If
you loved me you would have told me the fucking
truth, I shouldn't have to hear it from my brother"
"Yeah it seems like you didn't tell my big brother
that your moms is a junkie from Queens and she'll
fuck anybody to get high and that you been ran
through too. Or that you stole all my money from
my fucking stash. I had to fill him in on all that. He
was really acting like he was getting feelings for
your ass" Jr. said with a grin
"Fuck you!" Trish spat at Jr.
"Don't be mad because the little fucking life that
you made up is falling apart" Jr. laughed
"Look what do you want?"
"I want $250,000 and maybe I'll let you live"
"What? I don't have that kind of money" Trish lied
The truth was she did have the money but then she
would be broke and she be damned if she was going
to be broke again, she'd rather be dead.
"Well you better get that kind of money or else"
"How about $20,000?" Trish asked
Jr. looked at his brother and started busting out
laughing.
"This bitch really thinks I'm playing with her"
"Look I'm not negotiating with your ass. You stole
about $200,000 of my fucking money and I'm
tacking on interest"
"All that money wasn't yours" Trish screamed

"Oh so now you admit that you took my shit? I should kill your lying ass just for that"

"Some of that money was Mike's money!"

"Mike was fucking dead!"

"So what! That was still his money!"

"Look bitch I'm not arguing with you!" Jr. said as he pulled a gun from his waist.

Trish screamed.

"Yo what are you doing?" Jay asked his brother. This was not part of the plan they were just supposed to scare her and hopefully she would give Jr. the money so he could leave her alone.

"She's getting on my fucking nerves! She keeps running her fucking mouth!" Jr. pointed the gun at Trish

"Don't be stupid! This was not part of the fucking plan!"

"What? You catching feelings for this bitch now? She stole my fucking money and you gonna choose her over me?"

"Nah. I'm just saying don't be stupid"

"Fuck you" Jr. said as he pulled the trigger.

...

Harold looked at his watch it was 1:13am. He made a stop before he made his way over to Cindy's. He stopped at the bar on the corner by his job and got himself a few shots of Jack Daniels to put him in the mood. Now he was feeling good and ready to get nasty. He hoped she was as freaky as Crystal said. He circled the block a few times looking for a parking spot.

He finally saw someone pulling out and he pulled into their spot. By the time he was walking to Cindy's apartment it was 1:30am.

He took the steps up the second floor and stopped in front of apartment 2J. He took out the key that Crystal had given him and he looked at it for a few seconds. He got a little nervous and then he imagined a beautiful, freaky woman on the other side of the door ready to fulfill his fantasies. He gently put the key in the door and turned the knob. Once the door was cracked, he walked a few steps back towards the garbage chute and threw the key down the chute. He made sure to follow Crystal's instructions exactly he didn't want anything to go wrong. He tiptoed back to Cindy's door and walked inside. His heart was racing. He was scared and excited at the same time.

He gently closed the door and locked it behind him. He tiptoed and felt his way around the apartment. It was dark and he didn't want to knock anything over. He really felt like a burglar. He had such a rush. He walked to the back of the apartment to the bedroom and saw Cindy sleeping peacefully in the bed. Her hair was pulled back in a ponytail and he was amazed at how much she looked like Crystal, they looked like sisters. He walked over to her side of the bed and stared at her for a minute. Then he bent down and kissed her.

"Hey baby" She said as she kissed him back

Harold smiled because it was going better than he

thought. ' '

"Hey" Harold said back

Cindy didn't recognize the deep voice and she immediately opened her eyes. She screamed at the top of her lungs when she saw Harold standing over her.

She sat up and slapped him. She started kicking and screaming.

"Who the fuck are you? Get the fuck out?"

"Its me Joe. Relax baby" Harold said with a smile.

It was all part of the plan

"Get the fuck out! She began kicking"

She caught him a few times in the stomach

"Oh you like to play rough" Harold said with a smile

"What do you want?'

"You know what I want baby"

"Please get out! Now! Do you want money?"

"No I don't want money come over here baby" Harold said as he walked over to her and tried to kiss her.

She put up her fists and started punching. She punched him in the face twice and then she kicked him in the balls. Harold bent over in pain. *She's going a little too far.* He thought.

He reached out and grabbed her wrested and pinned her down on the bed. He laid a wet slobbery kiss all over her lips. He ripped her tank top open and revealed her perky breasts. He started slobbering all over her breasts.

She kicked and screamed.

"Let go of me! Get the fuck off of me you nasty pervert!"

"Calm down Cindy"

"Who the fuck is Cindy?"

She's really playing this part.

She kneed him in the balls again. Harold was in so much pain he screamed and bent over.

Just then she reached in the night stand and pulled out a small gun that fit in the palm of her hand. She shot him in the head twice.

"My fucking name is Christine"

...

Paulette was exhausted from another long night of wedding planning with her mother. She was amazed at how much energy her mother had when it came to planning a wedding. She was like the energizer bunny, she kept going and going and going. It was midnight and she had an 8am appointment tomorrow to look at centerpieces for the reception. She was beat. Paulette put her key in the door and was surprised to see Chris still up sitting in the living room watching T.V.

"Hey baby" She said cheerfully.

She was always happy to see her man.

"Hey" Chris said nonchalantly

"What's wrong?"

"Nothing"

"I'm so tired. I just want to get in the shower and go to bed, you know my mother will try to keep me up planning all night"

"Mmm"

"What's wrong with you?" Paulette asked with an attitude

Paulette could tell by Chris' one word answers that something was wrong with him and he didn't feel like being bothered.

"I should be asking you that?"

"What is that supposed to mean?"

"Your friend stopped by here today"

"My friend who?"

"Nina"

Paulette's heart dropped to her stomach, she felt like she couldn't breathe. *What the fuck did Nina stop by for?*

"And?"

"She wanted to speak to you and I told her you weren't here"

"Oh okay" Paulette took a deep breath, relieved that that was all she said.

"But then she had some interesting information to tell me"

"What?' Paulette asked like she'd seen a ghost

"Yeah she said she had to tell me something about you? So is there anything you want to tell me?"

"No" Paulette said

"Are you sure?"

"Yeah I'm sure" Paulette said nervously

"Are you fucking sure?" Chris said raising his voice

Paulette was startled she never heard Chris speak to her in that tone before, they never really argued about anything.

"Yes I'm sure" Paulette said like a small child

"Okay I gave you the chance to tell me the truth and you still want to fucking lie to me. You know what your fucking friend told me? She told me that you had warts, HPV!"

Paulette put her head down and started crying. She regretted ever telling Nina her fucking business.

"She's lying" Paulette screamed through tears

"Yeah that's what I thought too. I didn't think that the woman that I love so much, the woman that I'm about to marry, the woman that I share everything with could keep something this big from me and put me at risk, I knew she had to be lying"

"She is baby, I love you"

"And you're still fucking lying to me!"

"No I'm not"

"Yes you are! I found these in your gym bag. I'm leaving" Chris said as he threw a bottle of her medication at her.

"Baby wait, I can explain. Please don't leave"

Chris pushed past her and walked out the door.

"And the wedding is off!"

Paulette sunk to the kitchen floor and cried.

...

"Aaaaah" Trish screamed in pain as the bullet went into her thigh.

Jr. was aiming at Trish's head but Jay pushed him out of the way in enough time and the bullet went into her leg. Jr. landed on the floor and the gun flew out of his hand landing a few feet from Trish. Trish felt like she was going to faint once she saw the blood.

"Yo what the fuck is wrong with you?" Jr. screamed at his brother

"You wasn't supposed to kill her! You was just supposed to scare her! Don't you want your money? How is she gonna give it to you if she's dead?" Jay yelled back

"Fuck her! And fuck you too! You always putting a woman before me. You a bitchass nigga. I should fuck you up." Jr. said as he swung on Jay.

He caught Jay in the jaw and Jay immediately followed up with a quick punch to his face and then a blow to the stomach. That caught Jr. of guard and he stumbled trying to catch his balance.

Since Jr. and Jay didn't have the same mother they grew up in different households. But they did spend time together on holidays. Once Mike died Jr. really reached out to Jay because he felt like he didn't have anyone else he could trust. Him and Jay built up a friendship but over the years Jr. always felt like Jay was more concerned about the women in his life than being his brother. He couldn't stand his wife Linda and he hated Trish.

Jay caught Jr. with another blow to the face that knocked him out cold. Jay reached in his pocket and took out his blackberry. He dialed 911. He gave them Trish's address. He went over to Jr. and picked up his limp body and dragged him to the passenger side of the car.

He didn't want to have to explain this situation to the cops and he didn't want to be there when they arrived. He walked past Trish and bent down and picked up Jr.'s gun off the floor and he hopped in the driver's side of the BMW. He closed the door and pulled off. He didn't take a second look at Trish. She began crying.
She knew the love of her life was gone forever.
...

"Ring-Ring Ring"
Crystal looked at her digital clock on her nightstand. It read 4:23am.
"Who is calling me this late?" She said out loud.
"Hello?"
"He's dead! He's dead! Crystal what am I gonna do? What am I gonna do?"
She immediately recognized her mother's voice on the other end of the phone.
She could tell her mother was drunk and she had been crying, she sounded like she was in so much pain, now Crystal didn't know if she had made such a good choice.
"Mommy calm down. Who is dead?"
"Harold! Harold! He is gone!"
"What?" Crystal acted surprised
"They want me to come down to the hospital and identify the body, but I just can't do it! I just can't see him like that" Marie slurred
"Okay ma, I'm on my way over"

"Oooh Crystal what am I gonna do? He is my life"
Marie sobbed into the phone.
Crystal hung up the phone and placed it on the night
stand.
What did I do?
She knew her mother was going to take it hard but
she never imagined her sounding this bad.
Keith turned to face her and said
"What's wrong?"
"Nothing I have a family emergency I have to go
check on my mom"
"You want me to go with you?"
"No I'm okay, but I don't know when I'm coming
back so you should go"
Crystal hopped out the bed and looked in her closet
for a sweat suit. She found some sneakers under her
bed and put them on. She was in a daze.
Keith quietly got dressed.
In five minutes they were both dressed and walking
out the door. They were both silent.
When they got downstairs Crystal turned to Keith
and said
"Bye"
"Later" He said
Keith flagged a cab and Crystal walked to her car.
She got in the car and put her seatbelt on and cried.
She didn't want to have to face her mother. She
didn't factor this part into the equation. She started
the car and drove the twenty minutes to her
mother's house in Queens. She didn't bother turn on
the radio. She needed to think.

She found a spot directly in front of her mother's
house. The block was so quiet. She ran up the steps
and banged on the door, nobody answered. She
banged harder.

"Ma open up! Its me" Still no answer.

Maybe she's in the bathroom

She began looking through her key ring for her
spare to key to the house.

After a few seconds she found it and opened the
door. When she got inside. All the lights were on
and Marvin Gaye was blaring from the radio in the
living room.

"Mom!" Crystal called out

Still no answer

Crystal ran up the stairs.

"Mom!"

She didn't know why but she had butterflies in her
stomach.

She walked back to her mother's bedroom, the door
was slightly closed. She pushed it open and
screamed at what she saw in front of her.

Marie was laying on the floor with a gun in her left
hand and a small puddle of blood coming from her
head. Crystal saw a half empty bottle of Jack
Daniels laying on the floor next to her.

Crystal bent down and cried

"Mommy! Mommy wake up!"

Marie didn't move or say a word.

Crystal searched for her cell phone and couldn't
find it. She ran over to the nightstand and picked up
the phone and dialed 911.

"Please hurry! Its bad! My mother! She's hurt!"
Crystal held her mother in her arms and rocked
back and forth.
"I'm so sorry mommy, Please be okay"
In a few minutes the ambulance arrived and they
rushed over to New York Hospital.
She held her mother's hand the entire time while the
stretcher led her into the emergency room. The
nurses and doctors led Marie to the back and asked
Crystal to wait in the emergency room. In what
seemed like a few minutes a doctor came out and
told Crystal
"I'm sorry but your mom didn't make it. The wound
was to severe" Crystal's legs felt weak she had to sit
down. She fell back in the chair and sobbed.

What did I do?
I killed my mother.

Epilogue

A week later was Marie's and Harold's funeral.
Crystal decided to have them together. She didn't
know how she did it but she managed to plan
everything. She felt like she was having an out of
body experience the entire time. She couldn't
believe how everything had turned out. The only up
side was Crystal was happy to see her friends there
and have them around her.

Trish was right by her side on crutches, she
would be that way for a while until her leg healed.
She hadn't spoke to Jay since the shooting but she
was grateful to be alive and was taking it one day at
a time. She didn't tell the cops the truth, she told
them it was an attempted robbery.

Paulette was there too, or at least her body was.
It was clear that she wasn't the same Paulette she
was when she was with Chris, she didn't have that
glow anymore. She found out last week that she was
pregnant and her and Chris decided to be friends
and at least have a good relationship for the baby.
Paulette still wanted to be with him desperately but
she knew what she did was wrong and she was
happy to have his friendship. She just hoped one
day he changed his mind and forgave her. Michelle
was crushed when she heard the wedding was off.
Towards the end of the service Nina showed up.
She stood in the back quietly. She looked better
than they had seen her look in a while.
She didn't look like her old self but hopefully she

would get there soon. She had checked herself into rehab and had been clean for a couple of days now. Crystal was grateful to have all her friends there with her.

She loved them. They had been through a lot but they were her Girls.

The End... For Now

Shakeera Frazer is a graduate of Morgan State University and received her Master's Degree in Education from the University of Maryland. She has always been an avid reader with a great imagination. After teaching elementary school she decided to follow her dream and begin writing. *Fast Lane* is her first novel to date but stay tuned for the sequel. She currently resides in Connecticut.
To purchase the novel go to:
http://www.shakeerafrazer.com
www.amazon.com
www.barnesandnoble.com
www.twitter.com/msfrazer

Made in the USA
Charleston, SC
22 June 2010